1

June Gadsby was born in Felling, Tyne and Wear. Her first love has always been writing, though she is also an accomplished artist. She loves to cook, read and listen to music. She currently lives in south-west France with her photographer husband, Brian, and her miniature Yorkshire terrier. Her previous novels include *When Tomorrow Comes*, *The Jealous Land*, and *To the Ends of the Earth*.

VOICES OF THE MORNING

Patrick Flynn doesn't want another mouth to feed, so he endeavours to ensure that his newborn son Billy does not survive. But, helped by a warm-hearted prostitute and Laura Caldwell, the daughter of a wealthy local family, Billy does . . . Patrick deserts his family, leaving Billy to struggle for a living and to look after his alcoholic mother. He becomes obsessed with Laura, but she has other ideas, and it is with Bridget, the prostitute's daughter, that Billy joins the Jarrow crusaders marching to London to demonstrate against unemployment. Neither of them, however, is prepared for the reappearance of the evil Patrick Flynn . . .

Books by June Gadsby
Published by The House of Ulverscroft:

PRECIOUS LOVE
KISS TODAY GOODBYE
SECRET OBSESSIONS
THE ROSE CAROUSEL
THE IRON MASTER
WHEN TOMORROW COMES
THE SAFE HEART
THE MIRACLE OF LOVE
THE JEALOUS LAND
TO THE ENDS OF THE EARTH
VALLEY OF DREAMS
PRECIOUS MOMENTS
VALLEY OF BRAVE HEARTS

JUNE GADSBY

VOICES OF
THE MORNING

Complete and Unabridged

ULVERSCROFT
Leicester

First published in Great Britain in 2008 by
Robert Hale Limited
London

First Large Print Edition
published 2009
by arrangement with
Robert Hale Limited
London

Copyright © 2008 by June Gadsby

British Library CIP Data

Gadsby, June
   Voices of the morning.—Large print ed.—
Ulverscroft large print series: general fiction
1. Demonstrations—Fiction 2. Social classes—England,
North East—Fiction 3. England, North East—Social
conditions—Fiction 4. Domestic fiction
5. Large type books
I. Title
823.9'2 [F]

ISBN 978–1–84782–589–6

Published by
F. A. Thorpe (Publishing)
Anstey, Leicestershire

Set by Words & Graphics Ltd.
Anstey, Leicestershire
Printed and bound in Great Britain by
T. J. International Ltd., Padstow, Cornwall

This book is printed on acid-free paper

1

The herring gull flew upriver from South Shields, great wings beating silently over the deserted, frozen landscape. Then it turned, planing over the tidal mud flats, its grey and white plumage gleaming. Jarrow Slakes, as this long stretch of mud was known, looked almost beautiful, shining like pale gold in the morning light. The seabird soared, then circled over rows of slate-roofed houses that stood back to back with cobbled lanes in between. As it passed over the square tower of St Paul's Church, it gave a raucous cry before turning back in the direction of the oily, blue-black waters of the River Tyne.

Down below, Laura Caldwell was being dragged through the small north-east town of Jarrow at a breathtaking rate by her anxious mother. From time to time she raised her eyes to look at the moving silhouette of the seabird against a pale January sky. The raucous cry it gave echoed across the whole valley, the only voice to be heard heralding in the New Year. 1920 was only a few hours old and showing no sign as yet of awakening. The child gave a shudder. She would have preferred to be tucked up in bed instead of hurrying through empty streets on a pilgrimage that she didn't understand.

'Where are we going, Mummy?' she asked, not for the first time since her mother had washed and dressed her before daylight spilled over the rooftops. And all the while her father remained asleep, snoring contentedly, alone in the room he had occupied since the accident that had robbed him of the use of his legs.

'I've told you, Laura.' Elizabeth Caldwell's voice was terse. Her jaws were clamped tightly shut against the cold wind blowing in from the North Sea. Her coat was stylish and had been expensive when bought before the war, but was totally inadequate for the season. Even the Caldwells had been forced to economize during the long years of war and, two years after the much-longed-for peace, things were still tight. 'We're going to find Mrs Flynn. She didn't come to work this morning and . . . '

Elizabeth Caldwell's footsteps faltered. She skidded to a halt, catching her breath and tried to get her bearings. She was not at all familiar with this part of town, although it was a mere stone's throw from the smarter district where she and her family had lived comfortably for generations.

'Did she forget?' Laura's dark, nut-brown head and large spaniel eyes rose up again to the sky, following the gull's progress. It had changed direction yet again and was heading up towards the old Venerable Bede allotments. These plots of apportioned land covered the site of an old, disused mine. Her granddad lived near there, right over the place where the shafts had collapsed and killed a lot of miners. Some of them had been Gramps's friends. He always got a sad look in his eyes when he talked about it.

Elizabeth Caldwell quickened her pace to such an extent that the child felt as though she, too, were about to take off and fly like the gull. Her skinny little legs were going like pistons, tiny feet not even touching the ground.

'Do hurry up, Laura,' her mother said, not looking at the child, but glancing from side to side, with wary eyes that watered because of the icy bite in the frosted air.

'I can't go any faster, Mummy,' the eight-year-old protested breathlessly.

'You must. This is not a nice place and we don't want to stay here too long.'

Laura looked about her curiously, wondering what it was that made this place a bad place. And if it was bad, then why had her mother brought her here? The streets were unloved, scattered about with overflowing dustbins. An unpleasant odour hung in the air, causing her nose to wrinkle, but she couldn't see anything that made it a bad place.

'What place is it?' she asked, struggling to regain her breath.

'Never mind, Laura. Just don't tell anybody where we've been this morning. Especially not your grandma, do you hear?'

'But Mummy!'

Laura tripped over a loose cobble as they dodged around a lamppost to avoid a mangy dog and they both nearly fell. She heard her mother's impatient sigh and suddenly she was being scooped up and carried, clutched too tightly in Elizabeth's arms. She was a thin child and didn't weigh much, but there was a certain amount of humiliation at being picked up and carried at her age. However, she sat there, mute and brooding, in her mother's arms, hating being carried and hating her mother for embarrassing her in such a way.

Elizabeth Caldwell had never before found herself in the environs of the shipyard workers of Jarrow. She had been forbidden, as a child, to go near the place. Evil men and loose women resided here. She did not allow herself to think about it. It was sufficient for her that her own mother told her they were

4

wicked; folk who would undoubtedly go to hell when death finally overtook them. Heaven, surely, had no place for the likes of them.

Her thoughts were erratic today, swinging from the pathetic state of her marriage, her own miserable inadequacies and the frustration of employing a woman who was unreliable. Unfortunately, Mrs Flynn was too good at her job to let her go. It was really inconsiderate of the woman, Elizabeth thought, not to turn up for work like this. Elizabeth could not possibly cope single-handed with the preparations for the family luncheon. Especially on New Year's Day.

Mrs Flynn had claimed that she was sick, that her pregnancy was not going well. And that was a whole lot of lies, too, as Elizabeth well knew. That woman gave birth to children as easily as shelling peas. This was her ninth child, even though she wasn't much older than Elizabeth herself. She had buried four infants before their first birthday, and still she foolishly went on getting pregnant.

'Oh, Lord.' Elizabeth heaved a heartfelt sigh as they plodded on through dirty streets that were becoming narrow and gloomy, leaning in on themselves, cutting out the light. The cobbles beneath her feet seemed more treacherous with every step. 'How can people live in such squalor?'

Quite by chance she found herself in Dawson Street, where the Flynn family lived. The sickly-sweet stench of cabbage water was even more pronounced here, but there were other odours far more noxious that attacked her senses and sent her head reeling. She tried not to think about them and searched for number ninety-two.

A dark figure loomed out of the shadows as a man, shapeless and lumpy in worn-out workman's clothes, climbed the hill towards her. His head and shoulders appeared first, then the barrel chest and short, bowed legs that were the product of malnutrition and prevalent in the poorer working classes. Elizabeth kept a wary eye on the man as he approached. From a few feet away, he stopped staring at the ground and raised his head. He gave her a cross-eyed gaze and she caught sight of a dewdrop of mucous on the end of a thin, hooked nose before he sniffed it back loudly and wiped the offending nose on his coat sleeve.

'Mornin', missus,' he said, whipping off his grimy cap. 'Happy New Year to ye.'

He sniffed again, slurped at a globule of saliva that found itself on his bristly chin, then hawked and spat out a globule of mucous with apparent great pride and satisfaction. Elizabeth shuddered with revulsion and made to pass him, but he was in a convivial mood, it being the first day of the year and her being the only one about.

'Lost, are ye? Not from round here, I'll bet?'

'No . . . no . . .' Elizabeth stuttered, and thought how horrified her mother would be if she knew where her only daughter was at that moment in time. 'I'm looking for Mrs Flynn. Number ninety-two, I believe.'

He frowned, then scratched his baldpate that was mottled with moles, scaly blotches and grime.

'Would that be Maggie Flynn ye're on about?' he asked, and she detected the faint Irish accent that was more and more common in the area these days. The place was full of Irish navvies that drained the public houses dry of beer and spirits, and increased the population to satisfy the Catholic priests and the Pope in Rome.

'I think her name is Margaret . . . Yes, so that would be right, then . . . Maggie Flynn.'

The man sucked at the inside of his mouth and pulled at his bottom lip with grimy fingers that shook with the amount of alcohol he had drunk in the past few hours. It always amazed Elizabeth how well the poor could celebrate, even when they hadn't enough money to feed their children.

'Aye, well, just go down the hill a wee bit,' the man said, jerking his head over his shoulder. 'It's on yer left.'

Elizabeth thanked him and, lowering a relieved Laura to the ground, descended the hill with tentative, slithering steps, counting the numbers on the doors with their crumbling wood and flaking paint.

Before the war, even these working-class people had been able to afford a lick of paint, but the aftermath was still making itself felt. There was hardly a house that wasn't occupied by a widow and her children or a grieving mother. They had little or no money coming in, the men having gone, leaving nothing more than a name inscribed on a monument to the 'glorious dead'. Families, however, could not live on glory. It did not put food in their bellies or pay the rent.

As they neared number ninety-two, where she could already see that the door was wide open, despite the winter's cold, a piercing scream sallied forth. Elizabeth felt the grip of her daughter's hand tighten.

'What was that, Mummy?' Laura spoke in an urgent whisper.

'Nothing, sweetheart,' Elizabeth said uncertainly, licking dry lips. 'Just somebody being silly. They're probably still drunk after last night.'

Taking a deep breath, she forged ahead and by the time she had reached the door, other people had emerged on to the street, or were hanging from their windows, wondering what the racket was.

'Aw, Gawd in heaven, what a terrible noise,' said one woman, who stood on her doorstep, wrapped in a crocheted shawl, which she clutched about her with red, misshapen hands.

'Excuse me,' Elizabeth said nervously. 'I'm looking for Mrs Flynn . . . Maggie Flynn?'

The woman stared at her critically, taking in every detail as her enquiring eyes made a thorough inspection of the stranger. She might, Elizabeth thought, be aged anything from forty to sixty, but she was big and muscular, pretty much like the fishwives on the quay at Shields. One thing was certain. It was highly unlikely that she would suffer fools gladly.

'Who might you be, then? We don't often get your sort down here.'

'I'm Mrs Flynn's employer,' Elizabeth informed the woman stiffly and saw one ragged eyebrow rise as she became the object of close scrutiny once again. 'She hasn't turned in for work and she knows we're expecting twelve for lunch. I really can't manage without her and she's well aware of it.'

'I'm sure she is, hinny. Maggie isn't one to let people down.'

'Well, she has this time.'

Another scream assaulted their eardrums, exploding out of the Flynn household, and with it the same unsavoury smell that pervaded the air around the riverbank street.

'Hear that?' The woman pushed Elizabeth aside and stepped over the threshold of her neighbour's house. 'That's Maggie. She must be in trouble. There's been trouble ever since the start of this bairn.'

'She's in labour, do you mean?' Elizabeth asked, incredulous. 'But that's not possible. She can't be much more than six months — '

'Well, I wouldn't like to argue that point, but that's a labour cry if ever I heard one. Thought I heard the eldest daughter go off running hell for leather down the lane a few minutes ago.'

'For the midwife?'

The old woman gave a gruff chuckle. 'Eeh, lass, we can't afford no midwives here. No, that big lass of Maggie's can't stand pain or the sight of blood. She's no doubt done a runner. How about you?'

'Me?' Elizabeth drew herself up, thinking it

best to leave these people to their own devices, but before she could move, her arm was taken in a vice-like grip and she was being dragged, like it or not, into the dark interior of Maggie Flynn's house.

'Come on. She'll need all the help she can get. I don't see nobody else offering to lend a hand.'

'I really can't . . . ' Elizabeth's frantic mind was on the luncheon party still to be arranged, but then her mouth snapped shut with such force that she felt her jaw almost break as she took in the scene before her.

The light in the small living room glowed a dull, mustard yellow. Someone had knocked the gas mantle so that it swung over the bed of the woman who had just given birth. Elongated shadows cast themselves on to the browning wallpaper, and then shrank to dark blobs with every movement of the dusty fitment.

An older version of Maggie Flynn, probably her mother, had gathered together Maggie's children in a dark corner. She gave no sign of wanting to help. A young priest shuffled his feet at the foot of the bed, his expression a mixture of embarrassment and concern.

'Ah, Mrs Turnbull, thank goodness!' His face relaxed when he turned and saw the woman from next door, her sleeves already rolled up, ready for action.

'Out of the way, if you please, Father O'Rourke,' she said, pushing the priest to one side and pulling a reluctant Elizabeth Caldwell with her to the bed. 'This is women's business.'

Elizabeth gagged as the smell of warm, stale blood and perspiration wafted up from Maggie Flynn. At that moment in time, it was impossible to think of this woman cooking food in Elizabeth's pristine kitchen, six days a week, every week of the year.

'I think I'm going to faint,' she whispered and Mrs Turnbull gave her a withering look.

'You'll do no such thing. Anyway, the hard work is done for us. Would ye look at that now!'

Elizabeth kept her head averted, but couldn't stop her eyes swivelling in the direction of the bed. She had given birth to her own child in a clean house, in hygienic surroundings, with a doctor and a midwife present, and her mother to hold her hand. It had not prepared her for this kind of thing.

'Is it a boy, Mummy?'

Laura had been momentarily forgotten in the heat of the drama. The little girl was on tiptoe, peering curiously around Elizabeth at the gory mess that would haunt Elizabeth's dreams for a long time to come.

'Laura, don't look,' she hissed through clenched teeth and gave a pleading look at Mrs Turnbull. 'Please . . . You don't need me now, do you? I really must go.'

'Fetch me some hot water from the scullery,' the neighbour ordered, ignoring Elizabeth's feeble plea. 'Now, then, Maggie, lass. Ye can stop yer moanin'. Ye've a wee laddie here, though I doubt he'll see the day through.'

Elizabeth gulped and hurried off to the scullery, where she found a pan of water already simmering on the gas ring.

'Is he alive?' she heard Maggie ask, her voice void of hope.

'Just, but I'd say that it's a good job the priest is already here, for we'd have to send for him anyway.' She snipped at the umbilical cord, her hands working swiftly, then she began bathing the child and the mother with the water Elizabeth had brought her.

'So, what are you going to call this one, Maggie?' Her voice was rough, but kindly.

The priest's voice, by comparison, was low and guarded. 'Can we please move on,' he said, staring at his Bible rather than look at Maggie Flynn's weary face, or at the impossibly tiny bundle they placed in her arms.

But the mother was not looking at her newborn infant. She was looking, glassy-eyed, at the big man who had just entered the room, his square-jawed face flushed with fury.

'What does it matter what it's called, if it's not bliddy well going to survive?' he demanded and heads turned to look at him, bodies parted to let him through.

Elizabeth recognized the fellow as Mrs Flynn's husband. She had seen him only once before and hadn't liked him, even at a distance. According to her father, Flynn was a brutish rogue, in and out of prison. He found work where he could get it, but there weren't many places that would take him on, for he was incapable of holding on to his temper and settled arguments with his fists and anything else that came to hand.

Right now, he looked anything but happy and his voice was like sandpaper as he rasped out the words that were completely void of feeling. So, Elizabeth thought, this was the brute who constantly left his mark on her mild-mannered housekeeper. Mrs Flynn often bore the signs of his violence on her frail body, though if questioned she always claimed that she had fallen or walked into something.

'You've got to give the wee mite a name, Patrick,' Mrs Turnbull spoke up. 'They've got

14

to have a name to bury him with.'

Patrick Flynn curled his lip and snarled like a rabid dog, then he spotted Elizabeth Caldwell and shoved his face up to hers in such a manner she would have run from the place had she not been hemmed in by the neighbours arriving en masse to witness the spectacle. They crowded into the small space, using up the last vestiges of breathable air. This was as good an entertainment as they were likely to get for a while. It would keep their tongues wagging for months to come.

'What brings you here, Mrs Caldwell?' Elizabeth blanched at the fact that he knew who she was.

'I . . . I . . . ' Her throat tightened and she gagged nervously.

'Come to gloat over the likes of us, eh? Us what hasn't two pennies to rub together.' He drew in his breath and expanded his barrel chest. 'I daresay you don't have to worry, what with all the money that's coming out of that bliddy family of yours. It must be nice having a da with his own business. And that husband of yours did all right, didn't he? You go back and ask him about *his* war, eh? Ask him what kind of hero *he* was and see what kind of lyin' answer he gives. There's plenty what know the truth. Bliddy coward, he is, that's what.'

Elizabeth found her voice at last. 'I only came to see why Mrs Flynn hadn't turned up for work this morning,' she said with a proud tilt of her head, and as she spoke she pushed Laura behind her so that the child could not see the bed or the blood, or the dying baby, and was well out of the way of Patrick Flynn.

'Well, Maggie?' the priest pressed anxiously, interrupting strategically with an eye cocked in the direction of the clock on the mantelpiece. The clock had ticked its last tick years ago, but nobody seemed to have noticed. According to the bent hands on the fly-spotted face, it was always time for tea.

There was a long pause, then Maggie Flynn frowned deeply, took a deep, sobbing breath, and spoke.

'I want to call him William,' she said quite clearly and there were one or two indrawn breaths among the older members of the family.

'You can't call him William!' The old woman pushed herself forward and leaned on the rumpled bed, her face close to her daughter's. 'I won't allow that. Not William. Not that name.'

'If he's going to die, Mam, what does it matter?' Maggie said and turned her face away from the older woman's bitter eyes.

'Oh, for Gawd's sake, let the lass call the

16

bairn what she wants,' growled an old man from the back of the room. 'He won't be around long enough for anybody to care. Anyways, William Thomas could be a canny lad when he had a mind to be.'

'He was touched in the head!' somebody proclaimed and there were unintelligible murmurings among the others. 'If he hadn't hung himself he would have ended up in the lunatic asylum.'

'I'm still calling the baby William, after me brother.' Maggie was adamant. 'None of you knew him like I did . . . ' At that point in time there was a subdued titter of laughter, which she ignored, if she heard it at all. 'He was a good man. He looked after me, and I loved him for that.'

'It'll be written on the gravestone.' Maggie's mother pressed on with her objection to the name. 'I won't have it, I tell you. Any name but William.'

'The child's got to be named,' Father O'Rourke persisted. He was getting more and more anxious and impatient to get on with the baptism of the new infant before it breathed its last.

'William,' Maggie insisted and her husband growled disagreeably.

'Don't you start, Patrick Flynn!' Maggie said, dredging up her last ounce of strength.

'You never even met me brother, so how would you know anything?'

Patrick blinked down at his wife, so wan and fragile among the pillows and sheets that were so much askew a tornado might have run havoc through their cramped little house. He wasn't accustomed to having her speak to him in such a manner. She was usually acquiescent, to the point of being subservient. That was why he had married her, for he was a man who liked his own way and Maggie was easy to control.

'I might not have met the bugger, but I've heard how he used to lust after you, his own sister. And you let him have his way with you, didn't you? Everybody in this town knows. Why do you think nobody else would marry you, eh? It's a wonder they didn't lock the pair of you up.'

'My brother was worth ten of you, Patrick,' Maggie said, her strength ebbing away visibly. 'I'm still calling the bairn William. You know what you can do if you don't like it. And that goes for all of you.'

Patrick Flynn stared at his wife in disbelief and shook his head. He raised a dirty finger and pointed it at Maggie, the same finger he used to jab her in the chest when he needed to make a point. She looked at it in disdain, then he remembered the people gathered there, just waiting for him to live up to his reputation. With a sound like escaping steam, he lowered his arm.

'I really think,' said Father O'Rourke, 'that we must be getting on . . . '

So the new baby was expediently named William Flynn. A cardboard shoebox, lined with a discarded and discoloured pair of longjohns, served as a miniature coffin. Women wept openly and even the normally unemotional menfolk had eyes that were moist, though none of them would have admitted that they had been moved to tears.

'Give him to me, Maggie,' the exhausted woman's mother said, holding out wrinkled hands like claws.

'He's not dead yet,' Maggie objected sharply.

'He's too little to survive, Maggie. It's only a matter of time.'

Laura looked at the tiny object of their attention. The baby was no bigger than one of her dolls. And as she looked, she saw a tiny foot twitch, heard a whimper and a snuffle, making her draw in a sharp intake of breath.

'He's not dead, Mummy,' she said and winced as Elizabeth's fingers dug a warning into her shoulder, which she ignored. 'Why do they want to bury him if he's not dead?'

She was thinking of the kitten she had been

given for her fifth birthday, which had died the day after. There had been no twitching, no snuffling, no movement at all, even though she had willed the little creature with all her mite to live. This baby had the brightest blue eyes she had ever seen. They seemed to take in everything in that small, stifling room. Once, just once, they had sought her out as if they were trying to speak, plead with her to do something. But what could an eight-year-old do in a complicated world of grown-ups?

Maggie Flynn hoisted the baby up on to her exposed breast, kissing its golden head and pressing its lips against her large, brown nipple. There was a tiny murmur from the infant as the pink lips moved in a sucking motion, seeking nourishment.

'He's hungry,' Laura announced with a giggle and Elizabeth gasped to see her small daughter approach the bed without qualm.

'No, Laura,' she told her, pulling her away. 'Keep away now.'

'Let me have him, Maggie,' the old woman insisted yet again.

'No! I won't have you put him in that box as long as he's still breathing. And he is. Look! Look at that. He's feeding. I can feel the suck of him.'

'That's enough!' Patrick Flynn looked about him, a wild expression in his eyes.

'What's the use of wasting time? Put him in the box and let's get it over with. I've got to get back to work or they'll dock half a day's pay and I get double time at this time of year.'

The priest seemed to be more interested in the leather binding of his Bible than what was going on around him. He had witnessed this scene more times than he cared to remember in other families in his parish and it made him sick to his heart. However, the poverty and the ignorance that abounded in the working-class communities of northern England could not be fought with wise words. He decided that the only recourse was to pray. These people would at least understand that. He sank to his knees and bowed his head, one hand resting on the footrail of the bed. He made the sign of the cross and others did likewise.

Patrick Flynn swore loudly. He reached down and plucked the child from his wife's breast. She cried out and tried to grab the baby back from him, but he was too quick and she was too weak.

Then the strangest thing happened. The child's head went up and his gaze fixed on Patrick's face. For a long moment it seemed like the newly named William recognized Patrick, and didn't much like what he saw. He opened his mouth and let out a howl that was far bigger than his five pounds in weight.

'Dear Lord, he's a fighter, this one,' exclaimed the priest, jumping to his feet and taking charge of the infant before it was dropped. 'I think, Mr Flynn, we can rule out the cardboard box — for the time being. This little man is going to live after all, if I'm not very much mistaken. The good Lord be praised.'

Patrick turned to his wife, who was staring open-mouthed at the baby that had been pronounced on the verge of death such a short time ago.

'Maybe now you'll change his name,' he said roughly. 'That's the least you can do.'

'No,' she said, shaking her head and sinking back exhausted among her pillows. 'No, William it is, but I'll call him Billy.'

'Ah, God love 'im,' crooned Mrs Turnbull. 'He needs some booties for his feet. It's devilish cold in this house.'

'Mam's got a drawer of clothes ready in the dresser,' ten-year-old Collum Flynn said. He went to the drawer and rummaged about in it. 'They're not new. Nobody but me big sister got to wear new clothes. They've all been passed down.'

He turned and passed over a pair of knitted booties that all the Flynn children had worn when they first came into the world.

'Here ye are, Auntie Lizzie.'

Lizzie Turnbull sat down with the child on her lap and pulled on the booties, inspecting them with an amused smile.

'By God, them's mighty big boots for a little scrap such as he is. I reckon he'll be five before they fit him.'

There was a ripple of laughter, which the not-so-proud father did not join in. Instead, he barged his way out of the room and they heard his feet thudding angrily down the passage and the door banging shut behind him.

'Hello, little Billy!'

Everyone, but particularly Elizabeth Caldwell, gasped to see Laura go up to the child and kiss his cheek. The baby gurgled and latched on to one of her fingers.

'She's always wanted a baby brother,' she said, flushed with embarrassment.

'Ah, bless her!' somebody said.

'Don't hurt him, Laura,' Elizabeth instructed, her voice and heart full of anxiety, but not really understanding her emotions. 'He's only little, you know, and he's sickly.'

'Poor Little Billy Big Boots,' Laura said, smiling as the tiny, baby fingers curled around hers.

And that's how William Flynn got the name by which he was to be known for the rest of his life. And although he was never to be a big man, he soon outgrew the cardboard box his family had been so ready to lay him in the day he was born.

2

' . . . and there's this little baby that they said was dead, but I touched him and he's alive and . . . and . . . ' Laura halted her story-telling to gasp for breath. 'He's called Billy Big Boots because he's so small and they said his baby boots wouldn't fit him until he was five and . . . '

Laura always sensed when she had overstepped the mark. Her enthusiastic flow dried to a vague trickle. With an anxious glance at her mother, she bit hard on her lips. And waited for the telling-off she was sure would come.

'Laura!' Elizabeth shot apologetic glances all round and placed a hand on her daughter's shoulder. 'Such tales you do tell! I swear I don't know where she gets it. With an imagination like that she should be writing fairytales.'

Laura's grandmother squared her narrow shoulders and looked prim, as only she knew how. Her fingers tapped an impatient rhythm on the table, making small indentations in the highly starched cloth. Elizabeth gave a self-conscious laugh, and turned to the large but sad-looking pork joint gracing the centre of the table. It had been goose for Christmas and, as always, pork for New Year's Day, though it would have been a sight better had Maggie Flynn been there to do the cooking.

'But it's true, Mummy,' Laura cried out, mortified at being made out to be a liar, especially by her own mother. 'You saw him. He was like the baby Jesus born in the stable. Only it wasn't the Virgin Mary. It was Mrs Flynn.' She pushed out a brief sigh of indignation. 'And it wasn't Christmas either, but it was . . . it was . . . '

'All in her head! Take no notice of my fanciful daughter.'

Elizabeth laughed again, then frowned heavily at her husband, John Caldwell, who was reaching for the bowl of roast potatoes, but not quite making it from the low position of his wheelchair. He strained clumsily forward, succeeding only in upsetting the gravy boat on the pristine Irish linen tablecloth.

'Oh, John, really!' Elizabeth complained, unable to suppress her irritation at what she saw as his ineptitude, which she felt could be avoided but he did it anyway just to make her feel guilty.

'Leave the lad alone, Elizabeth.' Her father got up and filled his son-in-law's plate with food that was beginning to cool. 'There ye are, lad. You eat that up. God bless.'

Elizabeth and her mother exchanged glances. Each of them was thinking how humiliating it was to be married to someone who did not quite come up to the mark physically or socially. Her father, Albert Robinson, had at least started at the bottom, working on the docks at the age of thirteen. He now owned the biggest ship chandler's shop in County Durham. Albert was thought of highly, even though he didn't have a posh twang and, to this day, mingled with common dockers and miners, much to his wife's indignation.

John, on the other hand, had been a lowly clerk in Palmer's, the big north-east shipyard, before the war. He had never shown any inclination to rise to higher things. He was still a clerk when he married Elizabeth, but it wasn't long before his father-in-law took him on as assistant manager of the first chandler's shop, and then transferred him to the second in a growing chain of shops as manager. His rise to such exalted heights was the cause of much criticism and snide remarks about how useful it was to marry the boss's daughter. John Caldwell considered himself to be lucky. Elizabeth was, to all outward appearances, quite a catch as a wife. However, she wasn't the warmest person on God's earth. She was too much like her mother, steeped in Victorian, straitlaced propriety. John's bed had already been cooling down long before the debilitating paralysis had struck him.

'Sit down, Albert,' Mrs Robinson said, her jaw set firm. 'You're making the place look untidy.'

'Hmm?' Albert gave his wife a cursory glance, smiling vaguely. 'Are you sure you wouldn't like me to serve you too, eh?'

'Just cut a few more slices off that joint and be done with it.'

There was silence as they watched with rapt attention while Albert carefully but swiftly cut through the pale joint to its pink centre. The chiming clock on the mantelshelf above the open coal fire was the only thing to have a say in things. Unlike the clock in the Flynn household, this one still kept good time. The heavy brass pendulum swung to and fro and on the chimes of the midday hour it was everybody for themselves, but strictly under the critical eye of the matriarch of the family.

'Not too many potatoes, Oliver,' Harriet was quick to say when her portly, unmarried son took more than two. 'And don't give the child too much meat . . . No, Laura, you may not have onion stuffing . . .'

Eight-year-old Laura was the only one around the table who showed any spontaneous animation, and that was constantly squashed flat by the adults, who were of the opinion that children should be seen and not heard, if they were to be part of the proceedings at all.

'Do you think Little Billy Big Boot's family will be having pork for dinner?' Laura wanted to know as she stuffed her mouth full of meat and the gravy ran freely down her chin.

'It's not dinner, Laura,' her mother corrected her quickly. 'That's what the common people call it. We're eating luncheon.'

'Eeh, lass.' Albert gave his head a little shake. 'Where did you get that high-falutin' manner of yours from? The midday meal has always been dinner in my family as long as I can remember.'

'Albert, eat your dinner . . . lunch,' his wife instructed him, with a hot spot of humiliation appearing on each cheek at her blunder. 'Elizabeth is just trying to better herself and teaching her child to be the same.'

'Yes, I'll grant you that,' Albert said, sucking at his teeth and feeling in his top pocket for a spent matchstick that would serve as a toothpick. 'But there's no sense in going overboard, either. It's not as if she'd been born with a silver spoon in her mouth, or anything like that. We're just ordinary folk, Elizabeth. No need to put on airs and graces.'

'Oh, Father!' Elizabeth gave him a sickening look, and then turned to her daughter, who was tugging at her sleeve. 'Stop that, Laura, there's a good girl?'

'Mummy, how can you be born with a silver spoon in your mouth?' Laura's eyes were wide with disbelief.

'It's not quite what you think, Laura. Just eat your food and stop asking questions.'

'Billy Big Boots didn't have no spoon in his mouth. I saw right down his throat when he gave that big yell. There wasn't no spoon.'

'There wasn't *any* spoon, Laura.' Elizabeth took her napkin and wiped the gravy off the little girl's chin.

'Is that because they're poor?'

'Who the devil is this Billy character, anyway?' Oliver demanded, ignoring the grease that had dribbled down his own chin and on to his tie. 'Sounds like a blithering circus act.'

'Oh, dear, I really don't want to talk about it right now,' Elizabeth pleaded, her mind already replaying the scene that had taken place before her horrified gaze in that dirty, mouse-infested house. It had been quite sickening. Just remembering the smell that had emanated all around her that morning made her feel decidedly queasy. 'Laura, please, just eat your lunch and be quiet, there's a good girl.'

'This pork is undercooked,' her mother announced loudly, pushing her plate away from her. 'Where is that woman who works for you, Elizabeth? This is not up to her usual standard. You need to have words with her.'

Elizabeth bit down hard on her lip. 'I'm afraid that Mrs Flynn couldn't be with us today,' she said quickly. 'I had to do the cooking myself.'

'Good Lord, well, that explains it.' Her brother dabbed at his mouth and threw down his napkin. 'The woman hasn't left for good, has she? I hope not. Good cooks are hard to find at the best of times.'

'No, I don't think she's left,' Elizabeth assured him. 'She's just had a baby — today, actually.'

'Jolly good cook, that woman,' Oliver Robinson said, nodding reflectively as he sucked on a piece of pork crackling. 'This could be better, our Elizabeth, but it's not a total disaster. I seem to remember when you couldn't boil water without burning it.'

'Mrs Flynn has been giving Elizabeth lessons,' said Elizabeth's husband, who wasn't normally known for any form of conversation

31

since the war had robbed him of the ability to walk.

Not that a bomb or a bullet had put paid to his mobility. He had fallen from his bicycle while delivering a telegram to a bereaved mother. The army had rejected him on the basis that he suffered from 'nerves' and an erratic bowel syndrome. The Royal Mail, on the other hand, were glad to employ him, along with spotty-faced adolescents and conscientious objectors.

Elizabeth sat down and stared with brooding contemplation at the untouched food on her plate. She had been so angry with Maggie Flynn for not turning up as arranged. It had never crossed her mind that the woman might be ill. Nobody could have anticipated that a baby would come so far ahead of its time. She now felt terribly guilty for the uncharitable thoughts she had entertained before seeing the situation with her own eyes.

She glanced down at Laura. The child was tucking courageously into her food. There was no sign that she had been upset by what she had witnessed that morning. Elizabeth, on the other hand, could not get rid of the memory. It would certainly keep her awake for many nights to come, but then she never did sleep easily. She didn't know which was worse. Sleeping alone, or with John, tossing and turning, moaning and snoring loudly beside her.

'Please may I leave the table?' Laura put down her knife and fork on her empty plate, slid her bottom off her chair and stood to attention beside it, waiting for permission to be granted.

'But you haven't had your pudding, sweetheart,' Elizabeth told her, and saw the little girl's face twist in distaste.

'I don't like it,' Laura said, twisting her face even more.

'It's your favourite! Apple pie and custard.'

'No.' Laura shook her head adamantly, disturbing the thick, lustrous, brown curtain of hair that framed her sweet face. 'The custard has lumps.'

'How do you know?' her grandfather demanded with an amused twinkle in his eye. 'It's not even made yet.'

'Mummy's going to make it. She can't make custard like Mrs Flynn. Mrs Flynn doesn't make lumps.'

Elizabeth knew her daughter. She knew that if the child had made up her mind there was no persuading her one way or the other.

'Very well, Laura,' she said. 'You may leave the table.'

'Can I go out to play?'

There was a murmur of disapproval from

Harriet Robinson, but it had been a long, hard day, and Elizabeth knew that a little fresh air between Laura's luncheon and her afternoon nap would probably do her the world of good. In fact, she wished she dared accompany the child. The family festivities were always too suffocating for her delicate disposition. No doubt Oliver would, as usual, insist on playing games after the pudding dishes had been cleared away. Charades would be favourite, followed by pass the parcel and then a hand or two of dominoes or cards, where everyone would cheat and fall out and fight over who was the best player.

'Mummy?' Laura was waiting patiently for her decision.

'Yes, all right, but stay in the garden, do you hear? Don't go wandering off.'

'She shouldn't be outside on a day like this,' Harriet Robinson said sourly. 'She'll catch her death of cold.'

'Oh, she'll be all right, Mother,' Elizabeth said. 'Go on, Laura, but don't stay out too long. It'll be dark soon.'

Laura, however, had ideas of her own and it never entered her head that she was misbehaving. Well, not seriously, anyway. The grown-ups were busy talking about things that only grown-ups could understand. It was all too boring in the little girl's opinion.

Whereas things down at the Flynn house might be far more interesting, if only she could remember how to find her way back there, and be safely home again before the light started to fade. One way or another, Laura was determined to feast her eyes again on the squirming, red-faced, wailing little creature that they had pronounced dead.

But he hadn't been dead at all. He had grabbed Laura's finger as if it was the only thing that existed in this new world of his. He had looked up into her face with such an intent blue gaze that it made her quiver. She just had to see him again to make sure that he was real. In a funny way, she felt that this baby belonged to her. If they didn't want him down at Mrs Flynn's, she would bring him home for her mother and they could look after him together. She would love to have a little brother. She had asked for one time and time again, but they just looked sad or angry and shook their heads and told her to go away and play, like a good little girl.

The more Laura thought of the idea of seeing Little Billy Big Boots again, the more she liked it. She went off skipping gaily in the direction of the straggling streets where the Flynns resided.

Patrick Flynn paced the floor of the shabby front room in Dawson Street. His boots fell heavily on the floorboards, raising clouds of dust through the threadbare clippie mats that were strewn haphazardly about the place. They were so dirty you could no longer distinguish one colour from another in the tangled strips of rag woven into the hessian backing. He glanced frequently at his battered silver pocket-watch, the only possession that was entirely his when he met Maggie, and had taken her to be his wife. It was an act he had never ceased to regret.

'Well,' he said, stopping his pacing once and for all with an abrupt twist of his big body, his malevolent gaze sweeping over the occupants of the room, 'haven't ye's seen enough for one day? Divvint ye's have hames to gan to?'

There was a low muttering as people responded, making excuses, offering half-hearted apologies and help if needed. The only reply they got was a further narrowing of his pale, cruel eyes. Feet shuffled, anxious to be off. Patrick Flynn wasn't a man to mess with, especially when he had the drink inside him, and it looked as if he'd been drinking all night while he slaughtered the beasts down at Wilson's Abattoir. The blood from the animals was impregnated into his clothing and his unwashed skin, giving off a vile smell that made the strongest stomach heave just getting near to him.

He watched as, one by one, everybody except his wife's mother and the priest had gone. He jerked a thumb at the small cluster of children regarding him fearfully from the darkest corner of the room.

'Ye'll take the bairns to your house, Annie,' he said bluntly and the old woman nodded grimly, gathering the children to her and herding them out of the house with urgent, stumbling steps. 'No doubt our Maureen will already be there.'

He was speaking of his eldest child, a girl of limited brainpower, and the reason why he was rushed into marriage long before he was ready, and to the wrong woman. It had not taken him long to figure out that Maureen was none of his making. She was one hundred per cent Thomas, the result of Maggie's incestuous relations with her brother, if there was any truth in the rumours that had been rife at the time of her birth.

William Thomas had already hung himself from some scaffolding in the shipyard where

37

he worked. Given the unfortunate circumstances of his life, no one believed that any hand other than his own had been responsible for his tragic demise.

'I'll be back to see to Maggie,' Mrs Thomas called over her shoulder before the door closed on the agonized groaning of the woman who had just given birth, and the soft mewing of the infant in the shoebox by the side of the bed.

'You too, Father,' the big man said, fixing the priest with a mean, protruding eye. 'There's nothing more for you to do here.'

'Your wife needs comforting, man,' Father O'Rourke said, a pleading note in his reedy voice. 'And there's the child . . . Arrangements must be made . . . though it's still alive and only God knows why or how.'

'Ach, be off wi' ye, and yer religious bletherin'. What good does all that stuff do, eh?'

'Oh, come on, Patrick, man.' Father O'Rourke moved forward half a step and then backed off abruptly at a jerky movement of the irate man, whom he knew would beat him to a pulp with little or no invitation.

Patrick Flynn had a longstanding reputation for his brutality and it was a miracle he had not been put away in prison long-term before now. It certainly had nothing to do with the luck of the Irish, for even the other Paddies in the Tyneside docks area kept their distance from this one.

'Do ye not understand English, Father?' Patrick took a menacing step towards the priest and Father O'Rourke was out of the door quicker than he could say two Hail Marys. 'We don't need the likes of you and your black magic mumblings. What I have to do I'll do meself with no help or hindrance from nobody.'

The words of the big Irishman followed the retreating priest out of the door and could be heard all the way the length and breadth of Dawson Street, and probably one or two streets beyond.

Patrick's face twisted and he gave the door a hefty kick. So hefty, indeed, that it nearly came off its hinges and bounced open again a few inches. He ignored it and the cold that was blowing through the gap. Turning to the woman in the bed, he spat sideways into the embers of the dying fire. Sparks crackled up the sooty chimney and the baby gave the tiniest of whimpers.

'Right,' Patrick said, picking up the shoebox and staring down into it contemptuously. 'I've got things to do.'

'What are you going to do, Patrick?' The voice was urgent and Maggie's fear of her husband shone through it. 'For the love of God, give me the child. Let me have my baby.'

'You call this a babbie? Ach, ye're ramblin', woman. It's nothing but a scrawny, hairless rat wi' a red face an' . . . '

'He's your son, Patrick!' Maggie spoke in a soft, trembling whisper and her husband threw back his head and laughed raucously for a long time, until he stopped suddenly and his eyes blazed with liquid fire.

'So you say, woman, but I don't buy all this malarkey about him being born afore his time.' His voice was like broken glass. 'Besides, he won't survive but an hour or so. You heard what they all said. The miracle is he's breathin' at all. Even the bliddy priest thought that.'

'Give him to me.' Maggie stretched out long, skinny arms in his direction, her fingers plucking at the air between them. 'He must be hungry, poor little mite. I've got to feed him.'

Another laugh from her husband that was as cold as the air in the room.

'I'd say you've not got milk enough in those pathetic paps of yours to feed a mouse.'

'Please, Patrick . . . Oh, please give Billy to me. Let me love him before he's taken from me.'

Her husband hesitated, ruminating on whether or not it mattered one way or the other. He truly believed that the child would soon be dead, anyway, and right now Patrick would do anything to stop his wife's bleating. He felt like his head was caving in with the sound of her pathetic droning.

'Here, take it.' He thrust the shoebox at her and turned his back so that he didn't have to watch her lift the pathetic creature to her flaccid breast.

He tried to close his ears to his wife's crooning and the unbelievable yet distinct sound of the suckling baby. This wasn't supposed to happen. It was too weak, almost dead; *would* be dead soon. Yes, soon, please God. Patrick Flynn was fed up with being expected to provide for brat after brat, which Maggie produced as if he was some kind of money machine. And if this last one was his he'd be mightily surprised, for he'd only been demobbed six and a half months and even he could work that one out.

'Look, Patrick, look! He's taking it. He's sucking so hard on my tit I can hardly bear it. Dear God, he's a strong one, this, my bairn, my Billy. He's a fighter . . . just like his uncle was before he — Before they strung him up like a side of beef. That lad never took his own life. He wasn't made like that. I know it, and so do you.'

There was a palpable silence that fell over the room as the words left her lips, the force of them sapping Maggie of her last ounce of energy. Patrick's shoulders rose and fell and he gave a low, wolfish growl that grew in a great crescendo to an agonized howl. He turned, crazy madman that he had become, grappling hands going out to the child.

'That's it!' His voice was rasping, his eyes red with rage. 'I've had enough. Give it here.'

As he plucked the child from its mother's weak arms, neither of them was aware of the horrified gaze of the little girl who had crept, unnoticed, into the room.

★ ★ ★

In the Caldwells' warm, cosy front room, the New Year's Day celebrations were going along as well as could be expected for a family not generally known for embracing the frivolous on even the jolliest of occasions. They were, by chance or by design, rather staid in their approach to all things in life. Only Elizabeth's father, Albert Robinson, was aware that they had all been brainwashed over the years by the wife he had married in good faith because he believed himself to be in love with her.

42

He looked around the room now, studying them all, analyzing their natures, their moods. For much of the year he did not allow himself to ponder on the whys and the wherefores. He found it all too sad, this small group of good-living people, who were incapable of receiving any form of joy in their hearts. Smiling came hard to them. Actual laughter was non-existent, unless you counted Oliver's inane guffaws, inserted into the conversation whether necessary or not. Warmth and affection was something that occurred in other families. The Robinsons neither understood nor practised it.

What had he, Albert Robinson, done to deserve such a miserable, uncharitable lot? Laura was the only gem, but give her time and she would grow up to be just like her mother and her grandmother, no doubt. Their strict ways with the child were already tarnishing her, lowering her morale. His granddaughter was effectively constrained in an ever-tightening straitjacket of exigent rules and regulations passed down from mother to daughter. How much longer, he asked himself, would it be before that pretty, smiling face lost its innocent vitality?

His wife had inherited her rigid, maudlin personality from her forebears. Their daughter, too. He could only pray that his little

43

granddaughter would escape it. But he wasn't a praying man. Religious faith, all that stuff, was beyond him. The only thing he understood was work. That and being a clean, honest, decent man. It wasn't enough.

Albert gave a sound like steam escaping from a train. It was a suppressed angry, frustrated sound. He would like to give his wife a good talking to, shake some sense into her silly old head. But it was far too late for that, as it was for his daughter too. Instead, he picked up the poker and stabbed at the burning coals in the grate, making sparks, cinders and ash fly up the chimney and scatter on to the hearth, covering his slippers and burning tiny holes into his new knitted socks that Harriet had given him for Christmas. They were too big and curled up inside his shoes. And the wool made his feet itch. But he wore them because it was easier than facing his wife's emotions if he let it be known that he didn't appreciate her gift.

'Oh, Father! What on earth are you doing?' Elizabeth came scuttling over, a rattling tray in her hands, bearing tiny glasses of port and a platter of cheese. 'Look, there's some hot cinders on the rug. Oh, you are so careless. Mum gave us that rug. She'll go mad when she finds out.'

'Oh, God help us,' Albert said, though he

said it with no particular emphasis or feeling. 'Oliver, pass me the fire irons, will you? Quick, before your mother sees it.'

'Here, let me do it.' Oliver picked up the tongs and coal shovel and fumbled with the cinder that was already burning into the rug and causing the air to be filled with a strong smell of singeing.

'Too late,' Albert sighed when he saw the small but very obvious burn left by the cinder. 'I'm sorry, lass.'

'Oh, I'm sure you didn't do it on purpose, Father,' Elizabeth said tightly. She was doing her best to be forgiving, but her lips were drawn tight over her teeth and she avoided meeting his eyes.

'Put something over it,' his son-in-law suggested, handing over the thick book he had been reading. 'Take this.'

Albert gave John a grateful look and covered the burn with the book just as his wife entered, clean and neat, having changed her dress in favour of a tweed skirt and a beige twin set with amber beads. It wasn't unusual for her to wear two or three different outfits in a day. Even during the war she had managed to do it. She called it 'having pride in one's appearance'. Albert called it something else, but had never dared voice his opinion of such strangely obsessive behaviour.

But they should have known better than to try and fool Harriet. She sniffed at the air suspiciously and drew back her long chin, her small eyes darting this way and that.

'What is that awful smell?'

'What smell?' Albert said, trying to place himself between his wife and the damaged rug. 'I can't smell anything.'

'Something's burning!' She looked from one to the other of them.

'Maybe you've left the gas on in the kitchen,' Oliver said blandly, staring her right in the eye unwaveringly, but she wasn't taken in.

'Nonsense! I don't do things like that.'

'No, I suppose you don't, Mother. Quite right.' Oliver stood shoulder to shoulder with his father, happy in the knowledge that if there was to be a telling-off, he would not, this time at least, be in the line of fire.

'Perhaps somebody's burning some rubbish outside,' John said and they all turned to look at him, so he raised his eyebrows and shrugged his shoulders. 'Well, it's possible.'

Harriet was still sniffing the air, determined to find the cause of her displeasure. Albert decided that it might be better, after all, to come clean and get it over with. He could then make his escape up to his allotment and smoke a Christmas cheroot in peace with whoever else was there.

He and his pals had a few bottles stashed away up there. It was their crisis supply, saved and stored carefully out of the way of nosey wives. There were candles, too, for light, and enough old timber to make the odd fire for added warmth. Albert found that he was spending more and more time up there now that he was officially retired. He still showed his face down at the chandler shops, however. It kept everybody on their toes.

'What's that book doing on the floor?' Harriet asked, suddenly getting her eyes on the offending object as she peered through the space between Albert and their son. 'Goodness, why is everybody in this family so untidy? Pick it up, Oliver, and put it where it belongs in the bookcase.'

Oliver immediately obeyed, giving a quick glance of apology to his father.

'Actually, it's my book,' John said quickly, retrieving it from his brother-in-law. 'It slipped off my lap when I dozed off.'

'All right, Harriet,' Albert said quickly, holding his hands in the air. 'Mea culpa! I let a cinder roll on to the rug and it singed it a bit. Nothing too drastic, apart from the smell.'

Harriet's mouth opened wide, then snapped

shut, and they all heard her breathe heavily through her nose, making her nostrils flare. Albert had often mused on the fact that if she flared those nostrils any harder she would send out smoke and flames like a dragon.

'Nothing too drastic!' Harriet's flat chest was heaving with anger.

'It's all right, Mum, really it is,' Elizabeth chipped in, hoping to pour oil over troubled waters, but knowing that once her mother started there was no appeasing her. 'Anyway, it's my rug.'

'How can you say that, Elizabeth? It's the one I gave you!'

'Oh, Mother, don't! It's New Year's Day, after all. Let's not have any unpleasantness. I'm sure the rug will clean up.'

Harriet's shoulders flexed, but she said no more on the subject. Albert's low-throated growl went ignored. He got up and headed for the door, newspaper in hand, but his wife already had him in her sights.

'Where do you think *you're* going, Albert Robinson? Running away, are we? If you were thinking of sitting in the lavatory for the next hour reading your paper, you've got another think coming.'

On cue, Oliver came in with his two-pennorth and what he said was guaranteed to make them all forget the burn in the fireside rug.

'Speaking of running away,' he said, in his laconic style, 'does anybody know where Laura is? I've just looked out the window and she's nowhere in sight. It's getting dark. *And it's snowing.*'

Elizabeth gave a small cry of alarm, horrified that she should forget her daughter. It wasn't at all like Laura to wander off, but unless she had sneaked back into the house without them noticing she had been out in the cold for a very long time.

'I can't see her!' Already there was a rising panic inside her, making her voice come out an octave higher than usual. 'Oh, God!'

'You stay here,' Oliver volunteered. 'I'll go and look for her. She can't have gone far.'

'I'll come with you,' Albert said to his son, glad of an excuse that would get him out of the house.

They came back an hour later, cold and worried. Laura was nowhere to be found and it was dark outside. The snow had turned into heavy sleet, driven before an icy wind. Elizabeth burst into tears when she saw that Laura wasn't with them.

'We'd better call the police.' John, who had been silent during their absence, turned anxious eyes on his father-in-law, and nodded his agreement.

'Aye,' he said. 'There's a call box two streets away.'

'I'll go,' Oliver volunteered again and his sister ran over and clung to him, but he pushed her gently away. 'It's too early to panic, Elizabeth. You'll see. She'll come hopping back in any minute now with a great big smile on her face and we'll all be relieved and embarrassed for bothering the men in blue for nothing on New Year's Day.'

He left them all looking at each other helplessly. Even Harriet was bereft of words as they waited for Oliver to return from the telephone kiosk. Once or twice she looked down at the scorched rug and clicked her tongue, but said nothing.

3

Laura Caldwell, at eight, had a surprisingly mature intelligence for her age despite living the sheltered, coddled life of an only child. She knew that what she was witnessing in Dawson Street on that New Year's Day was evil and wrong.

When the big man grabbed the tiny baby in his rough hands and went off with it into the next room, a great fear came over Laura. Instinct immediately told her that something bad was about to happen. And she was the only person there who could stop it.

'No, no!' She bounded after him with terrified cries. 'Don't hurt him. Please don't hurt him!'

The woman in the bed hardly had the strength to lift her head, but she was observing the little girl intently. Her face contorted as she, too, tried to cry out, but she was too weak, all her strength, physical and mental, sapped from her.

Laura reached the bed and tugged at the grubby, stained bedcovers, wanting to rouse the woman into some sort of action, but it seemed an impossible task. Her fingers were

51

too small and she wasn't strong enough to shift the quilt, let alone the woman.

'Mrs Flynn, stop him!' Laura screamed at the top of her voice. 'That man's going to hurt Billy! We can't let him, we can't!'

Maggie Flynn raised herself on one elbow, and then sank back with a groan before she could get one leg out of the bed. She, too, was unable to push aside the top-heavy quilt that was pinning her down. She gave up the struggle with a grunt.

'But the bairn's dead already, pet,' she said wearily.

'No, he isn't, Mrs Flynn. He isn't!'

'He will be soon.' The woman sank further into the bed, then they both stiffened at the sound of a weak baby cry, no stronger than the mew of a kitten.

'See? I told you he wasn't dead, Mrs Flynn, but Mr Flynn's going to hurt him . . .' Laura gasped for breath. 'He might kill him, Mrs Flynn. Poor Little Billy Big Boots. You can't let him die. You can't!'

Maggie Flynn lay for a few long seconds, staring up at the ceiling, and then her hands curled into fists as she beat the bed on either side of her, magically regaining some of her lost resilience.

'Go for help, Laura,' she said finally. 'Get help, lass. Oh, for God's sake, get help!'

Before Laura could move, Mr Flynn was back, casting about him for something he desperately needed. He grabbed a pillow from beneath his wife's head and started with it back to the scullery from where there came more faint mewing from the newborn infant.

Laura followed the man, not knowing why she should do so, but it seemed the only thing to do. Mrs Flynn had begged her to go for help, but she didn't know anybody round here and the people spoke with such a thick accent she couldn't understand them half the time.

Patrick Flynn was standing at the deep stone sink, peering down at something that Laura couldn't see. He slowly raised the pillow and started to bring it down, an expression of determination fixed on his grizzly face. A soft whimper made him hesitate and it was then that Laura summoned all her courage and made her presence felt.

The little girl attacked the man from behind, pulling at his clothes, screaming at him to leave the baby alone. The assault took Patrick by surprise and knocked him off balance. He tried to swat her away as he would swat a bothersome fly. The damned little busybody had seen what he was about to do. He couldn't let her get away. She would tell on him and he'd land back in prison, where he'd already spent too much time.

Patrick threw the pillow to the floor and went for Laura, but he was a big, lumbering giant of a man and she was nimble enough to dodge his frantic lunges. She fled for the back door, which was the nearest exit to the street, but it was bolted and her child's fingers couldn't manipulate it quickly enough.

She felt his hands on her, gripping her, pulling her away and lifting her high off the ground. One of his forearms came around from behind as he struggled to keep the wriggling, kicking child still and quiet. Laura's sharp little teeth found purchase on a piece of his flesh. She didn't stop to think what she was doing or whether her mother or her grandmother would approve. She bit down hard, drawing blood, the taste of it like salty iron in her mouth. With a yowl of pain he dropped her on the hard flagstone floor.

Someone was banging on the door, the thuds so frantic that the worn wooden timbers moved and shed dust and flakes of paint. Laura screamed, but she still couldn't get the door open, so she was once more dodging the grasping hands of Patrick Flynn as she tried to get out of that nightmare house.

They both came to an abrupt halt at the

pale apparition standing just inside the scullery door.

'Let the bairn go, Patrick.'

Maggie Flynn, looking like a ghostly wraith rather than a human being, spoke in a hoarse whisper that had more menace in it than all the raised voices in the world could instil. Whether it was just the shattered emotion of the moment, or whether it was a temporary thing, the frail, subservient wife had gone, replaced by one of remarkable courage.

Laura's eyes were bright round marbles standing out on stalks as she watched the woman slowly raise her hand, and in it was a long, sharp carving knife. Laura had seen such a knife only half an hour ago when she watched her granddad slice through the pork with it.

'Aw, get away wi' ye, woman!' Patrick shouted in disbelief. 'Put the bliddy gully down afore ye hurt somebody.'

Patrick started to laugh, but he looked uncertain and Laura took the opportunity to slip through the doorway into the main room. At the same time, someone was coming in through the front door. It was a woman with an explosion of bright red hair and dressed in a way Laura had never seen before. She looked almost as crazy as Mr Flynn, the child thought, making her mouth into a large 'Oh!'

though no sound was emitted.

'What's goin' on here?' the woman shouted, looking beyond Laura to the scullery where there was some kind of scuffle taking place.

The woman teetered forward on shoes that weren't made for walking, but made her look taller than her four foot ten inches. Laura got a whiff of perfume as she went past. It was kind of sour and flowery all at the same time. Not at all like the fresh-smelling eau de cologne her mother favoured.

'What the hell are you doing here?' Patrick Flynn demanded as the newcomer, followed closely by the petrified Laura, entered the scullery.

Maggie Flynn was lying on the floor, trying to crawl up the wall. Her hands and her nightdress were covered in blood and the knife lay a few feet away from her under the sink. Her foot had knocked over the slop bucket and there was brown, murky liquid flowing over the floor, giving off an unbelievable stench. Patrick Flynn once more had the baby in his hands, holding the child as if he were about to throw him at the wall.

'No, Patrick,' the red-haired woman said firmly. 'Give the bairn here.'

He stared at her uncomprehendingly, as if turned to stone. None of them moved; none of them even dared to breathe.

'He's going to kill Billy Big Boots,' Laura murmured, clinging like a limpet to the woman's coat at the back, peering around her ample hips, and not believing her eyes. She wished with all her heart that her mother were there to put things right. Better still, she wished she had never come, and how was she going to be able to tell them back home what had happened without getting herself into a terrible lot of trouble?

'Is he, indeed?' The red-haired woman punched her fists into her sides and drew herself up another inch or two until her head came level with Patrick Flynn's shoulders.

'Divvint be daft,' Patrick said, his voice shaking as his Adam's apple moved up and down erratically. 'You don't want to believe what that little brat says. Who is she, anyway?'

'He put the pillow over Billy's face,' Laura insisted. 'Poor Billy couldn't breathe.'

'Did he now?' The woman held out her arms and never let her eyes stray from Patrick's face. 'I'll take that baby now, Patrick Flynn. We don't want no more trouble with the police, now, do we? There's been enough of that in this family because of you.'

Another long silence ensued and Laura could feel her own heart pumping away madly in her chest as she pressed even more firmly against this strange lady who seemed to be in charge of the situation.

Patrick threw back his head and gave a short, mirthless laugh. 'Colleen, Colleen! You're the last person in this street to get involved with the police.'

'I tell you, if you don't give me that bairn I'll shop you good and proper and to hell with the consequences.'

Laura winced at the use of a word she knew would have been frowned on by her mother and would have shocked her grandmother white-faced. But she continued to cling to the woman's skirts, not daring to move for fear that Mr Flynn would drop Billy and charge after her again.

'Oh, Patrick!' wailed Maggie Flynn from her slumped position on the floor, a stream of pee issuing from her and forming a steaming, frothy puddle as it mingled with the blood and the slops. 'Oh, Patrick, don't do this. I love you, Patrick. I'll do anything you want. Just leave the bairn be.'

But Patrick wasn't in the mood to listen to his wife's pleading. She could have promised him the moon and it would have made no difference. Not with Colleen Maguire standing there threatening to snitch on him. And knowing *her* the way he did, she wouldn't hesitate to carry out the threat, even if it did land her in a whole load of trouble. He wasn't going to take the chance that the police might not believe a common prostitute. If the truth be known, half the force could claim to be on intimate terms with the damned whore. She was curiously popular on all levels with her reputation of being an honest, caring soul, which was more than could be said for the majority of her fellow streetwalkers.

'Here!' he said, thrusting the infant at her. She took it and quickly cradled it to her bosom, rocking with it and pulling the loose edges of her coat around it to keep it warm in the unheated house. 'But don't think I haven't finished with you . . . or that little bugger either.'

He had addressed the last part of his sentence to Laura and she quivered with fright when she saw his great thick sausage of a finger jabbing the air in her direction. Her head was telling her to get away from the place as fast as she could. Her legs refused to move.

With one last disdainful glance at his prostrate wife, Patrick Flynn grabbed his coat and strode out of the room, anger stiffening his spine. Almost wrenching it from its hinges, he let the front door bang against the wall. The cold January wind immediately rushed in to fill the space that he had vacated.

'Shut the door for us, pet,' the woman said, giving Laura a little push, but it wasn't an unfriendly gesture. 'Ye're a good girl. What's your name, eh?'

'Laura Caldwell.'

Laura stood on tiptoe to push the bolt firmly into place after closing the door as instructed. Her heart was still beating fast and she was fearful of Mr Flynn returning before she could get away to the comfortable safety of her own home.

'That's a pretty name,' the woman said as Laura came back and stood before her. 'Now then, Laura Caldwell, can ye help us a bit more and take hold of this babbie till I deal with his poor ma?'

Laura's eyes widened. All she wanted to do right then was to leave Dawson Street and never come back. Not even to see Billy. She wasn't supposed to wander off. She knew that very well. Her mummy would be angry and worried and there would be trouble. And her daddy would go quiet and tight-faced, the way he often did. He would just wheel himself off to his room without saying anything. He did that a lot. And her mother would cry herself to sleep, which also happened a lot, whether it was Laura's fault or not.

'What do you want me to do?' she asked demurely.

She was looking in awe at the confusion of red corkscrew tendrils framing a face that was heavily painted with black and red and pink. Just like a clown, Laura thought to herself. She supposed this was what her grandma meant when she talked of women being 'all dolled up' and 'common as muck'. Her mummy only ever wore a little pale pink lipstick when she went out. Even then, Grandma Robinson criticized, but then she was old-fashioned. Grandpa Robinson called her 'straitlaced', but did it behind her back rather than to her face and risk being told off.

'Just sit down in the chair in the next room and take the babbie on your knee. Think ye can do that, me darlin'?'

Laura nodded uncertainly, for she had never so much as touched a baby before, and climbed on to the nearest chair. Baby Billy was placed on her lap and she tried not to hold him too tightly in case he broke. He looked so fragile and smaller even than Peggy, her favourite rag doll, though he was a good bit heavier.

'Like this?' she asked.

'Aye, hinny, like that,' said Colleen Maguire, and she touched a forefinger to Laura's flushed cheek. 'Your mummy must be very proud of you. I wish I had a daughter, but then, mebbe, in a few months' time I will have.' Colleen patted her swollen stomach and grinned. 'If it's a girl, what do you think I should call her, eh?'

Laura's eyes stretched some more as she stared at the woman's stomach, then at the painted face, thinking how pretty it was, despite the make-up. 'I don't know,' she said. 'My favourite name's Bridget, but Mummy says that's an Irish name.'

'Well, now, there's nothing wrong with bein' Irish,' said Colleen Maguire, herself born and bred in the shadow of the Ballyhoura Hills and proud of it. Though her life had taken a turn for the worse when her no-good husband had dragged her all the way to the north-east of England to find work in the mines or the shipyards.

So much for a man with foresight and ambition, she thought. With no jobs forthcoming, he had put his innocent young wife to work on the streets of Jarrow in order to pay their way. It was either that, he had told her, or starve. He had died without a penny to his name, six months later, struck down by the consumption he had brought with him. 'Bridget's a lovely name. How would you like it if I call my bairn Bridget, eh?'

Laura didn't say anything, but she smiled, and then turned her attention to the tiny baby moving feebly in her arms. She liked it fine that the lady would call her baby Bridget and she hoped she would get to see her one day. Maybe they could become friends, though if this Bridget were Irish, Laura's mummy and her grandma wouldn't like her to have anything to do with her. Well, she just wouldn't tell them, that's all.

'Come on, Maggie, darlin',' Colleen was saying, the words coming out on puffs of wind as she struggled to get Billy's mother to her feet. 'Back to bed wi' ye. I'll make ye a nice cup of tea to warm ye, then I'll take young Laura home.'

'Is she hurt?' Laura wanted to know, remembering the knife and the blood.

'No, pet. Just a cut or two on her hands where that bliddy husband of hers pulled the knife from her. It's to be hoped ye got him good, Maggie, and that it wasn't all your blood on his shirt.'

'I think I cut him bad, Colleen,' the woman whispered tearfully.

'Good! He deserved it.'

'Don't leave me . . . please don't go . . . ' Maggie gripped Colleen's wrists as Colleen deposited her as best she could on the big double bed in the front room that complained with a loud jangle of springs. 'I know what . . . who you are, but I beg of you, don't leave me. He'll kill the bairn.'

'He'll not kill the bairn. Trust me.' Colleen bustled about the place as if she was at home, boiling water in a big brass kettle on the stove and spooning tea into the brown earthenware teapot. 'He's killed once before and he knows I'll keep my word if he does it again.'

'W-what do you mean? Who did he kill?'

'Never you mind, but ye'er better wi'out the likes of Patrick Flynn. All of us are.' She turned her back on the woman in the bed and remained silent until the tea was mashed and poured. 'There ye are. Come on, Laura. Let's give Mrs Flynn back her babbie and I'll see ye home.'

Laura was appalled. 'But what if Mr Flynn comes back?'

'He won't. Believe me. If I know that sod, he'll be long gone, and good riddance.'

She lifted the baby from the child's arms with unexpected gentleness and her eyes became moist as she gazed down on the tiny scrap of humanity before returning him to his mother.

'Don't worry, Maggie,' she said, gently massaging the thin shoulder of the sick woman. 'I'll call on yer mam and tell her to come round right away. She'll take care of you and the new bairn.'

And then, taking Laura's clammy hand tightly in hers, she hurried the little girl out into the gathering dusk of the January afternoon. Once again, Laura found herself being transported at speed through the darkening back streets of Jarrow to the more sedate terraces where she lived. And where her mother was no doubt frantic with worry, not knowing where she was.

★ ★ ★

It was already dark when Laura's distraught family answered the door to Colleen Maguire's knocking. Elizabeth Caldwell took one look at her daughter and was overtaken with a great bout of weeping. Harriet Robinson, not one to show much emotion, sniffled into her hankie. Their eyes were already swollen and red-rimmed. It was Laura's grandfather who took control of the situation in his own inimitably calm way.

'Come in,' he said to Colleen Maguire, who hesitated, but he beckoned to her in a kindly manner, so she stepped over the threshold, appreciating the blissful warmth of a house heated with real coal and with no smell or feel of damp. 'Now then, young woman. Tell us what happened.'

'Albert!' his wife cried out, taken aback at seeing the likes of Colleen Maguire in the living room. 'What are you doing, asking this

. . . this *person* into our daughter's home?'

She looked at Colleen Maguire as if she were the lowest of the low. Colleen was used to such reactions from the so-called 'better' people of the town. She didn't flinch under the hateful scrutiny, but placed a hand on her hip and stuck out her chin defiantly.

'This *person*, as you put it,' Albert said to his wife, 'has brought Laura back to us in one piece. I don't know about anybody else, but I need to know what has been going on since the little one left this house two hours ago.'

'But, Father, she's . . . well, she's . . . ' Elizabeth's voice quivered in her throat as she gathered Laura up into her arms and glowered darkly at the red-haired woman who had delivered her. 'I'll take Laura to the doctor's in the morning and have him check her over. He'll know if she's been . . . ' She gagged, unable to say the words that were going round and round in her head.

'It doesn't matter what I am, missus,' Colleen said with a proud tilt of her head. 'The bairn saved the life of the Flynn baby today and I made sure she got home safely. That's all.' She gave a wry smile. 'Though you might want to wash her mouth out, for she bit Patrick Flynn as well as any dog could. He'll certainly not forget her in a hurry.'

The group in the hall separated as there

was the distinct squeak of a wheelchair and John Caldwell propelled himself forward. He and Colleen stared blankly at one another, and then John's expression froze.

'What's going on?' he asked, his voice so tight he might have had a hand strangling him as he spoke.

'Sure and I found the bairn at the Flynn house and himself ranting crazy-like, threatening to kill the newborn babbie. Twas Laura here that stopped him. She's a real heroine, this daughter of yours, John Caldwell. Any man would be proud of her. I know I would be, if I had one.'

Suddenly embarrassed by her own outburst, Colleen Maguire dropped her chin on her chest and stared at her feet that were ill clad for the time of year.

'Mrs Maguire's going to call her little girl Bridget,' Laura announced. 'It's my favourite name and she says it doesn't matter that it's Irish.'

'You're going to have a child?' Everyone stared curiously at John Caldwell, but he ignored them and continued to give all his attention to the red-haired prostitute.

'Aye, I am that.'

'John, you don't . . . you can't possibly know this woman,' Elizabeth muttered, lowering Laura to the ground and turning to

67

face her husband, hands clutched to her chest.

'Well . . . I . . . er . . . ' It was John's turn to be embarrassed, but Colleen caught his frantic gaze and gave a raucous laugh that brought back all the attention to herself.

'Sure and there ain't nobody what doesn't know Colleen Maguire!' She gave them all an especially bright smile. 'I get mesel' talked about all the way to the mouth of the River Tyne. Aye, and beyond, if I'm not mistaken.'

'Christ almighty, she's a whore!' Oliver exclaimed and moved closer to have a better look, reaching out a finger to flick at a gingery tendril of hair that curled over one of Colleen's flashing green eyes. 'Fancy that!'

The women gasped and Colleen slapped his hand away. 'As if ye didn't know, mister!'

'Dear God,' breathed Elizabeth as if struck forcefully from above. 'What in the world is a common *prostitute* doing with my daughter?'

'As I said, I've brought her back safely to you,' Colleen said, her eyes narrowing and passing from one to the other of the group of people that had gathered. ''Tis all I'm doin'. Bringin' her back. Nothing more and nothing less.'

'You'd better ask the lass in, Elizabeth,' Laura's grandfather said, and there were more shocked exclamations from the women present.

'I'll do no such thing, Father,' Elizabeth said, avoiding looking at the woman who had dared touch her precious daughter.

'Just give her some money and send her on her way,' Oliver pronounced, drawing deeply on a strong-smelling cigar and blowing out a cloud of blue-grey smoke that acted as a screen between them. 'That's what she's after. You can bet your life on it. These women will do anything for money.'

'I divvint want yer money,' Colleen told them, pulling her coat more tightly about her and shivering convulsively. 'I just wanted to be sure the bairn was home and safe. She's not been interfered with. Rest assured on that score. On the contrary. Tis her teeth marks that were left in that murderin' bastard's arm and I hope to God it turns septic.'

Elizabeth and her mother both looked as if they were about to faint.

'Go and clean your teeth, Laura,' Elizabeth instructed, but Laura held her ground firmly, not wanting to miss any of the fun. 'Do as I say. Quickly now, and rinse your mouth out well while you're at it.'

Colleen smiled at her, then turned and started to walk away, down the frosted garden path to the gate that hadn't been repainted since before the war and creaked agonizingly on its hinges.

'Just a minute!' John Caldwell called out after her, digging his fingers deep into his waistcoat pocket and drawing out a few pound notes. 'Take this . . . for your trouble . . . and your baby.'

She gave him a strange look, meeting his gaze, but not looking at the money he held out in his shaking hand.

'Keep it,' she said. 'That *and* a clear conscience.'

'What on earth did she mean by that?' Elizabeth asked her husband as they closed the door behind her and her parents returned to the lounge.

'How should *I* know?'

John was back to being broody. The money he had tried to give to Colleen lay crumpled in his lap.

'You knew her, didn't you?' Elizabeth was finding it difficult to get her words out. 'John, where does my father take you on Saturday nights?'

'Just down to the Swan for a pint.'

'I've smelled more than beer on you when you've come back, long after the pubs have closed.' Elizabeth reached out and held on to the wall as she stared down at her lame husband. 'Oh, God, he hasn't been taking you to one of those disgusting places, has he?'

'Albert?' Elizabeth's mother was regarding

her husband with revulsion, hardly able to voice her fears. 'Is it true? You've been going down to the Slakes? Paying for your pleasures, like common ship-workers?'

'You don't know what you're talking about, woman.'

Albert Robinson spoke to his wife more brusquely than she was used to. He pushed his way past the two women and headed back to the living room, where he threw more coal on the dwindling fire and stood silently watching the flames and the sparks shoot up the narrow chimney.

'Father . . . ?' Elizabeth was beside herself as she burst into the room after him. 'Say it's not true! It can't be. You wouldn't . . . John wouldn't . . . '

'This isn't something to be discussed in front of the bairn,' Albert said to the flames, having seen that Laura was also standing by his side, full of curiosity to know what the grown-ups were talking about.

'Laura, go to your room,' Elizabeth ordered, giving her daughter a persuasive push.

'But I haven't done anything wrong, Mummy!' was Laura's plaintive cry in her own defence.

'Yes, you have! I told you not to go away and you did. You disobeyed me. We were so worried we actually called the police, who are out there looking for you and they won't be pleased with you either. No more argument now. Go to your room at once.'

'I'll take her,' Harriet said, her eyes shooting daggers at her husband's back.

When the elderly woman and the child were out of hearing, Elizabeth placed herself between her husband and her father and resumed her questioning.

'Well?' she said, holding on to her composure with difficulty.

John glanced up at her fleetingly, licked his lips, then looked away, letting his eyes wander about the room, fixing on anything but his wife's unforgiving face. Eventually, he spoke.

'All right, I admit that your father did take me to the Slakes from time to time,' he said sulkily. 'What do you care for this pathetic body of mine these days? A man takes his pleasure where he can find it, Elizabeth.'

'Oh, John, how could you!'

Elizabeth's stern expression gave way to guilt and remorse. A river of tears flowed down her cheeks. She gave a choking gulp and ran off, almost bowling over her daughter, who had crept back, unseen, into the room. Laura's soft brown eyes rested enquiringly on her father's face.

'Grandma's crying too,' she said, confusion

softening her voice to a whisper. 'Did I do something terrible, Daddy?'

John beckoned to Laura and drew her on to his lap. 'Of course you didn't. Don't look so scared, sweetheart. Mummy's just a bit tired because she's had everything to do. And your grandma . . . well, she's just your grandma and you're too young to understand.'

'Will I understand when I'm a big girl?' That's what they usually told her when she asked questions they weren't prepared to answer.

John laughed and nuzzled his face into her neck. 'I'm all grown up, Laura, and I still don't understand, but you'll grow up to be a woman, so you'll have an advantage over me.'

Laura listened to her father's words and frowned deeply.

'What do you mean?' she asked.

He kissed her cheek and hugged her. 'Take no notice of me. I'm just being silly.' He raised her small hand to his lips and kissed the chubby fingers. 'Well, now, pretty princess, what's this adventure you've just had, eh? Are you going to tell Daddy what you've been up to?'

But Laura, for once, was bereft of words. Suddenly she was gripped by an unknown fear that seemed to squeeze the life out of her as she recalled the big, evil-looking Irishman and his hands reaching for that poor little baby. And in the instant before he ran out of the house, the raw menace in his face — and his finger pointing threateningly at her.

4

'Mornin', Billy. Is yer ma in?'

Billy looked down from the top of the slag heap where he was collecting a barrowful of coal bits to keep the family warm through the night. He had already been on his rounds selling kindling, a penny a bundle, but he wasn't saying nowt to his mam about the money. The pennies were secretly hoarded in an old jam jar, which he kept hidden in the outside lavatory. There was a convenient space for it beneath the broad wooden slats that served as a splintery seat for unwary behinds.

At the bottom of the slag heap, shading her eyes from the watery March sun, was Colleen Maguire. As always, her hair was a glowing furnace around her painted face.

'Aye, she's in, Auntie Colleen,' Billy said, surreptitiously wiping his nose on the sleeve of his hand-me-down grey jersey that let air in through the elbows and was frayed to ribbons at the edges. 'She never goes out.'

'Well, I was just wondering, like,' Colleen said. 'The door was shut and bolted and she didn't answer when I banged on it with me fist.'

'She's probably gone back to bed,' Billy said, with a characteristic twist of his face as if he'd caught a feather up his nose. 'She was feeling bad this morning.'

Billy looked across to where his family lived. Rows of dowdy streets spread away from the river like black spider's legs. It had rained in the night and the dark slate roofs were shiny as if oiled, disappearing into the morning fog at the far end where the Slakes oozed into the sea. At the opposite end, he could see the squat tower of St Paul's Church by the river and, swivelling around, his eyes sought out the tall spire of Christ Church. That's where he was headed next, once he dropped off the coal. It was Sunday and Laura would soon be on her way to the church with her family. He'd have to look sharp if he wanted to see her. The Caldwells were sticklers for being on time. In fact, they were sticklers for everything.

All except the old man. Old Albert Robinson lived life at his own pace and, since the death of his wife, he had slowed down considerably. In Billy's eyes, he was all right, was Mr Robinson. Always a smile and a kind word, and sometimes a penny or two for doing a small job, like helping him dig over his allotment or pull a few weeds. Last week Billy had earned a whole florin from Mr

Robinson and his gardening pals. This week he hoped to increase his earnings to half a crown.

'Gawd luv us, Billy, aren't ye cold wearin' so little?' Colleen Maguire rubbed at the gooseflesh on her own bare arms and stamped her feet, which, as usual, were inadequately clad. Even though it was coming up to Easter and the sun was shining, the air still had a sharp bite in it.

Billy gave a shrug and came slithering down the lethally sharp cinder slope, his boots, fortunately, taking the brunt of it. Only once did he sit down on his backside, adding to the collection of rips in his britches that were as big as his boots, but not long enough to hide his skinny calves.

'Did ye want her, Auntie Colleen?' Billy sniffed, wiping his nose again on his sleeve. 'Me mam, I mean.'

He skidded to a halt in front of her and exchanged grins with the girl at her side. She was the woman's spitting image, though she had the advantage of not having a face full of mascara, rouge and lipstick. The hair was the same colour, though, if not a richer auburn. It reminded Billy of the rust on the cemetery gates when the sun shone on them. It curled around her pretty face like a burning halo and her cheeks and nose bore a sprinkling of freckles much the same colour. But it was Bridget's eyes that gave Billy a warm feeling inside. They were the rich green colour of the sea on a warm, summers day.

Every time Billy looked into them, he remembered the time when the minister at the local church organized a day trip to South Shields for the children of the Jarrow shipyard workers. Billy wasn't sure why he had been asked to go along, since his dad had never been a docker, but then Bridget was there too, as were some of the children from a local orphanage. He had overheard the word 'under-privileged'. It was a big word and he didn't exactly know what it meant, but guessed it was something to do with him and children like him, from a poor background.

It had been a grand day spotting seagulls, chasing the waves and tasting the salty water. South Shields was just a few miles along the coast from Jarrow, but that day had been so special. Just like a real holiday. They had all been sad when it came to an end.

Just before they were herded on to the open-topped buses that would bring them back home, they were given a supper of fish and chips ladled with salt and vinegar. Billy thought he had died and gone to heaven and, judging by the moans of pleasure from Bridget and all the other children around them, he wasn't the only one.

On the way home, they sat on the upper deck of the bus, right at the front, waterproof aprons covering their laps, wind and rain driving in to their faces that were glowing with health and happiness. It was the happiest day of their lives and, Billy recalled now, not even coming home to his mother comatose on the floor surrounded by empty gin bottles had spoiled it.

Bridget Maguire and Billy Flynn had been friends all their lives, ever since Colleen had moved into the house next door just before her daughter was born. They were like brother and sister. Where Billy went, Bridget usually followed. They had crawled in the grass together when they were infants in nappies, had cried together when hungry or cold or, on occasion, lost. They had a tendency to wander off, hand in hand, in search of anything more interesting than chalking pictures on slate paths in the back lanes, or finding cheeky things to shout at the women hanging out their washing on lines strung from one street to the next, where backyard faced backyard, and ladies *directoire* knickers dried on a line between, flapping in the breeze, sometimes bearing the sooty handprint of the coalman, who had passed, making deliveries from door to door.

People always knew that if they saw Little Billy Big Boots — for the name had stuck — Bridget Maguire wouldn't be far away. And it was a good thing, too, for the girl looked out for Billy like a little mother. Because of that people forgave her for being the daughter of a whore.

Colleen reached out and ruffled Billy's fair hair, which was growing thick and wavy on the top, though his mother chopped the back and sides short and patchy with the kitchen scissors. And that was a sin, because he had a nice little face for a lad and those bright blue eyes of his would surely turn the heart of some lucky lass when he was older.

'I thought I heard a bit of a rumpus, that's all, Billy,' she said. 'It was probably nothing. Maybe yer mam was doing the housework and knocked something over.'

Billy pursed his lips, pushing them out until they almost touched the tip of his nose, then he chewed reflectively on a piece of twig.

'Nah, she doesn't do housework any more. She says she's too sick.' He gave a small, lopsided smile, which said it all.

'She's still drinking, then, is she, son?'

'Aye. Maybe it was our Maureen ye heard,' Billy said. 'Or one of me brothers. They're on nightshift at the pit, so they were all still in bed when I came out.'

'Does Maureen still work up at Mrs Caldwell's, Billy?'

Billy nodded. Maureen had taken over from their mother at the Caldwell house two years ago, when Maggie disgraced herself by being drunk on the job. It had made Laura's mother as mad as hell to be without her famous 'housekeeper', but Maureen had surprised everybody by proving that she could cook and clean as well, if not better than her mother. The fact that she lived in the Caldwell house during the week and only came home on weekends made it easier for everybody. Billy made it his business to go up there as often as he could. Especially on a baking day. Maureen always made extra so she could slip him the odd iced bun or treacle tart through the window. And Laura was there, of course, and not averse to chatting with him as if they were equals.

Laura Caldwell had just celebrated her eighteenth birthday, but age played no part in the feelings that ten-year-old Billy had for her. She was not only the most beautiful girl he had ever seen, she was special in so many ways. What's more, she always made Billy feel special too. He truly thought that he would never be able to love anyone quite the way he loved Laura and one day, he promised himself, he would marry her. He dreamed constantly of the day he would be old enough to look after the girl who had, according to rumour, saved his life.

It was a promise he kept a close secret, even from Bridget. And Bridget knew all his secrets. Sometimes, it seemed to Billy, his best friend in the entire world knew lots of things without even being told. When he questioned her on this, Bridget would simply laugh and tell him that it was maybe the Irish blood in her, and wasn't her great granny in Ireland a clairvoyant and could tell you a thing or two that would make your hair stand on end.

'I'd better hurry,' Billy said. 'I've got to light the fire for me mam and then old Mrs Davison said she'd give me sixpence if I'd do some odd jobs for her.'

'Well, off ye go then, Billy.' Colleen dug into her capacious bag that she took everywhere with her. 'Here. These are for you.'

Billy stared in awe at the highly polished black Sunday boots she held out to him. He'd never seen the likes of such smart footwear, except on wealthy gentlemen. Even the priest didn't wear quality like that on his long, splayed feet, that always appeared to want to go off in different directions.

'Where'd you get them, Auntie Colleen?' Billy wiped his dirty hands down the front of his jersey and took hold of the boots cagily, turning them over to admire every angle of them. 'They're brand new.' He lifted them to his nose and inhaled the aroma of the new leather that was still upon them.

'Aye, hinny, they are an' all. One of my . . . er . . . my gentlemen friends died a couple of days ago. He was old, but he had very good taste and small feet for a man. I didn't think he would miss these, though the family might not be too pleased. They were probably planning to bury him in them.'

All three of them laughed heartily, then Billy's attention was drawn back to the boots.

'I didn't know people got buried in boots,' Billy said, breathing on the black leather and polishing it to an even higher sheen on his sleeve. 'Me granny wore her slippers when they carted her off in her box last year.'

'Well, there ye are, but say nowt. And don't let yer ma pawn them like she does everything else. She'll only buy liquor with the money. When's the last time you had a proper meal, Billy, eh? You're lookin' as if you could knock back a meat pie or two.'

Billy's blue eyes shot up and grew bigger and brighter. 'Have you been bakin', Auntie Colleen?'

Not even his sister could beat Colleen Maguire at baking meat pies. Her pastry melted in the mouth and her fillings ran with rich, meaty gravy, oozing deliciously as you bit into them. There was nothing like it to bring an ecstatic roll of the eyes and 'oohs' and 'ahs' of delight between each munching.

'I have, but don't you tell anybody, cos it might ruin me reputation around here. They all think I'm only good for one thing. I'd hate to shatter their illusions.' She gave him a wicked smile before teetering away unsteadily on the slippery cobbles, then called out over her shoulder. 'I'm off to work now, but I'll be back by dinner time, being as how it's Sunday and me day off. Keep him out of trouble, Bridget, bonnie lass.'

'But what about the pies, Auntie Colleen?' Billy called out after her.

Colleen flapped a hand at him over her shoulder and wiggled her hips.

'What pies are these?' she asked, as if she didn't know. 'Just you be sitting at my table on the stroke of twelve and see what you get.'

The two children laughed and waved, then Bridget took charge of Billy's new boots as he trundled his barrow down through the back lanes that led to Dawson Street. As ever, she walked at his side, chattering away happily, whether he listened or not.

'They're a mite big for you yet, Billy,' Bridget said, comparing the size of the boots with the size of Billy's feet. 'Just shove some newspaper or some old socks in the toes and they'll do fine.'

'Nah.' Billy shook his head and grinned. 'I'm going to keep them for a special occasion. My wedding day!'

'When are you planning that, then?' Bridget giggled with embarrassment and her cheeks flared up. 'We're both too young for years and years yet. The boots will have turned to dust by then.'

'No, they won't. It isn't that long before I'll be old enough to get wed. Only another eight years or so. Dickie Carter got married last week and he was only eighteen.'

'You got somebody in mind, then, have you?' Bridget's cheeks had become scarlet and her eyes were a little too bright.

'Aye, but I'm not sayin' who it is. Not even to you, so don't go asking any more questions, cos I won't tell you.'

The scarlet paled and the eyes lost their lustre as Bridget realized that she was not the object of Billy's affections. Since she was with him most of the time, she couldn't begin to think who the lucky lass might be. The only other person Billy was friendly with was Miss Caldwell, who lived in that big house on Bede Burn Crescent, and she was far too old for Billy. And too tall, though Billy might grow a bit in the next year or two and catch her up. At the moment he barely came up to Laura Caldwell's haughty shoulder.

'Billy . . . ?' She started to ply him with questions, but his mind was already preoccupied with something entirely different.

'Listen to that!' He had stopped in his tracks and she almost collided with him as he let go of the barrow handles and spun around, his eyes searching the hill to the right of them.

Faint strains of brass band music floated down from the town on the breeze and Billy cocked his head to one side, the better to hear it.

'It's just the Sally Army,' Bridget said. 'They always belt out their hymns like that.'

'I haven't heard them play like that before.'

'I'd love to have a go on one of their tambourines. They make a lovely jingly sound, like me mam's bracelets when she dances around the house.'

'They'd never let you in, you being a Catholic and all,' Billy said, and saw Bridget frown. 'And they don't let girls into brass bands, anyhow.'

'I'm not a Catholic, Billy Flynn,' she said, her fists punched into hips that were far too shapely for one so young. 'Me mam says we're lapsed Irish Oranges. You're Irish too, though, with a name like Flynn, so you're probably the Catholic, not me.'

They stood there, blinking at one another. It was the first time the subject of religion had come up between them and rash assumptions were being made on both sides.

'I'm not Irish,' Billy told her firmly. 'I'm a Geordie.'

'That's not the same, silly. Geordie's not a religion.'

'Sammy Green's dad says it is. And he says we're a race apart.'

'What does that mean?'

'What?'

'A race apart.'

Billy shrugged his shoulders. 'Dunno. I'll ask Laura when I see her. She's going to be a teacher. She knows everything.'

'Huh!' Only Bridget could make that simple response sound so scathing and full of disbelief.

'It's true, Bridget. It was Laura who said you were a Catholic,' Billy said with a sniff. 'And her parents wouldn't let her have anything to do with you, even though she was the one who chose your name.'

Bridget looked thoughtful for a moment. 'If you're a Catholic, you can't marry a Protestant, you know.' She peered at him from beneath her gold-tipped lashes and saw his face twist as her words sank in.

'If I was a Catholic, I'd know it,' he told her sulkily.

'How do you know if you're Catholic?' Bridget's frown deepened.

'Dunno.' Billy shook his head, and then regarded her with his head at an angle. 'Does it have anything to do with what school you go to?'

'I don't go to school any more than you do, Billy-too-Big-for-yer Boots. The teachers wouldn't have me when they found out about me mam.'

'Auntie Colleen? Did she do something she shouldn't?'

Bridget's chin quivered perceptively and her green eyes turned into deep, dark saltwater pools as she shook her head, unable to answer Billy's question. She knew her mam wasn't a bad woman. Colleen Maguire was the best mam any girl could have. She was certainly better than Billy's mam, and heaps better than that snobby Laura Caldwell's mam. Bridget always had clothes on her back and hot food in her belly. And she wasn't stupid either, not since one of mam's friends had taken her education in hand, which kept the school board man from the door. And when she could, she tried to teach Billy the things Mr Smith taught her, though most of the time Billy was too busy trying to earn enough to keep the wolf from the door. His father certainly didn't do anything to provide for them, other than the odd five-pound note he sent from time to time, wrapped in a grubby piece of a foreign newspaper.

Nobody knew where Patrick Flynn was. He had disappeared into the wide blue yonder years ago.

'Come on, Billy,' she said. 'I'm cold.'

They walked on for a few minutes in silence, then Billy was back on the subject of Bridget's education.

'Bridget, how come, if you don't go to school, you can read and write and know so much?'

'I've told you, Billy. One of me mam's friends teaches me. He comes to the house and he brings all the schoolbooks and things and he talks to me. He's nice. Mam says he does it because he owes her a big favour, but we're not to mention it to anybody or there'll be trouble.'

'Why? What sort of trouble?'

Bridget shrugged. 'Just trouble. Do you always have to be asking questions, Billy?' She stopped and turned, realizing that Billy was no longer beside her. 'What're you doing now?'

Billy was standing with his head tilted back, cupping his hands behind his ears and listening for all he was worth, his face screwed up and his eyes half shut.

'Sssh!'

'What . . . ?'

'That's not the Sally Army band,' he said and smiled broadly. 'It's one of the shipyard workers' bands and they're marching. Listen, Bridget. What's that they're playing?'

Bridget gave a little giggle. 'It's Mr Smith's favourite song. He sings it to me mam every time he calls in.' She did a wiggle of her hips, exactly like her mother did, and twirled in front of Billy's amused grin, singing out a few notes of 'Oh, Lady Be Good'. When she had finished, they both fell about laughing.

'Who's Mr Smith when he's at home?' Billy snorted through his laughter. 'Is that your teacher friend?'

'No. That's a different Mr Smith, but don't tell anybody I told you their names.'

'How many Mr Smiths does Auntie Colleen know?'

'Oh, quite a lot. Some of her friends are called Mr Brown and there's even one called Mr White, which is daft when you see how black his skin is. He's from Africa and works on the boats that come into the Tyne.'

'Does he wear a bandage on his head?'

Billy asked innocently, not sure that he knew what a black man looked like, but there had been a brown one once in Jarrow, his head all trussed up in bandages.

'That's a Sikh, silly.' Bridget heaved an impatient sigh. 'And it's a turban, not bandages. They come from India.'

Billy narrowed his eyes and gazed thoughtfully out over the river, wondering, not for the first time, what lay in the world beyond the banks of the Tyne, apart from Newcastle city. He had seen a red and white, smoking funnel slide up between the banks only yesterday. It made a hell of a racket when it honked its foghorn. The sound of it gave him a creepy feeling inside, though he couldn't understand why. When he told his mam about it she seemed to get a similar feeling, because she dropped the glass she was holding, and it was half full and all, and that must have upset her more than hearing the boat.

'Dear God!' was all she could say for at least an hour afterwards and kept going to the window for the rest of the day, peeping out through the shabby net curtains every time she heard footsteps. 'Dear God, help us!'

She had been like that, all on edge, since that last letter with the foreign stamp on it flopped through their letterbox. Billy remembered how pale she had gone on reading the

91

contents, but she wouldn't tell him who it was from. She tore it into shreds and threw it into the fire.

The tramp of marching feet could not be heard above the stirring trumpet, trombone and French horn notes that sailed cleanly through the morning air. But Billy felt them. He felt their vibration through the soles of his old boots long before the band appeared, resplendent in their royal blue and gold jackets and black trousers pressed into knife-sharp pleats. And shoes, not boots, black and shining like polished coals.

'Cor!' he exclaimed breathlessly. 'Cor, I'd like to look like that one day.'

The band was approaching the two children, where they sat waiting on a grassy mound. Then they were abreast of them, the big bass drum banging away and sweet notes shooting like stars up to the wide blue yonder. Billy had heard nothing like it. The sound resonated in his head, throbbed inside his heart and made him tingle all over with an excitement that beat anything he knew any day.

'Aw, just listen to that, Bridget! That's grand, that is. Isn't it just?'

Bridget wasn't so impressed. The music was too different from the songs that her mam and their friends liked to sing. She would have been happier with 'Red Red Robin' and 'Five Foot Two, Eyes Of Blue', or her mam's favourite, 'Black Bottom', when she would shimmy all round the front room kicking her legs and showing an expanse of plump thigh for all to see. 'Come on, Billy, before yer mam wakes up and starts hollerin' because you're not there.' Bridget tugged at him, but he didn't budge; only a piece of disintegrated wool came away in her fingers.

'Watch me gansy, Bridget, man! It's me Sunday best.'

Bridget's cheeks fired up again and her eyes became mournful as she looked for a way to repair the gaping hole she had created. However, the jersey had long since been beyond repair.

'Gawd, Billy, I'm sorry,' she said, staring horrified at the damage. 'Maybe me mam can get you a better one. You know, from that friend of hers that died?'

'Hey, I'll put the deed man's boots on, but me Auntie Colleen isn't goin' to get me wearin' his gansy an' all.' As if a spectre had walked over his grave, Billy shuddered convulsively. 'Howay, let's go home. Put them boots in the barra and help us push.'

Bridget did as she was told, knowing that it was no good talking to Billy when he was in this overexcited mood. There was nobody

who could get quite as worked up as Billy
Flynn when something tickled his fancy.

★ ★ ★

'Billy? Billy, lad, is that you?'

He knew the minute he heard his mother's
slurred voice that she'd been on the bottle
again. He had no idea where she got the stuff,
but had an uneasy feeling about it. If she got
hauled in for stealing they would be in dire
straits. The authorities would split up the
family. They couldn't rely on Maureen to take
charge. Anyway, his sister had let drop that
she was engaged and planning to get married
as soon as possible. So she wouldn't be at
home at the weekends after that.

Billy was the youngest in the family, and
still only ten. His birth had never been
registered, but he was one of the bread-
winners and proud to be so. He only
managed a pitiful few shillings a week to
match what Maureen reluctantly chucked
into the kitty. It was never enough. Desmond,
unable to find work, had emigrated to
Australia. He had taken one look at the place
and its people and caught the next boat back
to England, broken in spirit and ill with the
shame of his cowardice. The two other boys
were working down the pit and dutifully

94

handed over their wages every Friday to their mother. Neither of them had any envy to travel.

It was Billy who furtively supported the family, buying food before his mother got her hands on his earnings and squandered them on drink. And when the pickings were too small, he swallowed his pride and begged for food for them. He'd even stooped so low as to pinch the odd item. A loaf of bread here, a few potatoes and a cabbage there. When you were starving, pride was something you couldn't afford.

It was easy going up to the allotments at night to pull up a strategic number of vegetables. He always worked twice as hard for the gardeners the next day to make up for it. He suspected that the old men knew all about his capers, but they just puffed on their clay pipes, patted his head and told him he was a good lad, as if they approved of his thieving ways. And they were honest men, every last one of them. Poor, but honest. Like his mam had been before she took to the drink.

Maggie never questioned him, never asked where he got the food. She probably realized that without it they would starve, though she ate hardly anything herself and looked like a walking skeleton with her clothes hanging loosely over her bones.

'Billy?'

'Aye, it's me, Mam,' he called out, quickly shoving his new boots under the horsehair sofa that was sprouting body hair as thick and as fast as his granddad did before he passed away.

There was a clatter from the back bedroom, where Maggie had taken up more or less permanent residence these days. Billy heard the roll of a bottle, the clink of glass upon glass, and a muttered curse, followed by a heavy thud and a grunt. She had obviously fallen to the floor and, even for Maggie Flynn, it was a bit early in the day to be reeling drunk.

'Did ye bring us a bottle, hinny?' she said in that special, whining voice she kept for pleading. 'I've got such a thirst on me. Can ye bring it in, darlin'? I can't seem to get me legs to work this mornin'. I think I must be comin' down wi' sommat.'

'I've just got coal for the fire, Mam,' Billy was quick to say. 'And a few sticks to light it with. It'll keep ye warm.'

'Oh, no, Billy. Don't say you haven't brung us a bottle. I need it, pet, I really do.'

The whining was getting higher and thinner and her voice cracked as if she'd swallowed a ton of gravel.

Billy's brow concertinaed as he tried to think of something. The last time she was in this state was in the summer when she threw off all her clothes and sang and danced in the street in the middle of the day, telling people she'd caught midsummer madness, inviting them to come and give her a kiss to see if it was contagious. Of course, nobody took her invitation seriously and Billy had been obliged to throw a blanket over her and drag her back inside. It was the first time he'd seen his mother's naked body, or the naked body of any woman, if it came to that. It wasn't a pretty sight.

But then, Maggie Flynn was old and sick. She had to be in her forties and he wasn't so young that he didn't guess that her body would be totally different to that of, say, Laura Caldwell. Laura was slim and pretty and he wouldn't mind betting that there wasn't a wrinkle anywhere. She certainly didn't have empty flaps where her bosoms were. They stood out all proud and perky like chapel hat-pegs beneath her gauzy blouses.

His mother's voice sallied forth again and he remembered what he was supposed to be doing, though he couldn't imagine that there was any liquor left to find in the house.

'There might be some beer left in the scullery,' he told her, going through to the back of the house to look, knowing fine well that all he would find was a mounting pile of empty bottles.

It was while he was rummaging about among the full bins and empty bottles under the sink that he heard the latch on the front door snap into place. He couldn't remember leaving it open, so it was probably Maureen. The other lads would still be in bed, where they would stay, dead to the world, until he came back later with food for the supper, which they would scoff down before rushing off to do their shift.

He retraced his steps, treading as quietly as he could in case there was an intruder. The room was empty. Or so he thought. There was a creak as something heavy got on a weak floorboard, then inch by frightening inch, a head appeared, then a face, deeply tanned and just as deeply lined. The shoulders followed, wide and well padded. Man and boy stared curiously at one another as the stranger unfolded and stretched up to his full height, which was considerable. Next to Billy, he was a veritable giant.

There was no recognition on either side and Billy wondered if it might not be one of his Auntie Colleen's Mr Smiths, having entered the wrong house by mistake. But none of those Smith men had keys and this

98

man had let himself in as if the place belonged to him.

'And who might you be, laddie?' The man's voice was gruff and the smile he gave was suspicious rather than friendly.

'I'm Billy Flynn, mister, and what are you doing with my new boots?'

The man did indeed have Billy's new boots in one big hand. He gave them a cursory glance and threw them on the table between them.

'*Your* boots, are they, midget? Well, I figured they would fit me better, though they might just cramp me toes a wee bit. I'll put up wi' that, though. What did ye say yer name was, laddie?'

'Billy Flynn. Who are you?' Billy could hear movement behind him and a quick glance over his shoulder confirmed that his mother was standing in the open doorway, clinging to the frame and looking at the man with glassy eyes and saliva dribbling from her open mouth.

Maggie screamed and fell to her knees. Billy didn't move and the man stared at him some more, but with deeper intensity as if he couldn't believe what he was looking at.

'Billy Flynn, ye say?' Billy nodded, his gaze travelling from the stranger to the boots and back again. 'Well, I never did. Who'd ha' thought that that scrawny little creature would survive.'

Billy jerked his head in an uncontrolled movement. 'Who are you, mister? And them are *my* boots. Me Auntie Colleen gave me them this morning.'

'Yer Auntie Colleen, is it? That wouldn't be that bitch of a whore Colleen Maguire with the red hair, would it?' Billy didn't respond; he had a weird feeling inside. His instincts were telling him that this man was trouble and Billy's instincts were never wrong.

'Aye, she's got red hair . . . pretty like.'

'Well, me lad, it just so happens that I'm Patrick Flynn . . . your da, in case you're wondering. I've been to sea and me boat docked in the Tyne yesterday. I've come home and it looks like it's none too soon, judgin' by the state of yer ma.'

5

'Will ye have another cup of tea, Patrick?' Maggie's hand shook as she poured the steamy brown liquid into the best enamel mug in the house and stood back while he picked it up and surveyed it with a mean eye.

The boys were lined up against the wall, sitting on a long, rickety form. It had once been a pew in the little chapel on the hill, which had been allowed to fall into ruin because no one worshipped there any more. This had more to do with the sinking ground beneath the ecclesiastical premises, due to over-mining, rather than a lack of faith in the community.

'So, I seem to have me a fine family,' Patrick said, breaking the uneasy silence at last. 'You'll have to tell me who you all are. It's been a long time. Speak up, now. You, lad. You with the glasses and the pasty face. Can't hear you, boy. What did you say you were called?'

'He's called Desmond.' Billy spoke up at last, seeing that his eldest brother was having great trouble finding his voice.

'Can't he speak for himself, then?'

'He's bad with his nerves, Patrick,' Maggie said in a hoarse whisper. She steadied herself quickly against the old Welsh dresser, making the pitiable collection of crockery rattle tonelessly. 'It makes him stutter.'

Billy watched his mother in awe. He had never seen her sober up so quickly. This man who claimed to be their father seemed to have miraculous powers over her. And judging by the look on Jack's face, Maggie wasn't the only one to succumb to them. Jack was usually garrulous to a fault, but he hadn't uttered a word since being ordered to come downstairs, tousle-headed and half-dressed. He just sat there, mute and shivering, although there was a good fire licking at the sooty chimney.

'A boy with nerves! I ask you. Can I have spawned that one? You must have gone with someone else on that occasion, Maggie, me darlin'.'

'No! Oh no, Patrick. Never. I would never do a thing like that.'

'You wouldn't, would you? That's not what I've heard. No sooner had me boat docked and I was hearing the name of Maggie Flynn. Fellas not fit to wipe their backsides on me shoes sayin' how cheap she was for them as can't afford the real thing. Would that not be you they're talkin' about, eh, hinny?'

For answer, Maggie shook her head vigorously and Patrick, whether satisfied or not, decided to ignore her and continue interrogating his four sons.

'You. The one with the squint and a runny rose. Which one of my offspring are you?'

'Thomas, mister . . . er . . . Da . . . I'm called Thomas.' Thomas rubbed his lazy eye as if trying to wake it up, then wiped his nose on the back of his hand and then on his trousers.

'He can't remember you, Patrick. It's been ten years.'

'Aye, it has an' all. And I feel every one o' them years weighing heavily in me loins. It's a long time for a man to be without his wife.'

Maggie tried to speak, but only succeeded in some unintelligible mumbling into the cupped hand she held in front of her quivering mouth.

'You.' Patrick pointed at the third boy in the line, whose head came out of his jumper like the head of a turtle and his eyes popped out on stalks. 'You must be . . . let's see . . . yes. You must be Jack. You've all grown, except this pathetic little tadpole.' He swiftly passed over Jack and fixed his eyes on Billy. Billy returned his cold blue stare, unwavering and apparently unafraid, though if truth be told, he was having to clutch his hands under the table to stop them from shaking.

'That's our Billy!' Maggie said nervously.

'Aye, so he said. Who'd ha' believed it. By rights you should be dead, son. If I'd had me way the day you was born . . . '

'Patrick!' Maggie interrupted quickly before he could go on and frighten her youngest child even more with his wild ramblings. 'Billy, go and ask Colleen if she has a few biscuits to spare, there's a good lad.'

Billy didn't rush away. He took his time, all the while keeping one eye on the big Irishman who smelt of fish and brine and engine oil all mixed up with acrid sweat.

Colleen refused to believe him at first when Billy told her that his father was back. Perhaps she simply didn't want to believe him. She made no pretence of the fact that there had never been any love lost between Patrick Flynn and herself.

'He must be mad,' she said, tapping her forehead and picking up a variety of biscuit tins and shaking them. 'What does he want to come back here for after all this time?'

'He says he's finished with the sea,' Billy told her. 'He says he's come back home to stay. Me mam's scared, and so are the others.'

'But not you, eh, big man?' Colleen gave a short laugh, shaking out her long red hair from her shoulders and running scarlet-painted fingernails through the tight curls. 'You, Billy, are the one person he didn't expect to find here. If I was you, darlin', I'd stay well clear of him. We beat him once. I don't think he'd let us get away with it again. Patrick Flynn doesn't forgive or forget. Whatever reason it was that brought him back here, he'll be out for revenge and he'll take it at the first opportunity, believe me.'

'Don't worry, Billy,' Bridget told him, giving him a sisterly hug that made him squirm with embarrassment. 'You can stay here with us if you want, can't he, Mam?'

'Aye, pet. Billy's always welcome here.'

Billy's brows lowered as he let her words sink in. He scratched his head, making a mental note to steal a bar of that special soap that killed nits, because he was infested again. Laura wouldn't let him near her if she thought he had nits. She'd caught a flea from him in the summer and her mother nearly had a thousand fits. Laura was thereafter forbidden to leave the house, except to go to school, for three months.

'Why should I stay away from him, Auntie Colleen?' he asked as she placed in his hands a tin with half a dozen dry biscuits in it. 'What's he done?'

'What's he done?' Colleen straightened her shoulders and shook out her rusty tresses again. 'What hasn't he done would be a better question, Billy. I suspect he's done a lot more than either you or I know about too.'

'I don't know nothing, Auntie Colleen.' Billy scratched again at his head and his stomach growled at the thought of the biscuits in the tin he held. 'Mam's never mentioned anybody called Patrick Flynn. Is he really me da?'

Colleen's thin, plucked eyebrows shot up and he heard her draw in a deep breath, then let it out slowly.

'Aye, lad. Well, he was married to yer ma when you was born, and he left her the same day. Your Maureen would remember him, and Desmond. The others would be too little at the time.'

Billy heard a raised voice penetrating the dividing wall between his mother's house and Colleen's. His eyes rolled like glossy marbles and he licked his lips, for they had become surprisingly dry.

'I'd better get back there,' he said and started to hurry out.

'Billy!' Colleen caught up with him, placed her hands on his thin shoulders and bent down so that her face was on a level with his.

'Aye, Auntie Colleen?'

'You listen to me, Billy Flynn. If he lays a finger on you, tries to hurt you in any way . . . well, you come round here, even if I'm busy, or if I'm out. There's a spare key always kept under the doormat for emergencies. Promise me, now.'

'Why? What would he want to hurt us for, Auntie Colleen?'

She stared at him for a long moment, then she cleared her throat, straightened her back and patted him on the head.

'Never you mind, son,' she said. 'But you have to promise me, eh? Just let yourself in and lock the door behind you. Is that clear?'

'Yes, Auntie Colleen.' Billy gave a tight, grimacing smile. 'Ta. And thanks for the biscuits.'

Colleen nodded, smiling back. He had no sooner crossed over the doorstep than she shut and bolted the door. She lay back against it, her heart pounding, her mouth cold with fear. Who'd have thought that Patrick Flynn would come back after all this time? And why had she been such a fool as to move into the house next door to his family? She would have been better off staying in the hovel she'd been in. Though, when she came to think about it, she wouldn't have been any safer there. Wherever she was, she knew that Patrick Flynn, if he had a mind to, would seek her out and . . .

The thought of what that man could do to her, if he thought about it, turned her blood to ice. Not just for her own safety was she afraid, but for the safety of her daughter, Bridget. That sweet, darling girl was the light of Colleen's life, and everything that was meaningful and precious. If Patrick ever laid a finger on the child she would swing for him. She really would.

Swallowing dryly, Colleen went to the scullery, feeling her fear attacking the pit of her stomach and her legs. When she reached into a drawer, her fingers trembled so much that she could barely grip the knife she drew out and held up before her face. The light from the small, square, opaque kitchen window glinted on the worn blade. It was her old mam's gully, passed down through three generations, but it was lethal enough to put paid to that murdering swine.

Looking about her, she located her bag and slipped the knife inside, placing it so that it was easily accessible. There wasn't a violent bone in Colleen's body, but she knew she would be able to kill to defend herself and her daughter. She was amazed that that murdering bastard Patrick had survived this long, for there were plenty who would like to see him dead.

* * *

Laura Caldwell trailed her feet as the family walked home from church the Sunday after Billy had told her that his father had mysteriously turned up. He had come to see her yesterday, on the pretext of delivering a message to his sister, but Maureen Flynn had taken the afternoon off. She was walking out with the baker's lad and sporting a tiny diamond chip engagement ring that she was so proud of showing it was becoming an embarrassment.

Billy was nowhere to be seen. Normally, he would be hanging around the church grounds and would pop up as if he was there just by chance. It both amused and vexed Laura. She did not exactly appreciate the attentions of this ten-year-old ragamuffin, but ever since the day he was born, she had felt a strange affinity with him. A responsibility that had arisen on that memorable occasion of his birth.

Laura often slipped him a sixpence from her purse rather than put it in the collection plate in the church. And she turned a blind eye when his sister baked extra pies and cakes and left them on the kitchen windowsill for him to collect, together with bags of fruit and vegetables. Her parents would have been appalled to think that their daughter was mixing with the likes of Billy. Only her grandfather would have understood, and approved. Like Laura, he was very fond of the little lad who had survived against all odds. He had an air about him that you couldn't ignore. A certain charisma that made him special.

But the news that Mr Flynn was back in Jarrow wasn't the kind of thing she wanted to hear. The man had a black reputation that made everyone shudder the moment his name was mentioned. Her grandfather claimed that he was surprised the fellow wasn't in gaol long before now and warned Laura about him.

'He's an evil bastard,' Albert Robinson had said when she whispered what Billy had told her as they sat in church, the whole family in a line on their own special pew. 'God forgive me for swearing in His house.'

'But what did he do, Granddad?' Laura asked curiously, for she was aware that the memory of how he nearly suffocated his newborn son wasn't the only terrible crime the big Irishman was connected with.

Albert thought about her question, probably weighing up whether or not she was old enough or mature enough to be given a truthful answer. The congregation was asked to rise in order to sing The Lord's Prayer and on the line 'in presence of His foes' he leaned heavily against her, his mouth pressed against her ear, and whispered so that nobody else could hear him.

'They say that he was responsible for the death of his wife's half-brother, though the police said it was an accident. They worked in the slaughterhouse together and William Thomas ended up with one of them meat hooks through his neck. Somebody must have seen it happen, but nobody would come forward. Too scared they are of him. He's a dangerous man is Patrick Flynn, so you keep an eye open for him. Just be thankful that he left when Billy was born. Happen he'll have forgotten it was you that said he put a pillow over the poor little mite's face.'

Laura felt a cold chill creeping through her as if her blood was turning to ice, starting in her extremities and ending up in her heart. Only her grandfather would be so honest with her. He was the only one who believed, finally, what she had told of that day more than ten years ago. Not many people would believe the fanciful tales of an eight-year-old girl, but he had.

She opened her mouth, listening to the introductory chords of the organ, but found that she couldn't sing a note. The thought of what might become of her if Mr Flynn took it into his mind to seek revenge made her feel physically sick. Suddenly, her knees gave way and she sat down on the shiny wooden pew with a thud, frightening her mother, who thought she was ill.

'Come along, Laura,' Elizabeth Caldwell said as the church emptied and she moved on ahead, pushing her husband in his wheelchair. 'Stop lagging behind. Maureen will have the dinner ready and you know how we all hate cold roast beef and gravy. Not to mention soggy roast potatoes.'

Laura no longer had an appetite. She slowed her pace even more and looked frantically around her, searching the faces of the congregation. Billy wasn't there and neither, thank goodness, was Mr Flynn.

★ ★ ★

It was on Good Friday of that year that Colleen had the misfortune to bump into Patrick. She had been so careful, hiding behind the locked doors of her house, scurrying like a shadow up and down dark back lanes and alleyways rather than be seen by the one man who had ever frightened her, though she would never admit it to anyone, least of all to Patrick himself.

She should never have taken the short cut past the Slakes, but it was late and she was tired. The shipyard workers were long finished their toil for the day and were ensconced in the nearest riverside pubs, drinking their overtime pay and putting the world to rights.

It was an eerie world after dark, especially when there was no moon. Only the breathy swish of the tide coming or going made any sound, apart from the slap of Colleen's feet on the wet, sandy mudflats. The silently watching trees and rocks the size and shape of great bears that seemed to rear up appeared ugly and threatening.

Colleen veered to the left where the path wound itself between flats and quarry. When it rained the water formed deep pools here where the ground had been blasted and dug away, or just eroded by the swirling eddies of the tidal river. There were pools deep enough for a child to drown in, which was why children were warned to keep well away from the place, and most of them did.

Colleen quickened her pace as much as was possible in that place where the mud threatened to suck her down. In the distance she could see tiny pinpricks of light as she neared the first streets of the town. Over and above the sound of her own steps, there was, suddenly, a heavier *splat, splat, splat*. A quick glance over her shoulder showed her nothing. The darkness was too dense and a thick mist was rolling in from the invisible sea. She prayed to God it was only a stray dog, but she didn't allow herself to slow up and plodded on breathlessly.

The other footsteps were gaining on her, overtaking her. She rounded one of the bigger boulders and suppressed a scream as a figure appeared before her. The figure, too, gave a sharp gasp of surprise, then she recognized the childish giggle that was tinged with nervous tension.

'Billy Flynn, what the blazes are you doing down here at this time of night, eh?'

Billy wiped his nose on his sleeve and glanced all around him nervously, though there was nothing to be seen.

'Me mam sent me to find me da,' he told her. 'He didn't come home th' night and his supper's goin' dry in the oven . . . and burnt black too probably.'

'Serves him right, then,' Colleen told him with a short, sharp nod, then she reached out and patted his cold cheek. 'Come on home, pet. He's not here. He's probably down at the pub or . . . ' She was about to say that Patrick was more likely than not comforting himself with one of the local women, but refrained.

'Come on, hinny. It's not good to hang about here.'

Everybody knew how the place was the haunt of tramps and perverts. Sometimes the gypsies hung out there and there were tales of children being abducted and never seen again.

'I promised me mam I'd not go home without him,' Billy said, his blue eyes shining like bright sapphires in a stray shaft of light as the moon peeped momentarily from behind a black cloud. 'I'm off to the Fiddlers to see if he's there. It's Friday night and he's supposed to be bringing us some fish and chips.'

'What about his supper in the oven, then?'

Billy grinned. 'Nah. It always burns. Me mam's not a very good cook. She gets drunk and forgets what she's at.'

'Well, all right, but you be quick and come back the long way round. It's safer than this hellhole.'

Colleen watched as Billy trotted away from her, thinking that she would have been well advised to take her own advice about going the long way round, but she was almost home now, so it didn't matter. Thankfully, it was only a few hundred yards to the bottom of her street. In fact, she could see the flickering, yellowish glow and the halos from the gas lamps.

And that's when she sensed, yet again, that she wasn't alone. Her mouth went dry as she turned and saw that it wasn't Billy who had decided to come with her after all.

'Hello, Colleen, darlin'. I've been hopin' to catch up wi' ye.' Patrick Flynn stepped out of the shadows, the mud making foul slurping noises beneath his boots. 'I've got something for ye . . . '

Colleen's blood ran cold, and then her whole body stiffened with absolute fear. The moment she had dreaded for as many years as she could remember had finally come. She knew it and so did he. It had been foolish of her to think that she could avoid him for ever.

Patrick Flynn took no prisoners when the mood for revenge was upon him. And no person, male or female, had the guts to bring him to justice. He was careful, aye, and a clever man, despite his illiteracy. He could strike and leave no clue, no witnesses, or none that would be believed, even if they could summon up the courage to shop him to the authorities. She had seen it happen before, on more than one occasion. Colleen was tough and no coward, despite her small stature. However, she knew well that common prostitutes had no legal rights. This, and the fact that she had a daughter to protect, had always prevented her from coming forward with damning evidence.

She had threatened Patrick with the police the last time she had seen him, the day he had done his best to put an end to the life of his newborn son. And she might have exposed him then, had he not disappeared without trace. Every day she had prayed for retribution, though she was not a devoutly religious woman by any means. The prayers had not worked. He had turned up once more, when least expected. Alive, filled with hate and twice as repulsive.

'Let me come by, Patrick,' she said, her voice quivering nervously in her throat. 'You can't afford to make a mistake at your time of life.'

'I'm not about to make any mistakes, Colleen,' he snarled at her like a rabid dog, ignoring the run of slimy saliva that dripped from his loose mouth. 'I've only ever made two mistakes in my life. The first was to get myself tied to Maggie, that useless, scrawny bitch. The second was to let that puny bastard of hers live when even the priest hisself thought it was God's will to let him die.'

'Aye, well even God makes mistakes. That little Billy was no mistake, though. The bairn is worth ten of you, Patrick Flynn, and always will be.'

'Not for long, he won't, when I gets me hands on 'im, thievin' little good-for-nowt.'

'If he steals, it's to put food on the table,' Colleen said, sticking out her chin with a surge of stubborn audacity. 'And speaking of thievin', where did you get them boots you're wearing, eh? I seem to remember that I gave them to young Billy, and right proud he was of them, too.'

'Too good for the likes of him. Let him gan barefoot like the rest of the bastards around here.'

Colleen shook her head in disbelief that any man could be so uncaring for children, whether they were his or anybody else's. Thinking that a more gentle tack might work better with him, she softened her voice.

'Aw, come on, Patrick, let bygones be bygones.'

She might have known that he wouldn't be fooled.

'Ach, is that what you think we should do, Colleen, me darlin'?' He was standing before her, legs splayed, fists punched into his thick waist, though ready to fly into action if she made any hasty move. 'How's about a kiss or two for your old pal, Patrick, eh? For old times' sake.'

Colleen's throat went peculiarly tight at the thought. She tried to swallow and ended up giving a choking cough that resounded in her ears. This was the most dangerous place of all, where the mud flats merged with the quarry ponds. People had died here. Children, tramps, drunkards. And prostitutes.

She backed away, scared now, as Patrick pressed his odorous body close, but he had her cornered, for there was nothing but a wall of sandstone behind her.

'Patrick, be sensible,' she mumbled with difficulty as one hand clamped tightly around her chin, forcing her head back until she felt her scalp graze the rock. 'At least let's find somewhere a bit more comfortable, eh? Come on, man!'

'What makes you think I want us to be comfortable, Colleen? You were all set, ten years ago, to see me in prison. I was a fool to run away, but me head was all confused.'

'That was a long time ago. If I'd been going to do anything, I would have done it long before now.' Colleen squirmed feebly as his fingers squeezed her flesh and his pelvis ground hard into her, making it impossible to move. 'Don't do this, Patrick. You'll not get away with it this time.'

A shower of dust and stones rained down upon their heads. Colleen cast her eyes up in time to see a movement, a small white face illuminated in a shaft of moonlight before it pulled back out of sight. Patrick looked up too, but she wasn't sure that he had seen Billy. She hoped to God he had not, for it would be the death of that poor little lad.

'Patrick, Patrick!' She tried to scream out his name to divert his attention, but the noise that emitted from her lips — already turning blue because of the pressure of Patrick's hands now around her throat — was no louder than the squeak of a frightened mouse.

He pressed into her even more, pushing her down, scouring the rock with her body until she was lying flat and he was on top of her, pressing her into the sludge. She couldn't fight him off, couldn't move her arms or her legs. She couldn't even feel them any more. All she could feel was the tightening of his hands as he strangled the life out of her. As her head seemed to grow and explode under the pressure of his iron fingers, she saw floating before her the faces of her darling Bridget and Billy, and she feared for them.

Then the darkness became full of blinding stars and even Patrick Flynn's foetid breath was gone, together with all his weight, and she was floating, like a feather in the wind and sinking in the dark mire until, one by one, the stars faded and total blackness took over.

6

Albert Robinson sat in his son-in-law's front room staring morosely out of the window. The newspaper he had been reading fell from his hand, the pages scattering at his feet. It was a terrible world, he thought, when people were murdered in a quiet, peaceable little town like Jarrow.

Of course, there were skeletons in most family cupboards, but they were usually kept locked away, brushed under the carpet. God knows, there were plenty in his family, but you just didn't talk about them. Nobody did.

The squeak of his son-in-law's wheelchair announced John's arrival. Albert stirred himself and bent quickly to gather together the pages he had dropped, but his rheumatism stopped him short and he gripped his back with a groan and straightened stiffly. He heard a familiar sound. The small click of his daughter's tongue on the roof of her mouth; Elizabeth was so like her mother it was uncanny. It was also very wearing for the old man, who had been looking forward to enjoying the rest of his days in peace and tranquillity, having finally retired from his beloved family business.

'Oh, Father! Really!' Elizabeth 'clucked' again and stopped to retrieve the newspaper sheets, which she attempted to put in order, but she was in too much of a hurry, as usual, and got impatient.

'I'll do that,' John said, reaching out and taking the pages from her. 'I'm sure you must have something more important to do, my dear.'

Elizabeth's nostrils flared as her patience ran out and anger set in. It was bad enough that she was married to a cripple without having him make sarcastic remarks about how she spent her time. There wasn't a moment when she wasn't working. Even with the help of Maureen Flynn, there were never sufficient hours in the day to keep this great mausoleum of a house clean and tidy.

'Give the paper back to me, John,' she said, her lips tightening as she held out a demanding hand. 'I'll go and put it in the bin.'

'I can do that, Elizabeth,' John said quietly. 'Besides, I haven't read it yet.'

Albert looked from one to the other of them and headed for the door.

'There's nothing worth reading these days. And half of what you read you can't believe. Them journalists! They're all a load of — '

'Father!'

'Ach!' Albert threw his hands in the air and shook his head as he marched out into the hall with a slight limping gait. 'I'm away off up to the allotments.'

Elizabeth sighed loudly, her exasperation with her father more than a little evident. She was fond of him, to a point, but they had never really got along too well. It had been a mistake to take him in after her mother had died. He hadn't been in favour of the arrangement but she had talked him into it. John had told her later that she had bullied the old man into doing what she wanted, just like her mother before her had been in the habit of doing. Well, the deed was done now and they had to live with it. All of them.

She pulled fretfully at her hands, then rubbed at a twitch that was attacking her right cheek. The iron tonic the doctor was giving her wasn't doing her nerves any good. All it had succeeded in doing so far was rotting her teeth.

She wasn't sure whether or not John had made a sound as his eyes focussed on the front page of the *Gateshead Gazette* he was holding, having carefully put the pages in order. Had he actually groaned? Had he called out in some agonized fashion? Elizabeth dragged herself out of the depths of her own misery to look enquiringly at her husband.

John's face had gone deathly pale. His eyes looked glazed at first, then they glistened with moisture. She bent and looked more closely at him and saw his mouth and chin quiver emotionally.

'John?' She touched his shoulder momentarily, then quickly removed her hand. 'What's wrong? Are you ill?'

The muscles in his gaunt cheeks became tense, and then he shook his head vigorously, more as if he were trying to rid himself of his thoughts than giving a sign of negation.

'It's nothing,' he said in a croaking whisper as he crumpled the newspaper into a ball. 'Just a twinge. Nothing for you to worry yourself about, Elizabeth.'

But Elizabeth wasn't convinced. They might not have a marriage any longer, but she knew her husband. She knew his every expression, could read his every thought. And John was more emotionally moved right then than she had ever seen him. And it had something to do with what he had read in the *Gazette*.

She retrieved the paper and smoothed it out so that the page he had stared at with such intensity was once again readable. And then she saw what the cause of his distress was and the implication she read into the signs made her feel unclean. Not to mention afraid of the consequences.

'It's her, isn't it?' she said, thrusting the paper at him, so that the photograph of the murdered prostitute rested squarely in his sickened gaze. 'That woman . . . a common whore. Well, she got what she deserved, if you ask me.'

'Nobody deserves to die like that, Elizabeth,' John told her softly, his eyes avoiding the newspaper and skimming over her face before being averted.

'She was a *prostitute*, for goodness' sake!'

'She wasn't a bad person. In fact, Colleen was as good a person as you'll find around here, including your fancy, bigoted friends who think they're God's chosen few.'

'You went with her, didn't you?' Elizabeth's face was screwed up in an expression of pure revulsion. 'Is that where you were when you came home late with my father, saying you'd lost track of time?'

'You didn't want me in your bed any more, Elizabeth. However, I'm still a relatively young man. I may be a cripple, but I have needs . . . physical needs. Colleen understood that.' John gazed off into the middle distance and gave a wry smile. 'Sometimes we just talked. In some ways, I liked that best. She

125

was a good listener, but she also needed somebody to talk to.'

'Oh, yes, I'm sure!'

'No matter what you or anybody else says about her, Colleen Maguire was all right. She didn't deserve to die.'

'Didn't she? I think that whoever did that to her did the world a service.'

'Where's your Christian heart, Elizabeth?' John's eyes flashed at her momentarily and for the first time she saw something akin to hate in his attitude. 'There are quite a number of suspects, as you can imagine, but at the top of the list is Patrick Flynn. Right now, however, he seems to have gone missing. Him and that little lad of his. The one they call Billy Big Boots.'

'Billy?' At last some warmth of feeling stole back into Elizabeth's cold heart. 'Dear God, you don't think the man would harm his own son, do you?'

John slowly shook his head and wiped a hand over his face. 'I don't know. Remember when Laura was little, the day Billy was born? She came out with some ridiculous story about Mr Flynn trying to suffocate the baby.'

'Oh, that was nothing, John. Just childish imagination. You know what Laura's like, even now. She scribbles away at every spare moment, writing fairy stories. They read them out at the school. The children love them, but they're not true. They're just a product of Laura's fertile imagination.'

'I wonder. Maybe she really did see that bastard try to murder Billy. Remember, Flynn went missing around that time too, then turned up again years later. The priest had moved on, the grandparents were all dead. The incident had been forgotten. Not even Laura mentioned it any more.'

'I can understand a man like Patrick Flynn going with whores,' Elizabeth said suddenly through gritted teeth. 'Look at his wife.'

'Maggie Flynn gave our household many years of good service,' John said in the woman's defence. 'It was a pity she ever left. Her daughter will never be a patch on her.'

'Oh, don't! The last I heard Maggie Flynn never takes her head out of the gin bottle. They're a fine pair, I ask you, and still breeding if the size of her is anything to go by.'

A scuff of feet announced the arrival of Maureen Flynn. There was a timid tap of knuckles on the door and there she stood, cowering fearfully, her face sheet-white and lips compressed.

'I'm sorry, Mrs Caldwell, but . . . '

'Maureen?' Elizabeth frowned at her young housekeeper. 'What is it?'

'I . . . I . . . ' The girl stuttered and couldn't get the words out, so Elizabeth took it to mean nothing at all but a lapse on Maureen's part.

'Bring us some tea and cake, would you? And don't take all day about it.'

'Yes, Mrs Caldwell.' Maureen started to go, then she turned back and rested a doleful look on her employer. 'Mrs Caldwell, can I take the rest of the day off, please? Me mam's bad and we don't know where our Billy is and . . . and . . . I'm not feeling well mesel' like.'

Elizabeth's brows lowered. The girl had no brain and was lazy, but she wasn't one to take time off that wasn't owing to her. And she did look rather ill.

'Very well, Maureen,' she said, 'but bring the tea first and see if you can manage a few salmon sandwiches. I do believe there is a tin in the pantry. Red salmon, mind.'

'Oh, but . . . ' Maureen thought better of the argument that had risen like bile in her throat. 'Yes, Mrs Caldwell.'

★ ★ ★

In the kitchen, Laura was as pale as Maureen. Two broad-shouldered policemen in plain clothes were standing near the back door. She had taken pity on their plain and simple housekeeper when Maureen had begged her not to inform Elizabeth Caldwell of their presence or of the reason for them being there.

They had swaggered in through the back door, long overcoats flowing, big black shoes polished and creaking with every step they took. Laura had been scribbling furiously in one of her notebooks, rushing with enthusiasm to the end of her latest children's story. One of the men had rudely picked up the notebook and read a few lines before either of them thought of showing their identity cards.

'Oh, I'll get my mother, shall I?' she asked them hesitantly, but they didn't need to see Mrs Caldwell, they said.

'We've come to see Maureen Flynn.' The older and more senior of the two turned to Maureen. 'That would be you, miss?'

Maureen's eyes grew very wide. 'What have I done?' She looked frantically at Laura and shook her head. 'Honestly, I haven't done nothing!'

'No, no, Miss Flynn,' the more fatherly of the two detectives said kindly. 'I'm afraid, lass, you've got a bit of trouble on your doorstep.'

All the time they were talking, the service bell was ringing and Maureen was looking more and more frightened and confused.

'Perhaps you'd like to answer that,' the senior man said, 'and tell your employer that you'll be taking some time off. As quick as you like, now.'

Maureen's mouth opened as wide as her eyes, then she gave a little nod and rushed off to answer the impatient bell.

Now, she was back there, trembling from head to foot as if her whole body had turned to jelly.

'Mrs Caldwell . . . she . . . she wants tea and cake . . . and sandwiches and . . . ' Her eyes locked with those of Laura's. 'I . . . I can't do it . . . I . . . What's happened? Has there been an accident or something?'

Laura took one of the girl's ice-cold hands and squeezed it. 'Never mind the tea, Maureen,' she said, then turned back to the policemen. 'Can't you tell us what's happened, Sergeant? I may be able to help. I'm a friend of the family, you see.'

Maureen shot her a surprised and grateful look.

'All right, miss. I suppose it won't do any harm and you'll find out soon enough. There's been a murder, you see. A neighbour of Miss Flynn's here. We went to question Mr Flynn because . . . well, no matter. He wasn't there. It seems he hasn't been home since Friday night, according to his wife. The thing

130

is, Mrs Flynn is in rather a . . . well, you might say, a delicate state of health.'

'You suspect . . . ' Laura gulped audibly, remembering that day ten years ago and seeing Patrick Flynn in her mind's eye, a pillow poised over poor little Billy's face. 'Did he . . . did he murder Colleen Maguire?'

'Miss Maguire is indeed the victim,' the sergeant said. 'However, we can't point the finger at Patrick Flynn, though he's high on the list of suspects. Trouble is, miss, we can't find him. And his youngest son seems to have gone missing too. Billy Flynn, that is.'

'Billy didn't do anything.' Laura was quick to Billy's defence. 'He's only ten . . . '

The inspector held up his hands. 'Now, now, miss, I didn't mean to imply that the lad had done anything wrong,' he said, patting her shoulder in an avuncular way. 'It's just that he's the only one who can deal with his mother, it seems, and nobody knows where he is.'

'Oh, he hasn't hurt Billy as well, has he?' Laura's dark eyes were frantic. 'Mr Flynn is a bad man . . . an evil man. He . . . ' She heard a gasp and remembered the presence of Patrick Flynn's daughter. 'Oh, I'm sorry Maureen, but you didn't see him that day when Billy was born. He was going to put a pillow over Billy's face. Everybody said the poor baby wouldn't live, but he did and he's a good boy.'

The younger but senior policeman was listening intently to her words and came closer, drawing himself up to his full six feet and expanding his broad chest beneath the stiff mackintosh he wore.

'And who told you that, Miss Caldwell?' The other policeman stepped forward, regarding her from beneath thick, wire-wool eyebrows. 'About the business with the pillow, eh?'

Laura's head snapped round and she blinked at him, slightly shocked at her own outburst.

'Nobody told me,' she said in a half-whisper, afraid that he might take her words wrongly and arrest her for telling lies. Slander, they called it. Her grandmother had warned her over and over again about telling tales. 'I . . . I saw him.'

Out of the corner of her eye, Laura could see Maureen's pale face staring at her in disbelief. The inspector and his colleague were both now giving her their full attention, eyes narrowed, mouths tight and grim.

'You saw him do what, young lady?'

Laura swallowed and cleared her throat. 'It was a long time ago. I was just a little girl, but I was there when Billy was born and . . . ' She looked about her, fearing that her mother might come in and tell her to forget that silly story once and for all. 'I went back later. I saw Mr Flynn standing over the baby with a pillow and he was going to smother the poor little thing. I shouted for him to stop and . . . '

'And?'

'And then, the woman with the red hair came in and there was an argument and Mr Flynn ran out of the house.'

'The woman with the red hair being Colleen Maguire?'

Laura nodded. 'Yes. She was kind to me. She brought me home, but nobody would speak to her and they didn't believe me when I told them. About Mr Flynn and Billy, I mean.'

The inspector turned back to Maureen Flynn. 'Is this true, Miss Flynn?'

'I don't know.' Maureen shook her head vigorously. 'I wasn't there. Mam had sent me for help when the baby started to come. I went for me granny, but I was too scared to go back home, so I stayed with her that night.'

'It is true,' Laura said plaintively, every bone in her body sagging with the frustration of not being believed yet again. 'Mrs Maguire said that I had saved little Billy's life that day.

133

She said that Mr Flynn would have killed the baby. I tried to tell everybody, but I was only eight. Nobody believed me. They still don't.'

The inspector exchanged a glance with his sergeant and then smiled kindly at Laura. 'Well, Miss Caldwell, I think perhaps I do believe you, but we can do nothing without proof. I suggest you call in at the station and make a statement and we can keep it on record, but don't you go telling people what you saw. If Flynn is guilty of murder, I'd feel a lot happier if he was behind bars before he knows you've pointed a finger at him.'

There was a suppressed whimper from Maureen and he gave her a sharp look. 'Miss Flynn, can we trust you not to mention what you've just heard? He may be your father but he's a nasty piece of work, and I daresay you already know that.'

'Yes, sir,' Maureen said and scrubbed at her red, watery eyes. 'I don't live at home no more, anyway, so I never see me da. I won't say anything to nobody, I promise.'

'If he's done a runner you might never see him again,' the sergeant said pointedly.

'I don't mind that,' Maureen said, tenderly rubbing her arm where Laura knew there was a scar. She suspected that Patrick Flynn had inflicted it on his daughter. That and many other injuries, mentally as well as physically.

With the police officers gone, none the wiser about the whereabouts of Patrick Flynn or his youngest son, Maureen turned mournful eyes on Laura.

'Do you know where me brother is, Miss Caldwell?' she asked.

'Why do you ask me that?' Laura felt she had to be on her guard from now on until the suspected murderer was caught.

'Because you and Billy have always been thick as thieves. He's always hanging around you.'

Laura chewed on her mouth and gave a deep frown. 'Yes, I know. I don't know why he does that, but he's always popping up, wherever I go. It's irritating.'

'He worships you, miss, that's why. Our Billy knows that you saved his life, so he kind of thinks of you as his own special angel . . . Well, you know . . . ' Maureen hung her head, embarrassed at her own words. 'Something like that.'

'Oh, I see.' Laura bit down on a smile, thinking how nice it was to be worshipped, even from afar. She did so wish, though, that the one doing the worshipping were some-what older and wiser than ten-year-old Billy Flynn. Someone like David Simpson, the minister's son, or . . . Well, anybody that her parents would approve of.

She and David had been going out for a few months but she wasn't sure where she was with him. He was tall and dark and handsome and he treated her like a precious piece of porcelain. Whenever she thought of him, her heart did a little flip. Seeing him, even at a distance, lit her body up as if she were filled with electricity. So far, however, he had done nothing but hold her hand gently when they were alone together and, in church, he would send her that special secret smile of his across the aisles while his father gave the sermon. One day, she hoped, she would be walking down the aisle on David's arm, the new Mrs Simpson.

'Go on home, Maureen,' Laura said, suddenly realizing that the girl was waiting anxiously for an order. 'I'll explain things to my mother.'

'What about tea?'

'Goodness, I think we can manage just this once. Off you go and . . . Maureen?'

Maureen halted in her swift tracks and looked questioningly over her shoulder. 'Aye, miss?'

'Be careful.'

'Aye, I will.'

'And if you find Billy, tell him . . . tell him to come here. It'll be much safer for him than in your house.'

'Eeh, me mam wouldn't like that, miss. She goes daft if Billy's not around to handle her.'

'All the same, tell him. Until your father is found, I'm afraid for his safety.'

Maureen nodded slowly as Laura's words sank in, then she was gone, her flat feet slapping the pavement as she ran down the road in the direction of Jarrow Banks and Dawson Street.

★ ★ ★

It did Albert Robinson's old heart good to hear the laughter of the group of miners who had gathered up in the top allotment. They met there, rain or shine, to practise. Forty members of the pit brass band, some of them so keen they still bore the coal dust on their faces and on their clothes.

As he approached, he heard them warm up, and smiled genially as the odd discordant note sallied forth. Albert was no musician, but, by God, he liked the sound the band made. It could relieve tension better than any of those hocus-pocus medicines the doctor could dole out. And, unless you were too near and deafened by the blast of the ensemble, the music was sweet and soothing to the ears, or rousing to the heart. And definitely good for the spirit.

'Hey, lads!' He greeted them with his usual jovial smile and a wave of the hand, which had known toil as tough as any of them had known.

They were gathered around the long shed that the pit manager had loaned to them and at the sound of his voice multiple salutations issued forth. Albert Robinson was a man well liked for his easy nature and his fair dealings with the men in his charge and his reputation had filtered through from the most junior brickie to the most senior miner in the region.

There were greetings all round, then Joseph Coates, the bandmaster, came forward to exchange a few words with his old friend.

'Good to see you back,' Joe said with a slight nod of his bald head. 'We thought maybe you'd given up the allotment after moving in with your daughter.'

'Never!' Albert told him, shaking hands firmly. 'I just needed a bit of space. You know what it's like, losing somebody close, like.'

'Aye, course I do, lad.' Joe had lost his wife two years ago.

'Well,' Albert said, rubbing his hands together, the skin rasping like sandpaper, 'I figure it's time to get back to the things I enjoy doing. What are you and the lads going to play for me that'll set me off digging this blessed plot of mine, eh?'

He cast his gaze around the quarter-acre plot that had miraculously been engulfed by weeds in the months he had not been in the mood to tend it.

'It looks like you haven't come back too soon, man,' Joe said. 'How about we play you something cheerful, like a Sousa march?'

'Aye, that'll do me fine.'

'And I'd take a look in your shed, Albert.' Joe indicated the small wooden structure behind them that Albert had spent many an escapist hour in the past. 'I think you'll find you've got a lodger.'

'What?'

But Joe just touched a finger to his forelock and went back to his lads, who immediately picked up their instruments and started to play.

Albert noticed that the lock to his shed had been broken into. It was hanging loosely and the door was slightly ajar. Even before he pushed the door open, he had a gut feeling that he knew what to expect.

'Billy? Is that you in there?'

A small, white, heart-shaped face appeared through the dusky light. Albert closed the door behind him and stood regarding the boy.

'Aye, Mr Robinson. I'm sorry.'

'Ye're sorry, are ye? Well, I don't know what

for. Come here and tell me what this is all about, laddie. Come on. You know I'm not goin' to eat ye, goodness' sakes.'

'Have they caught him, Mr Robinson?'

'Who's that, then?'

'Me — The man that killed me Auntie Colleen.'

'If yer talkin' about that father of yours, Billy Flynn, the answer's no. It seems he's disappeared into the wide blue yonder.'

'Is Bridget all right?'

'Aye, she's being looked after at the orphanage, according to the newspapers.'

'Is that good?'

'It's better than your dad getting her hands on her, aye.'

'I'd never let anybody hurt Bridget. Especially not me da. Never!'

'Ye're a good lad, Billy. When did you last have something to eat, eh?'

'Dunno. Me belly's as hollow as one of them holes in the quarry.'

'In that case, come and share me bait. I've got half a roast chicken here and some apples that need eatin'. You gonna help me?'

'Aye, thanks, Mr Robinson. I will, an' all.'

7

Billy missed having Bridget around. It was like a part of him had died. Her absence opened up a deep hole inside him that he couldn't explain. Not to anybody. All he knew was that on those rare occasions when he caught sight of her when he hung around the church on Sundays, it gave him a nice warm sensation that crept up from his toes to his ears.

Sometimes she would smile and wave and break away from the tangle of orphanage girls in their cheap orphanage clothes. The dreary-faced woman who accompanied them always called Bridget back to lecture her on obedience, but Bridget wasn't one to let a sharp telling-off get in the way of their friendship.

One day, the first Sunday after Billy's thirteenth birthday, Bridget proved herself to be particularly disobedient. It was a cold January day and the ground was covered in glistening frost. Even the air seemed to be frozen and there were flurries of soft white snowflakes, despite the blue sky and a sun that was golden, but sadly without heat.

Billy was hovering, as usual, waiting to see if Laura Caldwell might pass his way, for he hadn't seen her in a long time. She was all grown up now and working as a teacher at the local school. Any other girl might have been too full of self-importance to stop and speak to the likes of Billy Flynn, but not Laura. She wasn't nearly the snob people made her out to be.

'Billy!' Bridget hailed him just as he spotted Laura and her family coming out of the church and his mind was going haywire, wishing he could turn to both girls at the same time, but he wasn't that clever.

'Bridget Maguire, you get back in line this minute!' The stern voice of Bridget's 'keeper' rasped through the space between them.

Bridget, as usual, ignored the poker-faced woman and charged up to Billy. There wasn't much difference in their heights. Bridget, a few months younger than Billy, won by an inch. Her cheeks were rosy from the wind, and her eyes were like shining emeralds. And her hair, which had started out that morning in the regulation tight braid down her back, was flying about her face in curling tendrils. Nobody was ever going to tame that flaming bonnet.

Billy loved Bridget's hair. It was as fiery as

her temper and as warm as her heart. He had touched it once on a day when a bee had got tangled there. Maybe one day he might get to touch it again, because it was a pleasant experience. Very pleasant. And very different from the satiny smooth helmet of dark hair on Laura's head, which Billy hadn't felt — but he had dreamed of running his fingers through her tresses more times than he could remember.

'She doesn't look very friendly,' Billy said now as Bridget skidded to a halt on the other side of the white-painted fence that separated the tiny graveyard from the road.

'Who?' Bridget struggled vainly to push most of her hair beneath her crocheted beret. The hat was a rather vivid puce colour and clashed horribly with her colouring, but orphanage children had to take what they could get. Bridget no longer had a loving mother to look after her.

'That old hag that shouted at you.' Billy swiped his sleeve under his dribbling nose and then felt ashamed when Bridget handed him her hankie. It was probably the only one she had and she would get into trouble for giving it to him, but he kept it anyway. It smelled nice and clean, a bit like Laura Caldwell often smelled. Sort of soapy and lavenderish.

'Oh, that's Miss Simpson.' Bridget grimaced over her shoulder at the woman standing fifty yards away, hands on her hips and, no doubt, her flat bosom rising and falling with the frustration of having to shepherd a bunch of unwanted, wayward girls back to the cold, prison-like walls of Peel House, which had once been grand but was now a charity orphanage for parentless children and those in a state of absolute poverty.

'Isn't she married, then?' Billy wanted to know, for the woman seemed far too old not to have a husband and children of her own.

'No. That's why she's so miserable. Anyway, she doesn't like children, so what's the point of her getting married?'

Billy's eyes and mind had wandered, because Laura, the last of her family to leave the church, was having a few words with the vicar.

'Hmm?'

'Billy Flynn, don't ask questions if you're not going to listen to the answers. It's bliddy rude.'

That got Billy's attention back. He stared at Bridget hard, then grinned cheekily. 'Does your Miss Simpson let you use language like that, Bridget?'

Bridget frowned at him, then she too was

grinning. 'What she doesn't hear won't bother her,' she said. 'Are you going fishing next Friday?'

'Aye, o' course. You comin'?'

'If I can slip out without being noticed I will, but let's go somewhere different next time. The last place was stinking and those fish you caught looked like they'd been dead before they took your bent nail in their mouths.'

Billy gave an amused snicker, but refrained from mentioning that the supper he had provided for his family last Friday night had rendered them all so ill they thought they were dying. He was the only one that the food poisoning hadn't attacked, because Billy didn't much care for fish. Not, that was, when he saw where they came from and how his hands had stunk for hours after handling them.

They had fetched up at a part of the Tyne where the sewage went into the fast-flowing river. The water was a muddy brown with oily swirls and greyish foam. It smelled a bit like the mop he used to clean the kitchen floor after it had been sitting dirty in a bucket for a week.

'Mr Robinson's going to show me where to catch the best fish,' he said, looking back in the direction of the Caldwells and Mr

Robinson as the family walked sedately towards the lychgate a few feet away from where he and Bridget stood chatting.

'Are you still working for him?' Bridget wrinkled her snub nose and closed her eyes to slits as the sun blinded her.

'Aye.' Billy nodded proudly.

Mr Robinson had more or less taken Billy under his protective wing ever since the day he had taken refuge in the allotment shed. The old man was Billy's unspoken hero. If Albert Robinson had asked him to walk to hell and back for a penny-farthing, Billy would do it. But the wages Laura's granddad paid him were a lot more than a penny-farthing, and the work wasn't work at all. It was a pleasure to be out in the allotments, digging and planting, never mind the weather, for as long as he pleased. And it pleased him a lot, especially when the lads from the shipyard band gathered to blow their horns and beat on their drums.

Billy had begged them to let him join, but he couldn't play any of the instruments to save his life, so Mr Robinson gave him a penny whistle and showed him how to play that. And he wasn't half bad at it. Just for the fun of it, the band would let him join in, though they made it clear that he didn't qualify to play with them officially, him not being a shipyard worker.

'Why have you gone all red in the face?' Bridget squeaked in surprise suddenly, then pointed at him and laughed loudly. 'Billy Flynn, you're blushing!'

'No, I'm not.' Billy's eyes flickered from the approaching Laura Caldwell to Bridget and back again. He could, indeed, feel the heat mount in his cheeks and his mouth had gone dry. He cleared his throat and spoke out clearly, not wanting the opportunity to be missed. 'Hello, Laura!'

Billy had waited until the family had walked on. Laura, for some reason, seemed to be lingering behind. When she heard Billy's voice she looked startled, so he guessed that her lingering was nothing to do with him, though he tried to pretend that it was.

'Oh, hello, Billy.' But Laura then stopped and turned her back on him as if searching the departing parishioners for someone in particular.

'Silly sod, Billy Flynn.' Billy heard Bridget's criticism through a haze, for he now saw what was taking Laura's attention.

A tall young man had broken away from a group of people milling around the vicar and ran, on long legs, down the hill to where Laura greeted him with open arms and a smile that Billy would have killed for. The couple embraced, right there in front of him, arms and lips, everything touching.

The pleasurable heat in Billy's cheeks had turned to a burning humiliation. He turned away, trying not to listen to the soppy, romantic words the young man was uttering. Words that Billy wouldn't dream of saying to anybody, though he wished he were the one saying them.

'My dearest, darling Laura!' the young man said, lifting Laura off her feet and swinging her around. 'There, it's done at last. Bans read and everyone happy. And in a few short weeks you'll make me the happiest man alive when you become my wife.'

'I can't wait!' Laura said breathlessly, clinging on to her hat and apparently not caring that she was showing a good length of calf before her fiancé put her back on to terra firma.

Billy watched, stricken, as Laura inspected a sparkling diamond on the third finger of her left hand, the prisms glinting expensively in the sun. He didn't even notice when the skinny, wretched Miss Simpson came and dragged Bridget away with surprising vigour. Nor did he hear Bridget call out to him, ridiculing him for having a fancy for a girl so much older and taller than he was, and Billy still only thirteen with no prospects to offer.

Something inside him, a feeling like a stone sinking in murky water, seemed to drag him down. He felt all dull and heavy inside, like the day his Auntie Colleen died. His head wasn't quite on straight and his stomach churned. How could Laura marry that man? How could she do that to him, Billy, who loved her to distraction?

Aye, yes, that's what it was. He had never really been able to put a word to what he felt about Laura Caldwell, but it was, without a doubt, the deepest love any boy could have for the first girl who touched his heart. All the time this love was growing inside him, it never occurred to him that Laura's life would go forward. He honestly and truly believed that when he was old enough she would be there, waiting for him. And those lovely nut-brown eyes, the full pink lips like velvet cushions, would belong to him. He had dreamed of what it would be like, snuggling up to her, touching her, running his fingers through that long, thick, dark curtain of hair that was the colour of the old mahogany dresser his mam polished with so much vigour when she wasn't lying comatose with the drink inside her.

Billy turned and leaned heavily against the fence for a few minutes, staring blindly into the distance. He didn't regain his senses until a mangy dog came and sniffed around his ankles. Without thinking, Billy kicked out at the mutt and the dog leapt away with a surprised yelp. Billy felt a lump rise in his throat and he swallowed it back with difficulty, scrubbing desperately at his damp eyes. Silly sod, he told himself. Boys his age didn't cry. Only girls cried. In fact, Billy couldn't remember ever crying and didn't know why he should do so now, except it wasn't like him to hurt a poor defenceless animal. Billy loved animals, and especially dogs, and this one had just been trying to make friends.

Full of remorse, he sank to his knees and held out his hand in the direction of the dog. The animal hadn't gone too far and was still taking an interest in this soppy lad with tears rolling down his cheeks.

'Here boy,' Billy said, his voice a low croak. 'I'm sorry, lad. I didn't mean to hurt ye.'

The scrawny mongrel hunkered down fearfully for a moment, then crept tentatively forward. Billy saw how the dog's ribs were showing and that the soft black muzzle was sucked in with starvation. Billy knew that look well, for hadn't his whole family looked like that many a time. He delved into his pocket and found a crust of stale bread he was saving for the pigeons that roosted in one of the sheds up at the allotments. They could do without their treat for one day, he decided, as the crust was ravenously grabbed from between his finger and thumb.

'Gawd, ye must be hungry, fella. Yer belly touching yer backbone, is it? Come on, let's see if we can find you something else to eat.'

The dog looked at him suspiciously, so he ignored it and headed off up the hill to the vast field that was used by the local populace as gardens. They grew vegetables, mainly, but there was always the odd old lady up there tending flowerbeds. And where you had old ladies you usually had biscuits, scones and jam sandwiches, which they liked to have with their cold tea in between weeding, planting and gossiping together like clucking hens.

But it was Sunday and all the old ladies were at home cooking the Sunday roast for the family. Not much chance that Billy would find his mother basting a bit of beef or pork or even a chicken. Food wasn't only scarce in Maggie Flynn's household, it wasn't considered a priority. As long as Maggie had enough drink to keep her in a mindless blur she was happy, though she never stopped whining.

As luck would have it, the big long shed the band used for their practice sessions had a window with a faulty catch. Billy had learned long ago that with a bit of poking and twiddling he could get it open and climb inside. Once in, he waited till his eyes became accustomed to the dark, then he mooched about until he came up with a treasure that would seem like gold to any starving dog.

Billy opened the door and wasn't too surprised to see the poor creature outside, shivering convulsively and giving tiny, pathetic whimpers. When he clapped eyes on Billy, one paw rose and wavered a second or two, then the sad, hound-like eyes looked from side to side, watching for danger, but also drooling over what Billy had in his hand.

'Look what I got for ye, fella,' Billy said, proffering the half sausage that somebody had left behind. It smelled all right and Billy remembered his own hunger as he gave it generously to the dog, which sniffed at it warily before devouring it at speed, scared that it might be stolen from him before he could swallow it.

'You got yourself a dog, then, Billy?'

It was Mr Robinson who came strolling round the corner of the building. Man and dog eyed one another. The dog licked grease from its mouth and as Mr Robinson came closer, the top lip quivered, the rose up, showing a set of strong canine teeth. A low growl issued forth.

'It's all right, lad,' Mr Robinson said easily. 'I'm not going to hurt you. Where'd you get him, Billy? He looks like he's been through the mill, poor old boy.'

Billy shrugged. 'He just turned up outside the church when I was . . . ' His words tailed off. The dog had effectively helped him forget his anguish over losing Laura to another man. Maybe it was a lucky omen or something, like a gift from God. Colleen Maguire had told him about these gifts that came when you least expected them but most needed them. He still missed Auntie Colleen, and no doubt always would.

'It looks like he's been badly treated by the amount of scarring on his side and on his head.' Mr Robinson scrutinized the dog more closely and shook his head. 'Aye. Looks like somebody's been beating the living daylights out of him for a while.'

'Do you think I could keep him, Mr Robinson?'

'Oh, well, now. I don't know about that. He might have a vicious streak in him.'

'Nah.' Billy smiled and then grinned broadly as the dog came and licked his fingers and nuzzled against his thigh. 'He's just scared and hurting, is all.'

Seeing how well dog and boy were bonding, Mr Robinson gave a short sharp nod of his head and headed off to his allotment.

'You'd better bring him to my shed, Billy. I've got some iodine in there. We can clean him up too. He's probably running in fleas, so the minute you get him back home with you, give him a bath with carbolic soap. That should do the trick.'

'Thanks, Mr Robinson. Come on, fella.' The dog trotted obediently after Billy as he followed Mr Robinson.

After a minute or two, man and boy drew abreast as Mr Robinson's old legs tired. He rested a hand on Billy's shoulder for support.

'Ye make a good walking stick, lad,' the old man said, his chest wheezing from the exertion of going uphill too fast when he was of an age when most men put their feet up, or curled up their toes. 'How old are you now, then? Eleven?'

'I'm thirteen, Mr Robinson, as of today.'

'Thirteen, is it? Quite a young man. You'll be going off to work in the mines soon, I'll wager, eh?'

'No! Never! I'll not go down no mine, not even if they pay me.'

Mr Robinson's brows furrowed deeply.

'It seems to me, Billy lad, that you've been improving yourself lately?'

'What do you mean by that?'

'You're losing that thick Geordie accent of yours. Did that happen by accident? Or by design?'

Billy stared at the toes of his boots as they continued to march up the hill together. He hoped he hadn't blushed again like a silly girl, but his face did feel awfully hot.

'Dunno,' he muttered into his chest.

'I hear you're often up at my daughter's house,' Mr Robinson said, puffing and panting as the climb became steeper. 'But then your sister, Maureen, works there. She quite takes after your mother for her cooking. Mind you, if she marries that lad she's going round with I daresay the family will soon be looking for another cook.'

But Billy's mind was on the wander and his brain was getting confused. It was with a vague, pained expression that he asked: 'Will she really get married to that man?'

'Best ask your sister that? I have enough trouble keeping track of my own family.'

'Not our Maureen. Laura . . . I mean . . . your granddaughter, Mr Robinson.'

'And why would you want to know that, young fella?'

Billy slid his eyes up to the piercing ones of his companion and gave a small shake of his head. 'No reason. Just being nosey. You know me.'

'Aye, I do an' all, Billy Flynn. I also know that you don't ask questions just for the sake of it.' Mr Robinson stopped in his tracks to get his puff back. 'Out with it. What do you know about my granddaughter's fiancé? He appears to be a fine, upstanding young man with very good prospects and an excellent background.'

'Nothing!' Billy's eyebrows shot up into his hairline as he realized he'd got himself into a bit of a tricky situation. 'Honest, Mr Robinson, I just . . . well, I don't think she should marry him, that's all.'

'Well, I daresay that's something for Laura to decide.' Mr Robinson patted Billy's head, and then did the same to the dog. 'It's not for the likes of us to judge, eh, Billy?'

'No, Mr Robinson.'

'So, what are you going to call this new pal of yours, eh?' Mr Robinson was, five minutes later, dabbing on strong-smelling iodine to the sores and weals the dog sported, thanks to the cruelty of an uncaring owner.

'Dunno. I've never had a dog before. There was one once that bit us. It was called Rover. I couldn't call this one Rover, not after a dog like that.'

'There now.' Mr Robinson got up from his knees, straightened his back with a slight groan and returned his first-aid items to the white tin box with a red cross on its lid. 'All patched up.'

'That's what I'll call him!' Billy cried out, then softened his voice as the dog cowered nervously, tail between its legs. 'I'll call him Patches. Is that all right, Mr Robinson? Is that a good name for a dog?'

'Aye, son. It's a grand name for a dog.'

Billy bent down and was pleased that Patches allowed him to throw his arms around its furry neck, because he was suddenly overcome once more with emotion and he needed to hide his tears. He may be all tough and brittle on the outside, but Billy had a soft centre and right now he felt more like a little lost child than a 'man' of thirteen.

★   ★   ★

Bridget closed her ears to the scolding she was getting from Miss Simpson, and closed her eyes to the angrily wagging finger at the end of her nose. She didn't even make a sound when the woman gave her a hefty slap, leaving red finger-mark welts on her cheek that stung for a full ten minutes after. What did bother Bridget was not being able to spend time with Billy, who was like a brother to her, even more than a friend. And she loved him dearly.

Her disobedience earned Bridget a few hours in solitary detention. Most of the girls had learned how to avoid being dragged kicking and screaming up to the dusty attic of the orphanage. Bridget accepted it almost willingly, rather than be part of a simpering group of children who dared not breathe out of tune with the harsh supervisor's rules.

She didn't mind the mice and the spiders and the odd rat that scampered about among the rafters that were festooned with cobwebs hanging like soft gauzy curtains, wafting in the breeze through the gaps in the tiles above. She had even secreted some candles and some Vestas. The matches were contained in a tiny silver case that had dropped from some visiting dignitary's watch-chain.

Oh, the fuss that was made when the illustrious gentleman had stormed back into the building the next day, accusing Miss Simpson of harbouring common thieves under her leaking orphanage roof. It was only when another girl, a pathetic creature with a concave chest and a cough that produced blood among the green phlegm, was accused of the theft that Bridget stepped forward. Bridget's strong sense of justice always came to the fore, making her popular with the victims, but very unpopular with Miss Simpson and the orphanage governors.

'Leave her alone! Sally didn't have anything to do with it!' Bridget had screamed out, as Miss Simpson's heavy hand descended on the bowed head before her. 'It was me. I stole the bliddy Vesta case.'

'Where is it, girl?' Miss Simpson had spoken through gritted teeth, her face becoming more and more like one of the stone gargoyles that were to be found over the entrance of the church. 'Hand it over.'

'I can't.' Bridget stood her ground and braced herself for another beating. 'I found it on the ground and threw it away. It wasn't worth anything, that bit of tin — and it smelled horrible.'

The honourable gentleman, whose Vesta case it was, regarded her with one very arched and disbelieving eyebrow. Bridget's face twisted slightly beneath the gaze, then she ignored him and kept a wary eye on the hand of Miss Simpson, who had enjoyed torment-ing her from the day they had placed her in the orphanage's care.

'Honest, it did, Miss Simpson,' she said with a rueful smile, then turned her emerald eyes back to the man. 'I don't know why you're so bothered, mister, over an old thing like that, but I'm sorry if I did wrong.'

Out of the corner of her eye she could see Miss Simpson's flat chest filling out and her lips pulling back, ready to breathe hellfire and damnation.

'How did you come to be in this place, child?' The man was looking at her through half-closed eyes, his gaze fixed on her face. Beside him, Miss Simpson deflated like a pricked balloon.

'Somebody killed me ma,' Bridget told him, then quickly added, 'sir.'

His head jerked. He blinked just once, then glanced at the supervisor, who gave him a look that could have meant anything. Then Miss Simpson tossed her head haughtily and pretended to be distracted by two of the other girls who were whispering behind their hands.

'Come here, child . . . Bridget, is it?' Bridget nodded and stepped forward, flinching in surprise when the man's gloved fingers hooked beneath her chin and tilted her face up so that she could see the hairs growing inside his nostrils. 'Your mother . . . could she have been called Colleen, by any chance?'

Bridget swallowed, which wasn't easy with her head tipped back like that, so she pulled away from the tenacious fingers and glowered at their owner.

'What if she was?'

He gave a loud, amused guffaw. 'No need to answer my question. I can see that you are your mother's daughter. Colleen was full of light and fire and she had those same sea-green eyes, only yours are brighter — and even more beautiful.'

'Did you know me ma, then?' Bridget's forehead wrinkled, remembering how the supervisor had introduced him as Sir Reginald Burnleigh. She didn't recall any of her mother's friends being called that. Most of them were called Smith or Brown.

'You might say that I was a friend of hers, my dear, yes. A long time ago. Long before you were born, I daresay. How old are you, Bridget?'

'I'm thirteen.' It wasn't quite true — there were a few more months to go yet — but it always felt better saying you were older than you really were.

'Ah, I see.'

Bridget wasn't sure what Sir Reginald saw, but he looked kind of relieved. Afterwards, when Miss Simpson called Bridget to her office, she did not get the telling-off or the beating she was expecting. Far from it, in fact.

'I don't know what you've done to deserve it, Bridget Maguire, but Sir Reginald has asked me to set up a fund for you. A small sum of money for the rest of your life. I must say it's highly irregular and we must not let any of the other children know or . . . '

Miss Simpson's voice droned on, but Bridget had switched herself off from the old dragon's reflections. She couldn't believe what she had just been told. She was to have some money, all her own, for ever and ever! This Sir Reginald must have been a very good friend indeed of her mother's, even though he was as old as Laura Caldwell's granddad. The words that she had so often heard her mother speak when astonished at anything kept repeating in Bridget's head. *Well, I never did!*

'Bridget, close your mouth, girl, and stop staring into space like that with your eyes out like chapel hat-pegs!' Miss Simpson's voice finally got through the confused haze of her thoughts. 'Are you listening to me? You are to receive a weekly allowance of five shillings a week, effective immediately. This will be paid into an account for you and you will receive a lump sum on your fifteenth birthday, which is when you will terminate your stay here at the orphanage. It's enough to live on, if you live frugally, but in order to earn the money, you must stay clean and honest.'

'What does he mean by clean and honest, miss?' Bridget demanded, ready to defend herself if this so-called gentleman dared to suggest that she was or ever could be otherwise.

'He means, Bridget, that you will not choose the same occupation as your mother, who was a prostitute.'

'Is that the same thing as a whore?'

Miss Simpson looked as if she might faint. 'Yes, but you're far too young to understand what that involves, Bridget, and I am not prepared to try and explain it to you.'

Bridget shrugged. At least she understood what frugal meant. Having five shillings coming in every week would be a bliddy luxury, she thought, then cast her eyes up to heaven and apologized to her dead mother's soul for swearing. From now on she would try to be better and speak more like a lady, because one day she would like to find this Sir Reginald and thank him properly and show him that she was worth every penny of the money he had invested in her.

That night Bridget had tied her blankets together and escaped from the dormitory room she shared with a dozen other girls. She shimmied down the makeshift rope, dropped lightly to the ground and ran off in the direction of Dawson Street. If she told no one else about her famous legacy, she had to tell Billy. Maybe he would be so happy for her he would forget Laura Caldwell and his silly dreams about her, whatever they were. Billy never had to tell Bridget anything. She could see inside his mind as if it was all printed on his forehead. Sometimes, she thought she could see inside his heart too, but Billy himself didn't seem to understand what was going on in there. She could hear her mother's voice as clear as if Colleen was standing there beside her, sharing her thoughts.

'*Och, it's a male thing, Bridget, me darlin'. They think they know all about love, bless their cotton socks. In reality, they wouldn't recognize it if it hit them in the chops. Sure and the only romance they understand goes on in their pants . . . and I shouldn't be talkin' like this to me daughter, though I say it meself. Anyhow, you'll find out for yourself soon enough.*'

8

Billy stood for a while, watching the abortive attempts of his mother trying to get up from the floor. She had spent the night there, clutching the empty gin bottle to her chest. He had come down in the early hours and found her. She was too heavy for him to lift, so he simply covered her over with the quilt from her bed.

'Aw, Gawd, our Billy, don't just stand there!' she yelled at him. 'Give us a hand, will ye.'

Her vibrant voice penetrated his thoughts, which were straying, as ever, in the direction of Laura Caldwell. News had filtered through to him, via Laura's proud grandfather, that Laura and her handsome fiancé were to be married in a month's time.

It had been a long engagement and for a while Billy's hopes had risen high, thinking that the marriage wasn't meant to be. He willed it to fail. They should have been married shortly after the bans had been called. The day he had found Patches. However, something must have happened, because no wedding took place. The waiting had been excruciating for young Billy, forever hopeful that Laura would change her mind and turn to him for solace. At sixteen he considered himself to be no longer a child. He'd been doing the work of a man for three years or more and although he could never be called tall or brawny, he was muscular and wiry, and as strong as the next man any day.

Having refused adamantly to go down the pit, Billy had turned to the shipyard for employment. They took him on reluctantly in a time when men were being laid off. Most of Billy's childhood friends could be found in the dole queue and it was understandable that they were bitter towards him. Billy took it all in his stride. They wouldn't have done his job anyway, brushing out the workplaces, running and fetching for management and general mucking out when required. He was never in any doubt that he had been taken on because of a strong word in his favour from Mr Robinson, who had friends and ex-colleagues in high places at Palmer's.

In old Albert Robinson, he had found a mentor, and a good friend in Patches. The dog was his constant companion. Wherever Billy went, Patches was never far away, always keeping a watchful eye on his young master. Only once did one of Billy's workmates try to bully him, using a bit of unnecessary physical violence. Patches was straight in with teeth bared and made a hole in the stupid fellow's dungarees. And probably left a reminder of the attack in the man's flabby buttocks too.

As it was Sunday, Billy was due to meet Mr Robinson in half an hour when the sun was almost up. While most folk in the vicinity went to church or stayed in bed on a Sunday morning, Albert Robinson and Billy, accompanied by the faithful Patches, escaped the hawk-sharp eyes of their womenfolk and went fishing.

'Aw, howay, Mam!' Billy's tone had changed towards the mother he had loved all his life. 'Why do you have to drink so much?'

It was a question neither of them could answer. Maggie because she was too far steeped in alcohol all the time to know which end was up; and Billy because he was too young to know the workings of his mother's mind. What he did know was that he wasn't ever going to touch a drop of drink like that, having seen what it turned people into. The demon drink, the vicar would call it in breathing hell and damnation from the pulpit to his parishioners. Aye, it was a demon all right. A monster of a demon that had the power to ruin people's lives. Well, his mother could rant and rave, but Billy had had enough. Let her rot in her alcohol-soaked flesh. *See if he cared!*

'Bottle's empty, Billy!' Maggie cried. 'Go and get me another one from the off licence, eh? You know I can't get through the day without a drop passing me lips. Go on, laddie. Take pity on yer poor auld ma. If ye bang on the back door of the corner shop, Alec'll let yer have something for us. Gan on, pet.'

'No, Mam! I've bought you your last bottle. You'll have to face life without it from now on. I don't care any more. Your drinking has destroyed this family. It's got to stop.'

'I can't stop!' Maggie wailed. 'It'd kill me, son, it'd kill me.'

'Ye're killing yersel', Ma,' he shouted back at her, feeling an uncomfortable lump rise in his throat. 'Ye blame the drink, but it's not that. It's you that lifts the glass to your lips.'

As far as Billy was concerned, his mother might as well be dead, for she certainly wasn't alive, even though she moved and breathed, but was most of the time staggering or comatose. He was her youngest child, yet he had never known her as a mother. For as long as he could remember, Maggie had leaned on him. He had been her prop, her provider, but now he felt awash with guilt at having been a part of her downfall. He should have been tougher with her, but he had been nothing but a bit bairn when it started.

Her behaviour had driven the rest of the family away. The boys had drifted from the mines to the sea. Desmond had gone down with his ship in a storm. Jack had married and emigrated to Australia, where he was doing his best to follow in his mother's alcoholic footsteps as he wandered like a nomad from bush town to bush town. Tom had just walked out one day and never come back. God alone knew where he was. And there was the baby that was born after Patrick Flynn had committed murder and fled. The poor little thing had been all grotesque and mangled. It died the next day and that, at least, was a blessing.

Only Billy stayed on. He could have walked away from the situation on many an occasion but he always had the desperate hope that things would improve. Now, he knew they never would. Maggie had the appearance of an old hag. Her skin was like yellowed parchment, all dried up and wrinkled, and there were pouches under her eyes like sacks of coal. He had seen her naked, had washed her down when she was covered in her own vomit, pee and shit. He had put her to bed, fed and clothed her; listened to her moanings and her complaints for as long as he could remember.

He looked at her now and was sickened by what he saw. Sickened to the point of hatred. How dare she be so weak, so pathetic? How could she expect him to be her prop when she had never been there for him, except during a time when he was too young to remember or be aware that she cared for him? Even though she had apparently watched the man she married attempt to suffocate him, or so the story went, she had taken Patrick back and seen him beat his children senseless, and her with them.

Billy gave a convulsive shudder at the thought of his father and the spectre of that detestable individual floated through his mind, the way he had appeared through the darkness of the mud flats as he murdered Colleen Maguire. The police had searched for him, but he had vanished without trace.

Maybe he was dead, as many people seemed to suggest. Billy hoped they were right, but retained that nagging dread in his mind that Patrick would turn up again sometime, somewhere.

'I'm going now, Mam,' he said in a low voice that she probably did not hear, for she was grovelling about and mumbling to herself, hopping on one leg as she struggled into her pants. 'I don't know when I'll be back.'

'Go then!' she screamed at him as he went through the door. 'You're no son of mine. I want nothing more to do wi' ye, d'ye hear, Billy Flynn!'

'Aye,' he called out over his shoulder. 'Just like me dad, am I? Maybe ye should have let him smother me when I was born, like he tried to do.'

'You're no son of Patrick Flynn either, so don't blame him.' She was hanging on to the corner of the kitchen table, swaying perilously, her eyes covered in a pale film that gave her a blind look. 'It was my fault ye was born. I couldn't wait for Patrick to come home from the war, so I went with another man. Why d'ye think he hated ye so much, eh?'

Billy hesitated, pondering on her words, then continued on his way. So that was what it had all been about, he thought. Patrick had always been harder on the others, in a way, than he had been on Billy. Billy, he just ignored most of the time, eyeing him hatefully and suspiciously, as if he was cooking up something really bad for him and didn't want to touch him until the plan gelled in his brain.

Well, whoever Billy's real father was, it wasn't Patrick Flynn, and he thanked God for that. It was as if a huge weight lifted from his shoulders. If it hadn't been for Laura and her impending marriage, he would be a happy man this day.

Billy called to Patches. The dog was waiting for him eagerly, pink tongue lolling, eyes bright and hopeful. Together they sauntered through the back lanes of Jarrow, heading in the direction of the River Don where they would pick up Mr Robinson, who had promised to let Billy try his hand with his best fishing rod. There was a big pike out there somewhere that had been taunting Albert Robinson for years. A giant, by all accounts, and the old man was determined to catch the slippery devil before he was too old and feeble to reel him in.

As the sun rose up over the Tyne Valley, bathing the land in a rosy glow and gilding the swollen waters of the Don that slid by, Billy stuck his hands in his pockets and whistled a merry tune. He felt as new as the day itself and he was determined to enjoy his Sunday out with Albert Robinson in their hunt for the big pike.

'Ah, there you are, Billy!'

Albert Robinson was waiting at the arranged spot where the undulating river banks met a densely wooded area that was a tangle of blackthorn, hawthorn and oak, and the occasional Scots pine reaching majestically to the sky. Somewhere in the middle of it was the pond the locals called the Witch's Cauldron, because of its dark, mysterious depths. It was even more dangerous than the Slakes, but it held no fear for Billy.

'Hello, Mr Robinson,' Billy greeted his friend, his ready grin quickly put in place. 'I'm not late, am I?'

'No, son, but let's get a move on, eh? It's just the kind of morning that brings old Neptune out of his hiding place. This could well be my lucky day.'

Neptune was the name Albert Robinson had given to the big fish that had been his rival for years. He was quite convinced that it was the same fish that got bigger and bigger every time he saw him. Albert enjoyed entertaining his pals down at the Venerable Bede public house about how he 'almost snagged him' and he must have been 'this big' — the arms stretching as wide as they could get. It was a standing joke, this mythical creature, for no one really believed that the pike existed. And if it did, no one would dare try to catch it. It was Mr Robinson's fish and woe betide anybody who thought differently.

'Right now,' Mr Robinson said after they had been walking for about half an hour. 'This is the place, Billy, but we have to be very quiet. Just pick yourself a spot and relax. That old devil's in for a bit of sport today. I'll show those unbelievers down at the pub. They'll have to eat their words good and proper when I present them with Neptune. That fish has been escaping my hook for too long. It's time the battle was won.'

'Do you think I'll catch anything today, Mr Robinson?' Billy asked, his cheeks already flushing with excitement. 'You did promise that I could use your best rod.'

'Aye, I did that.' Mr Robinson looked momentarily troubled, but then he smiled broadly and handed over the rod. 'And I'm a man of my word. Here you go, Billy. A box full of fresh gudgeon. Fished them out myself before the light was up. That should make the old bugger's mouth water.'

Billy couldn't help thinking that all those gudgeon, small though they were, would have made a tasty meal for him and his mother, with enough left over for the next day. The thought of Maggie brought back the memory of how things had been between them earlier. For a moment, he felt heavy and sad, but then he pushed it to the back of his mind and concentrated on the business at hand. He picked up one of the gudgeon, asked God for one of his miracles, praying that Mr Robinson would bag his prize fish and they would both go home happy.

'Like this, Mr Robinson?'

Albert Robinson looked on proudly as Billy set up his rod and his bait. Then he supervised the casting of the line so that it fell just right.

'There you are, Billy. Just the ticket. We'll make a fisherman of you yet.'

There was no mistaking the pride and the enthusiasm in the boy's eyes as he sat, his gaze fixed on the rod and the line and the bobbing sinker with the rippling water going out from it in circles. Both his mother and his hunger were secondary to the pleasure and the anticipation that this day was bringing him. Until today, he had never managed to catch anything bigger than the small fish he was now using for bait. Usually, Mr Robinson made him throw the fish he caught back into the river, saying they were too young to be taken. However, Billy never went home empty-handed. There was always a decent-sized fish or two donated to him from Mr Robinson's catch. Something told Billy, though, that he would not be given as much as a scale from Neptune's huge body, even if the creature was unlucky enough to get caught. There would be grand celebrations at the Venerable Bede, then the fish would be stuffed and mounted above the bar as a lesson to all unbelievers.

Mr Robinson, as usual, had brought a

chunk of crusty bread and a wedge of Cheshire cheese with two blood-red tomatoes, a hard-boiled egg each and some fruit. By the time the sun was well up in the sky, Billy's hunger had returned, but Mr Robinson was concentrating too heavily on the waters of the pond to worry about eating. Billy continued offering up prayers that old Neptune would come and take the bait, but Neptune was playing hard to get, as usual, like the king that he was.

A church clock began to strike the midday hour, its tinny gonging sound reaching out from across the river. Mr Robinson checked his pocket watch and heaved a deep sigh. Just as he put his rod down, wedging it secure with a large stone, there was the sound of voices. A man and a woman were arguing as they came closer and closer to the little fishing party.

'Oh, now, that's all we need,' grumbled Mr Robinson, squinting in the direction of two approaching figures.

Keeping his eye on his line, Billy suddenly caught sight of a movement in the water a few feet in front of where he was still sitting. A dark shadow, then a form, solid and silvery turning to green and gold in the sunlight, the long, sleek back rising above the surface, and then turning with a

176

flash of a ridged dorsal fin and tail.

'Mr Robinson!' He hissed out a breathy warning. 'Is that Neptune? Look!'

Mr Robinson looked just in time to see the fish emerge again, then plunge with a challenging flick of the tail, sending up spray and bubbles like a line of diamonds following him down to the bottom of the pond.

'Dear God, it's him all right, laddie!' The old man was almost overcome with excitement, but he needed to forestall the couple coming their way or all would be lost. Neptune would take fright and disappear. 'Keep your eye on him, Billy. Don't let him get away. Guard him for me, eh?'

'Aye, Mr Robinson,' Billy said, not quite sure how he was going to persuade the great pike to hang around until the old man was ready for the kill. He didn't think, for one minute, that a pike could be sweet-talked into staying put.

Mr Robinson started to climb the bank towards the quarrelling pair, waving his arms about like a shipwrecked sailor hailing a passing vessel. The two people took no notice of him and continued their dispute, which was extremely heated. The woman sounded as if she was close to tears.

At last, the quarrelling stopped. Billy gave a quick glance over his shoulder and saw that the man had gone, leaving the woman in tears, hurrying towards Mr Robinson, who was speaking to her in soothing tones, his important mission momentarily forgotten.

'There, there, sweetheart,' he was saying, holding out his arms for her to run into, which she did. 'It can't be as bad as all that, surely?'

That was when Billy realized that the woman was none other than Laura Caldwell, Mr Robinson's granddaughter. He froze, not knowing quite what to do. It was bad seeing Laura so devastated, but then she hadn't even looked his way for months, always too busy making cow's eyes at that arrogant fiancé of hers.

'It's over, Granddad,' he heard Laura say as she sobbed into Albert Robinson's old tweed fishing jacket. 'I've told him I can't marry him and that's that.'

'Come on, love,' Mr Robinson said gently, putting his arms about his granddaughter and hugging her briefly to him. 'It's not worth getting yourself all worked up about. It was the right decision you made.'

As they spoke, the old man drew Laura towards the river where Billy was standing, holding his rod in a grip so fierce that his knuckles shone white. He couldn't believe his ears. Laura was no longer tied to that idiot of a man. She was free. She could marry somebody else now. She could even . . . He dared not even think it. Him and Laura Caldwell? What a laugh! There wasn't a cat's chance in hell that a lady like her would see anything in a sixteen-year-old boy, even if he had loved her for as long as he could remember.

'Do you really think so, Granddad?' Laura was saying, her voice full of tears. 'That it was the right thing to do, sending him off like that? I thought . . . I thought that you approved of him.'

'Aye, lass, I did. Maybe not quite as much as your parents, but then it wasn't for me to say anything. A girl has to make up her own mind. Aye, and make her own mistakes too. I knew my little Laura would see sense in the end. It never looked to me that you really loved the lad.'

Laura raised her eyebrows at the last remark and turned her head, the action of which led her eyes to rest on Billy. A slight frown creased her forehead, but she effectively ignored him and continued talking to her grandfather.

'I did love him,' she said, her breath catching in her throat as she spoke. 'At least, I thought I did. But maybe it was the wrong kind of love . . . you know . . . ?'

Mr Robinson gave a short chuckle. 'Aye, lass, I do know, and many a marriage has floundered because of that. There's love and love . . . and then some. Most of us live as best we can with the bed we make. The lucky ones are the ones, like yourself, who recognize that the bed in question is all wrong.'

'Mr Robinson!'

Billy wanted to hear more of their conversation, but an urgent situation had arisen and he had to attract the old man's attention. Something was tugging sharply at his line, taking it out into the middle of the pond where the water was deepest. It was Neptune. It had to be. The big fish had finally taken the bait, but it had taken Billy's gudgeon and not Mr Robinson's.

'What is it, lad? Oh, my giddy aunt, you haven't gone and hooked Neptune, have you?'

Mr Robinson surged forward, old legs going like stiff pistons, and arrived at the water's edge, red-faced and puffing. He stood there, panting and gawping at the rippling rings going out from the spot where Billy's line entered the water. Laura hung back at first, then joined them, her face still streaked with tears, her eyes red-rimmed. Billy stared at her and felt an unaccustomed blush creep up from his neck when she forced a smile in greeting.

'Hello, Laura,' he said, and his voice was a mere croaky whisper.

'Billy, what are you doing?' Laura pointed to where the pike had risen to the surface and was thrashing about in an attempt to dislodge the hook from its mouth. 'Look out. You'll lose him if you're not careful.'

That's exactly what Billy wanted to do. He couldn't possibly catch Mr Robinson's prize fish. The old man would never forgive him. But the temptation of hauling in such an impressive creature before the eyes of Laura Caldwell was suddenly stronger than that to let the thing go. Not that he knew how to free the fish without first pulling him on to the land.

'Steady, lad, steady!' Mr Robinson shouted and reached out as if to take the rod and reel in old Neptune himself. 'You've got him, but play him wisely. Reel him in slowly . . . no not like that . . . give him some slack now . . . '

Mr Robinson's hand was on Billy's shoulder as the lad concentrated for all he was worth on the task before him. He allowed himself a quick glance over his shoulder to see if Laura was still there and watching. Satisfied that she was, and looking halfway to being interested, he gave the finale all it needed to impress the woman of his dreams.

'Gently, Billy, gently . . . ' Mr Robinson's hand was once again hovering as he fought not to take over the rod.

Every muscle in Billy's sinewy body was straining to breaking point as he pitted his strength and his wits against the king of the Witch's Cauldron. He dug in his heels and sank into the mud up to his ankles, but he didn't care. The tug on the line was so great that he felt himself being dragged towards the edge of the pond, his feet leaving deep grooves.

'I can't hold him, Mr Robinson!' he yelled, but didn't take his eyes off the silvery back of the pike for a second.

'Yes, you can, Billy. Go on, lad, put your back into it.'

'Come on, Billy!' Laura's voice broke through the sizzling whine in his ears and he knew this had to be the proudest moment of his life. 'Come on! You can do it! Oh, yes, yes!'

Just when Billy thought that his muscles would pop like pricked balloons, the pike gave up the battle. As the line went slack, Billy fell on his back, but never let go of his rod and started reeling in the fish with a passion he hadn't known he possessed. There was no going back now. He had to catch that blessed monster fish. And he had to do it for Laura.

Minutes later, Neptune was lying on the grassy bank, being admired by Mr Robinson, Laura, and a group of local fishermen who had heard the commotion and come running. Billy was dripping with sweat and muddy water, so breathless he could hardly speak.

'Is that Neptune, Mr Robinson?' one of the fishermen asked. 'Have you caught him at last?'

'Aye, that's Neptune.' Albert Robinson nodded and his face seemed softened by sadness as he bent down and gently removed the hook from the pike's mouth. 'That's my old arch enemy, lads.'

'Congratulations,' another fisherman said with a touch of astonishment in his voice. 'Most of us lads down at the pub didn't believe ye. Well, now ye can boast and crow like a ruddy rooster, eh?'

'Well, it's not me who caught him, so I'll not be doing the crowing,' Mr Robinson said, picking up his gaff. ''Tis Billy here that reeled him in.'

It went strangely silent, for there wasn't a man in Jarrow who didn't know Albert Robinson's famous dream about catching the biggest pike ever.

All eyes were cast down to where the fish lay panting, its mouth opening and shutting, its body still writhing with the last vestiges of strength that remained. Billy imagined that a round, glassy eye looked at him accusingly, then watched plaintively as the old man, who had not, after all, been the victor, offered him the gaff.

'Go on, lad. The honour's yours fair and square, but don't let the bugger suffer.'

Billy shook his head. 'No, Mr Robinson. I caught him with your rod. He's still your fish. You finish him off.'

There was a moment's hesitation, then Albert Robinson raised the gaff over his head, hovering for a brief second as if paying his final homage to the king of the river, and brought it down with all his might, killing Neptune in one clean blow.

★　★　★

There was a riot of cheering and back-slapping as the men in the Venerable Bede took in the news that Albert Robinson's 'mythical' fish had finally been caught. Mr Robinson and Billy had been hoisted shoulder-high and carried to the public house and it had taken two men to carry the pike with ease. It was still early, but the landlord tipped the local bobby and everyone entered by the back door, too excited to worry about the fact that they were breaking the law. Besides, PC Humble wasn't averse to being slipped the odd ten-shilling note just to look the other way. Indeed, on this occasion, he had joined them and was already knocking back a half pint of Newcastle Brown.

Laura had accompanied them to the door of the pub, but being a female and not officially allowed inside, she had kissed her grandfather and beamed a tremulous smile in Billy's direction.

'Well done, Billy,' she told him. 'Your mother will be proud of you.'

'I dunno about that,' he said, twisting his face and wrinkling his nose, which he often did when embarrassed. 'I didn't do it for her.'

'Oh, who did you do it for, then?'

Billy shrugged and no more was said. Laura gave him a curious smile and headed back for home, still looking dejected and still with an unshed tear in her eye. It would be a while, Billy thought, before she stopped thinking of the fellow she almost married. By which time, Billy might be in a better position to speak to her about how he felt.

His name was being called, so he stopped watching Laura's elegant back disappearing away down the street and went to join the others.

'Hey, Albert, he certainly is a big fella,' Cedric Small, the landlord, was saying, eyeing the fish on the bar counter as he pulled pints and offered them all round. 'What are ye goin' to do with 'im, eh? Fish and chips for the family for the next fortnight, eh?'

'It's not up to me, that,' Albert said, rubbing a rough hand around his bristly chin. 'It's up to Billy here. He's the one who caught old Neptune.'

Billy noticed just a bit of an edge in Mr Robinson's voice, though the man was smiling genially enough at him.

'That's only cos I used your best rod, Mr Robinson,' Billy said in a loud voice so that everybody could hear above the cacophony that was going on. 'You would have caught him if . . . if it hadn't been that you were called away . . . you know . . . talking to Laura, like . . . ?'

'Still, Billy, lad, you were the one who got him, good and proper. And you hauled him in without any help from me. You deserve all the praise you can get for doing a thing like that.' Albert turned to the men gathered around him. 'He's not only a good lad, this one, he's mightily strong with it, mind and body. Come on Billy, let's buy you a drink to celebrate, eh?'

'Thanks, Mr Robinson, but I don't touch alcohol.' Billy shook his head positively. 'Not me. I've seen what it does to people.'

There were murmurs of surprise and one or two guffaws of sarcastic laughter, but Albert Robinson held up his hands and the look in his eyes made them fall silent.

'The lad has good reason to be tee-total,' he announced. 'And we all know that reason. Now, Billy, lad. How about a sarsaparilla or a dandelion and burdock?'

'Can I have a lemonade, please?' Billy gritted his teeth and waited to be ridiculed, for some of the men in the pub were his workmates from Palmer's and he didn't want them to think that he was some sort of pansy.

'A lemonade for our hero, landlord.' Mr Robinson slapped the palm of his hand on the bar counter. 'Billy Flynn's a bigger man than any of us gave him credit for and no mistake. Anybody disagrees with that, he'll have me to answer to.'

The landlord raised an eyebrow, polished a tall glass and poured in a generous measure of lemonade. Still nobody spoke or jeered, so Billy took it and sipped the refreshing liquid.

'Now then, Mr Robinson,' the landlord said, looking pleased with himself. 'What will it be? Your usual poison, eh?'

'I think, Cedric, today calls for a change. Pour me a double whisky, will ye? Let's celebrate in style.'

The drink poured, Albert Robinson suppressed whatever disappointment he might have been feeling at that moment in time and raised his glass to make a toast.

'Here's to Billy Flynn,' he said. 'Once too small for his boots, but now a real big man.'

'Aye,' the cry went up. 'Good on ye, Billy Big Boots. Ye're all right, son. Here's to ye.'

Then the men started to sing to the tune of 'The Sun Has Got It's Hat On': Good old Billy Big Boots, hip-hip-hip hooray. Billy bagged old Neptune and it's such a happy day!

The voices penetrated the walls of the pub, reverberating out into the morning sunshine.

'Come on, Billy. Get out yer penny whistle. Give us a tune to sing to.'

Billy obliged and as he played he thought to himself that if only he didn't feel so guilty over catching Mr Robinson's pike, it just had to be the happiest day of his life so far.

9

'This is not the time to bring shame on your family!'

Laura sucked in her lips and bit down on them hard, determined not to give way to the emotion that was boiling up inside her. Her mother had been shouting at her for an hour or more, while her father sat slumped and without words, not even bearing to look at his only daughter who was the object of the family shame.

She had hoped, week after week, that it would come to nothing. A mistake in the dates, a physical dysfunction. Her monthly periods had never been very regular at the best of times. It was only when she started feeling sick every morning, her breasts hurt, and her clothes pinched around her waist that she allowed herself to accept the fact that she was pregnant.

'I'm sorry,' Laura now murmured and, her knees giving way from standing in the same spot for so long, she collapsed into a nearby armchair. 'I'm really sorry, but . . . '

'This kind of thing does not happen in respectable homes,' Elizabeth Caldwell continued,

189

her voice vibrant with anger and mortification. 'Your grandmother must be turning in her grave at this moment. Laura, how could you cheapen yourself, going with somebody before you're married?'

'It . . . it was only the once,' Laura pleaded, as if it would make things better.

'Who was it?'

Laura bent her head over her lap, her cheeks suffused with the crimson colour of shame.

'Charles Dawson,' she whispered.

There was a stony silence before her mother went on. 'But . . . but he's married to someone else now. I've seen them in church on Sundays!'

Laura's face puckered up and her eyes filled with tears. One warm salty tear plopped on to the back of her hand. She stared at it hard as if it were a crystal ball that might tell her where her future lay.

'Yes.'

'Oh, my God, Laura! Why didn't you marry him three years ago when you had the opportunity? John, say something to your daughter, for goodness' sake.'

John Caldwell shifted uncomfortably in his chair. His pale, lifeless eyes drifted from his wife to his daughter and then dropped to the floor between them.

'I've heard of a woman who takes care of these kind of things,' he said. 'A Mrs Tanwell in Brook Street. Maybe Laura should go to see her.'

'Lord in heaven, John, what are you suggesting? Butchery? I've heard that some girls die after getting rid of babies like that.'

'What choice do we have?' John flapped at the air with a lily-white, bony hand and his head sank down between his shoulders, making him look like an elderly tortoise. 'It's either that or raise a bastard in your home.'

Laura looked up and drew in a sharp breath of stale air since it was summer and warm outside, but her mother refused to open windows to allow flies to come in and private matters to be overheard.

'You can't make me have an abortion,' she said vehemently, jumping once more to her feet, clamping her hands protectively over the tiny unborn infant in her womb. 'I won't do it, I tell you.'

'And what are you going to do, Laura?' Elizabeth's eyes narrowed and her thin lips became even thinner. 'Don't think you can bring an illegitimate child into this house. I would die of shame. How far on are you?'

Laura swallowed with difficulty and did a rapid calculation, surprising herself at how far advanced her pregnancy was. How could she not have realized?

'About four months,' she said. 'Maybe more. I . . . I'm not sure.'

Elizabeth's expression was wild as she glared first at her daughter and then at her husband. She shook her head as if trying to dislodge the problem from her brain, then ran out of the room in floods of tears.

'Father?' Laura stood there helplessly, palms turned towards her father. Short of sinking down on to her knees before him and begging his support, she didn't know what to do. 'Please, Father . . . I don't know what to do.'

John Caldwell averted his gaze. His hands gripped the wheels of his chair and he started out of the room in the footsteps of his distraught wife.

'I'm sorry, Laura,' she heard him say in muffled tones. 'I can't help you. Please make arrangements to leave this house and . . . well, just go away somewhere. I'll see that you have sufficient to live on until . . . '

His words trailed off behind him and Laura was left standing in the silent room, echoes of her mother's sobbing over her head and the squeak of the wheels on her father's wheelchair fading away down the hall.

There was only one person she knew she

could turn to, but even her grandfather might not wish to know about her unfortunate condition. And seeing the disapproval in the old man's eyes would be too hurtful; far more hurtful than that shown to her by her parents. Laura heaved a sigh and regretted that one act of madness that had led to the conception of an innocent child. People always said you should never go back and they were right. She had never been able to get over losing the one man she believed to be right for her. Despite his many infidelities, Laura was still desperately in love with Charles. She had foolishly chased him away and he had paid her back by marrying the first woman who came along. It was far from being a match made in heaven. Eleanor Blenkinsop was years older than Charles, a widow with three children of her own. Everyone knew she was desperate to find another husband. Charles had fallen into her net, still bruised from getting his marching orders from Laura.

If only he had not come into the little haberdashery shop where she was buying some embroidery silks, Laura thought time and time again. It was looking up and unexpectedly seeing him standing there, gazing down at her, as startled at the encounter as she was. He had forgotten completely what he was there for — probably to buy something intimate and flimsy for his wife for Christmas. Anyway, their eyes had met, their fingers touched, and Laura was lost.

They had continued to meet, discreetly, over a number of weeks. Laura knew it was wrong, but she couldn't help herself. The last time, when she had given herself to him fully in the back of his big Austin automobile, he had told her, on parting, that he couldn't see her again. His wife was carrying his child.

How ironic was that? Laura was too shocked by this revelation to consider the possibility that she, too, might be carrying his child. She had been a virgin and that had been her only physical encounter, apart from passionate but hurried kisses and unbearably urgent fondlings. If only she had been strong enough to withstand his more pressing advances that one time. If only! Life, Laura thought wryly, was so full of 'if only'.

Laura glanced around her at the room she had known all her life. It was her home, yet there was no warmth, no welcoming feel about it. It belonged to her mother. Not even her father fitted in.

She picked up her hat and her scarf and walked, with heavy feet, into the hall. A cool breeze was wafting through the place, bringing the faint sound of people enjoying an amicable conversation. One of the voices belonged to Maureen Flynn. Or Mrs Hedley, as she was now.

Suddenly the solution to all Laura's problems seemed to cry out to her. Maureen was a rough-and-ready character but she understood about life. She was just her mother's cook, but was always on hand with good advice and friendly support when needed. Which was why the kitchen at Elizabeth Caldwell's home was rarely empty, for people came to visit Maureen constantly. She was a long cry from the skinny little schoolgirl who had run off petrified at the sight of blood when her little brother was being born.

The doors between hall and kitchen were ajar and as Laura picked her way down the long corridor between her mother's domain and the domestic part of the house, where her mother never went, she smelled freshly baked bread and cakes. Normally, it would have made her mouth water, but today she felt too queasy to appreciate it.

They didn't see her enter, the three people sitting at the kitchen table clutching steaming mugs of tea, laughing and talking together. Laura felt a twinge of envy. She had never had a special friend to call her own; never felt the need for one, until now.

As she stepped further into the room, the door creaked and her shoes scuffed on the rough stone floor. Three heads shot up, their conversation suspended, the laughter frozen on their jolly faces.

'Oh, Maureen . . . ' Laura gulped and fixed her eyes on the cook as pleadingly as possible. 'I'm sorry to interrupt, but . . . '

'It's all right, Miss Caldwell,' Maureen said, taking off her small reading glasses and giving them a wipe on her pinafore. 'Come on in. Would you like a cup of tea? I could bring it to you in the lounge, if ye like.'

'No . . . no, Maureen, thank you.'

'A piece of cake? It's carrot and cinnamon. Your favourite.'

'Thank you . . . no.' Laura's eye flickered over the other two occupants of the room, recognizing Maureen's brother, Billy, and the prostitute's daughter, Bridget Maguire, who had done so well for herself, despite being dragged up by a woman with no husband and no morals.

'What's the matter, hinny?'

Maureen was on her feet and coming over to her, arms outstretched, ready to comfort her. It was only then that Laura was aware of how wretched she must appear. She felt a sob start deep in her chest and surge to the surface and then, as she fell against Maureen, the floodgates opened and she cried like a little lost child.

Behind them, chair legs scraped on the floor as Billy and Bridget got up and came over to see if there was anything they could do to help. Laura Caldwell had always struck them as being a strong person, not given to fuss or over-sensitive behaviour, so it must have shocked them to see her like this. Laura now wished she had simply left the house, alone in her misery.

'Oh, Maureen,' she gasped, meaning to break away from the woman's hold, but found herself blurting out the reason for her emotional state. 'I'm in such deep trouble and I . . . I don't know where to turn.'

'Oh, aye? Come on, pet, tell us what's troubling ye?' Maureen pushed her into a chair at the table and pulled a second chair close to her, then sat there waiting, grasping both of Laura's hands in her own.

Laura glanced up at Bridget and Billy and bit down on her lip. She didn't say a word, but it was obvious that she didn't want them to be there. Billy just stared at her, not budging an inch, until Bridget thumped his shoulder and pulled him away.

'Come on, Billy,' she said, pushing him out through the back door where the sun was shining on the little vegetable garden that

Billy helped Maureen with. 'It's women's business and Miss Caldwell needs a bit of privacy.'

★ ★ ★

'What's happening, Bridget?'

Billy was rocking from one foot to the other and trying to peer over Bridget's shoulder as she listened at the door they had just come through. She had left it open just a crack, obviously with the intention of listening in to Laura's conversation with Maureen. Now, Billy's own curiosity was getting the better of him. He hadn't seen Laura Caldwell for months and he was shocked at how thin and deathly pale she had become.

'Ssh, Billy. How can I hear anything with you muttering in me ear, eh?' Bridget gave him a thrust with her behind because he was leaning on her heavily and there was a danger of them both falling headlong back into the kitchen.

Billy took a step back, but stood impatiently clenching and unclenching his fists, wishing he could be a fly on the wall. Wishing even more that he could be in there now, holding Laura's hand, instead of his sister.

'Oh, my Gawd!'

Bridget turned from the door and put her hands up to her cheeks. Her green eyes were wide with disbelief as she stared at Billy.

'What?' Billy had had enough waiting. 'Bridget! What's wrong? She's not ill, is she?'

'You could say that,' Bridget said through her fingers, then grimaced and walked off down the garden path to the gate that led into the back lane and the wooded area that went down to the river.

Billy gave a quick glance towards the house, then followed her.

'Tell me, Bridget,' he said, tugging at one of her arms that were swinging characteristically at her sides. 'Oh, come on. It can't be that bad . . . can it?'

Bridget stopped in her tracks and he bowled into her, nearly knocking her off her balance.

'It depends who you are,' she told him with another grimace. 'Laura — Miss Prim — Caldwell has got herself knocked up good and proper. Can you imagine how her parents took the news?'

Billy shook his head and frowned at her. 'What do you mean by knocked up?' He couldn't believe it meant what the lads down at the shipyard talked about when they got a girl into trouble. 'Not . . . ?'

'Bun in the oven, so-so ... ' Bridget stopped and grinned. 'You *are* innocent, Billy. She's with child, as the posh might say. Laura Caldwell is, you know — so-so. What's worse is that she can't marry the man in question.'

'Oh, no!' Billy's eyes widened in shock as Bridget nodded slowly. 'Not Laura. Are you sure that's what she said?'

'Not in so many words,' Bridget informed him, picking up a twig with some dead oak leaves on it and flicking them off one by one. 'She says she hasn't seen anything in four months or more and her father's ordered her out of the house. Don't look at me like that, Billy. It's not my fault your precious Laura's going to have a baby out of wedlock. Serves her right for being so snooty, that's what I say.'

Billy glared at her reproachfully. It wasn't like Bridget to speak ill of anyone, except jokingly. But she wasn't joking about Laura and he wondered why. There had never been any bad feeling between the two of them to his knowledge. And yet there had been times, he recalled now, when Laura's name was mentioned, that sparked something off in Bridget. Billy shook his head. He would never understand women.

'I'm going back inside,' he said, brushing past Bridget, who spun around and caught the tail of his shirt that had escaped from his dungarees.

'Hey, Billy, what are you going to do? She doesn't want the likes of you around when she's talking about private matters. It's family business and nothing to do with you, anyway.'

'Isn't it?' Billy struck out for the house in long strides, Bridget running to keep up with him.

'Billy? What do you mean? How's it got anything to do with you?' Then she stopped dead in her tracks and blinked at his disappearing back, all the colour draining from her face. 'Eeh, dear God, Billy, it wasn't you who fathered her bairn, was it?' He didn't stop; just waved a hand briefly. 'Billy! Billy, tell me it wasn't you!'

When he burst into the kitchen, Bridget's words were still ringing in his ears. Until she had called that out to him, he had had no idea what he was about to do. Comfort Laura in some small way, hold her close and tell her that he would make everything all right, no matter what it took. But Bridget had planted the seed of an idea in his head and it was with this in mind that he burst through the kitchen door, snatching his cap from his head and standing stiff to attention before the two women.

'Laura,' he said through gritted teeth, and

his sister and the woman he had always loved took a startled step back at the suddenness of it. 'I know I'm younger than you, but at nineteen I'm a man and although I've been finished at the shipyard like all the others at Palmer's, I've still got all me other bits and bobs that I do and I don't mind working even harder. I already earn enough to feed a family on and . . . well, if you're willing, I . . . '

'Billy Flynn, what on earth are you on about?' His sister was regarding him with a bemused expression, but he wasn't interested in what Maureen said or thought.

Ignoring Maureen, Billy fixed his eyes unwaveringly on Laura and spoke out loud and clear from a heart that was nearly bursting with anticipation.

'Laura, I'll marry you, if . . . if that's all right with you, I mean . . . ?'

As quickly as his courage had mounted, it was now departing as he saw the look of horror in Laura's eyes and the way her mouth twisted as if he had suggested something vile. For a long while they stood there, staring at each other, and Maureen staring just as hard at the pair of them, not knowing what to make of the situation. Then Billy swallowed hard and the noise of it could be heard by all.

'Well, I just thought I'd ask,' he said numbly. 'It would be better than you struggling to raise a bairn without a man, even if it isn't mine.'

Still Laura held her silence, and Maureen with her, though his sister made one or two small sounds as if she were bursting to laugh or cry or both — he didn't know which, nor did he care.

He screwed his cap up in his hands, straightened it out again, then placed it awkwardly on his head and walked back outside, giving another gulp as he closed the door firmly behind him.

Down by the river, he could see Bridget sitting on a fallen tree. She was dangling her legs and dipping her bare toes into the burbling waters. Making diamonds, she used to call it when they were children together. The sun was filtering through the greenery above, turning her hair into flame and giving her a kind of halo of gold. Billy went to join her, sitting as close to her as he could get. He always found comfort in her closeness.

'So what did she say to your grand proposal, then?' Bridget asked, staring down at her fingers, which lay entwined in her lap.

'Nothing,' Billy said, smoothing out the stiff material of his dungarees over his thighs, the roughened skin of his workman's hands rasping like sandpaper. 'At least she didn't laugh.'

'Maybe she needs time to think it over, eh?'

'Aye. Maybe she does.'

'It was probably a bit of a shock for her, you asking her to marry her like that. I mean, it took me by surprise and I thought I knew everything there was to know about you, Billy Flynn.'

'Aye, there's not a lot you don't know, Bridget.'

'Do you think she'll say yes?'

'Dunno.'

'Will it bother you if she doesn't — you know — say yes?'

'Aye. Aye, Bridget, it will an' all.'

Bridget's arm slid out and went round Billy's slumped shoulders. She pulled him against her and he buried his face in her shoulder, breathing deeply to keep himself from crying, because real men didn't cry. He didn't see the tears that ran down Bridget's cheeks that she swiped at surreptitiously, not wanting to give herself away.

Silly bitch! She chastised herself silently, then she whispered into the top of Billy's fair head: 'Silly sod. You're worth better than Laura Caldwell. A lot better.'

'Thanks, Bridget.' Billy sniffed and raised his head, looking at her with glistening blue eyes. 'I doubt anybody would agree with you, but thanks, anyway.'

'Hey, come on.' Bridget gave him a playful dig in the ribs. 'It could have been worse. It could have been me up the spout instead of Laura. How would you have liked being landed with me on your plate, eh?'

Billy didn't say anything. He just stared at her for a long time, then blinked once and looked away into the middle distance, a small frown creasing his forehead.

★　★　★

'Just listen to that! Who'd have thought a little pint-sized woman could make such a racket?'

Billy grinned at the man who had spoken. They were standing at the back of a crowd of unemployed workmen, craning their necks to see the tiny, elfish Ellen Henderson, well-known Member of Parliament, who had taken up their cause. Even if they couldn't see her too well, they had no problem hearing her, for she had a forceful voice that carried right across the square.

'This town has been murdered!' she was crying out. 'There's not a man in gainful employment anywhere in Jarrow. Who among you can afford to feed your children? We have to let the government know that they are not doing enough to help the working men of this country, and in particular this town that should stand proud, not hang its head in shame . . . '

It was just one of the many speeches, some of them ad hoc, that 'Red Ellen' had made. A great roar went up as she made her closing statement, calling for the men to take action, promising that she would be behind them all the way.

'In fact,' she said, 'I'll do more than that. I'll march with you!'

'How about it, Billy lad? You going on the march?'

'Where to?' Billy asked, for he had been distracted at the crucial moment of the MP's speech, having caught sight of Laura Caldwell walking by, trying to hide her pregnancy behind a shopping bag.

'Why, London, of course. We're all going to march to London with a petition and show the bloody prime minister that we mean business.'

'Think it'll do any good?' said another man.

'Red Ellen seems to think so.'

'What! I can't see her making any impression on anybody. She's not the size of two pennorth of copper. Funny-looking little thing.'

Billy looked across to where he had a better

view of Ellen Henderson as she walked across the square and climbed into an official-looking black car — probably the mayor's. He had to agree that she wasn't anybody's idea of a raving beauty, and she was a bit lame too. That flaming mop of hair didn't do anything for her either, with her pale complexion and pointed elfin features. But she was game, he would say that for her.

'Give her a chance, lads,' he said, and just for a split second the MP turned a bright blue gaze on him and gave him a radiant smile. 'She looks to me like she's made of stern stuff.'

Ellen Henderson's smile broadened. She nodded at Billy and raised a hand in a kind of salute, and he knew that whatever happened, he just had to be among the 200 men who would be marching to London.

Taking leave of his pals, Billy headed to Bridget's house. She had bought the upstairs flat above the cobbler's shop in Staithes Terrace and he often stayed there with her rather than go home to his mother and her drinking. She was more and more abusive towards him these days, though she still relied heavily on him for financial support. He hated the time he spent there in the old family home. It didn't smell clean and fresh like Bridget's place. There were no real home comforts left. Maggie had pawned them, all but the beds they slept in and a table and two chairs in the kitchen. If he'd had his head screwed on the right way he would never have gone back there, but she was his mother, after all.

'Bridget!' He clumped up the stairs, enjoying the meaty aroma of whatever Bridget was cooking for dinner. 'Hey, Bridget!'

Bridget was in the living room and turned to greet him with a face that he didn't recognize. She looked guilty, embarrassed. Then he saw the reason why. There was someone else in the room. Laura Caldwell.

Billy stared in silence at Bridget's visitor.

'Miss Caldwell's my new tenant, Billy,' Bridget informed him.

'Hello, Billy,' Laura said, smiling shyly as she pulled her coat around her distended belly where her baby was residing, waiting for its time to present itself to the world. 'I hope my presence won't . . . I mean . . . ' She gave a huge gulp and looked to Bridget for support.

'She had nowhere else to go, Billy,' Bridget said. 'Her landlady turned her out because she couldn't afford the rent.'

'My . . . my father died,' Laura said huskily, 'so the money stopped.'

'Couldn't your mother take you back?' Billy said, his brain both seething with anger at the injustice of Laura's situation, and frozen solid because of what had happened at their last meeting.

'My mother isn't very strong,' Laura said with a quick glance at Bridget.

'Mrs Caldwell,' said Bridget, with little sympathy in her voice, 'is having a nervous breakdown and can't see her way clear to put a roof over the head of her only daughter.'

Billy had never heard such bitterness coming from Bridget. He had always understood that she had no liking for Laura. They were like chalk and cheese, these two young women. He still thought of Laura as young, though she must be in her late twenties now. There was, however, something very childlike about her. An innocence and a beauty that still touched him, despite the difference in their ages and despite her condition.

'I'm so grateful to Bridget,' Laura was saying. 'I've promised to pay her back. Every penny of the rent I owe. Just as soon as . . . well, as soon as I can find a job and earn some money.'

Billy gave a short laugh. 'Don't bank on it,' he said. 'There aren't any jobs to be had, even for working men. And then there's talk of another war with Germany. This country is going to the dogs.'

'Oh, let's not get maudlin, Billy,' Bridget said, bustling about in the way he liked, looking happy and bright-eyed, though today her eyes were perhaps a little too bright. 'I've got some lovely lamb stew on the go. Let's all sit down and enjoy it.'

'Before we do that, Bridget,' Billy said, 'I've got some news.'

'Oh, aye? You've not found a job, have you?' Bridget turned to Laura with a proud smile. 'Billy will never be destitute. He's one of those *entrepreneurs*. Isn't that the right word, Billy? While all the men in Jarrow are doing nothing and feeling sorry for themselves, Billy Big Boots here is working and earning. It might not always be exactly legal, but we'll not say anything about that, eh, Billy? There's men who do a lot worse and get away with it.'

Billy gave a half-hearted smile. 'I stay inside the law,' he said. 'Well, sort of. Anyway, that Ellen Henderson — you know, the MP? — she's organizing a petition against the unemployment around here in the north-east, Jarrow in particular. There's going to be a march. Two hundred men marching from Jarrow to London with a petition for the prime minister. I'm going with them.'

All the time he was talking, Billy was aware that Laura took no interest. She looked as if she was withdrawn into her own little world, building walls up around her too solid for anyone to penetrate. Besides, he thought, he could hardly expect to impress her now that he was unemployed like everybody else around here. The other lads on benefit didn't get enough money to feed their families on. At least he had his scrap business that he had built up since he was a nipper, and it was still going strong. It was amazing what people would pay for somebody else's rubbish.

'I've heard about this march,' Bridget said. 'They're raising a thousand pounds for the men to keep them in food and clothing.'

'It's all that Ellen Henderson's doing,' Billy told her. 'She's pretty strong in parliament, always fighting for the underdog.'

'What's she like, then?'

'Well, I expected somebody big and bolshy, but she's tiny and walks with a bit of a limp. Mind you, she's got red hair, which is why they call her 'Red', and she's as fiery as a fire cracker. Reminds me a bit of you, Bridget. You can be a bit explosive when you get going.'

Bridget frowned and made a derogatory sound.

'I don't like the idea of you going all that

way down to London. It'll take days, two hundred men walking two hundred miles, sleeping rough and starving most of the way. And what if the weather's bad?'

'Well, then, we'll get wet,' Billy said with a laugh.

'Maybe I should come with you to make sure you look after yourself,' Bridget said thoughtfully and Billy was surprised to hear her sound so serious.

'Nah, don't be daft. Anyhow, women aren't allowed. This is a man thing.'

'And what's Ellen Henderson, if she isn't a woman?'

'Aye, but she's different. It's her that's in charge. She says she'll march with us to show the prime minister that she means business.'

'If she can march with you, then so can I.' Bridget got that determined light in her eye that Billy knew of old. 'Right. That's settled. You let me know when we have to start off and I'll be ready.'

'They won't let you, Bridget, honest,' Billy said, shaking his head. 'It's going to be just us men.'

'What does your mam say about this march, Billy? How's she going to cope with you missing for days on end? Weeks, maybe?'

Billy chewed on his mouth as he thought about the plight of his mother. Maggie hadn't been well lately. In fact, she had been so ill that she hadn't even touched a drop of alcohol for over a week. Nor had she eaten anything, so she looked like a skeleton and he fair expected to hear her bones rattle when she walked. Not that she did much walking. It was all she could do to find the strength to get out of her bed these days and a lot of the time he had to help her to the lavatory out in the back yard. She had no pride left in her. She couldn't afford to have any when she was incapable of even wiping her own backside.

'I'll have to think about that,' he said. 'Maybe our Maureen could see to her while I'm away.'

'Oh, it might never happen,' Bridget said, bustling in and out of the kitchen and getting a tasty meal on the table that made Billy realize how hungry he was. 'Come on, let's eat. Miss Caldwell, I've set a place for you, if you don't mind a bit of Irish stew, though I have to admit there's more potato in it than meat.'

Laura roused herself enough to reply, but her voice seemed weak and her eyes far away.

'Thank you, Bridget, but I'm not hungry. I think I'll just go to my room, if you don't mind?'

'You got that back pain again?' Bridget asked. 'Maybe you should see the doctor.'

'Oh, it's nothing, really. I'm just tired.'

She got up, dragging her heavy body wearily to the open door into the passage. Billy received a pointed look from Bridget and he grabbed Laura's suitcase, which she was struggling to pick up.

'Here, let me do that,' he said and saw a fleeting look of gratitude, though Laura remained silent as he accompanied her to her bedroom and placed the case on the bed so she could unpack it without having to bend.

He hovered in the doorway, the memory of that day when he had proposed marriage to her still fresh and bothersome in his mind. But Laura was already ignoring him and opening the case, her movements slow and laborious, and he couldn't help thinking that the illness that reflected in her face was the same as he saw every day in his mother's regard. He had never seen a sadder woman than his mother, until now. Depression, the doctors called it, and short of sending patients to the lunatic asylum there seemed to be no cure for the disease.

Billy started to say something, offer her some kind of comforting word, but she turned a dark gaze on him and whatever he was about to say died in his mouth.

'Thank you, Billy. I can manage now.'

It was totally dismissive. He nodded,

backed out of the room and closed the door behind him.

Back in the living room, Bridget was ladling out her Irish stew into two large soup plates.

'Come on, Billy. I can't let you go back to that house of yours without something hot in your belly, even if it is summer.' She sat down and shoved a plate towards him, so he did as he was told and sat down opposite her. It never took much persuasion on Bridget's part to share a meal with her, or just sit with her in front of the coal fire in the winter, or on the front step downstairs when the sun shone. Sometimes, they went for walks together, and that was good too. In fact, everything was good about Bridget. One day she would make a fine wife for some lucky fella.

He looked up at her and grinned.

'So what's that grin for, Billy Flynn?' she asked, compressing her lips so that her dimples showed.

'Ach, I was just comparing you with you Mrs Henderson.'

'You were, were you?' Bridget's head went on one side and she regarded him closely, one golden eyebrow raised. 'And what conclusion did you come to?'

'I think you'd make a fine politician, Bridget Maguire, with that tongue of yours,'

Billy said, scooping up a spoonful of stew and swallowing it with an ecstatic groan of appreciation. 'And you've got the right colour hair, I'd say, but I bet Ellen Henderson can't cook as good as you can.'

'Really! So, with my tongue and my hair I'd be good at politics? Is that what you think?'

'No, Bridget, because you haven't got the hard-faced look to go with it.'

'What's that supposed to mean?'

Billy hesitated, not sure if she would take his remark the right way, but he felt the need to say it, so he did: 'You're far too pretty.'

He continued to scoop spoonfuls of stew into his mouth, concentrating his gaze on the plate before him. For some unknown reason he felt embarrassed and he didn't understand why. He didn't understand at all. This was Bridget he was talking to, and nobody was closer to him than she was. She was more like a sister than a friend and his life would never be the same again if he ever lost her.

Eventually, Billy looked up, because he wasn't used to being in the same room with Bridget and not have her voice in his ear for what seemed a long period of time. He found her staring at him curiously.

'Do you really think I'm pretty?' she said huskily.

'Aye, of course I do.'

'I'm not used to compliments,' she said and started to clear the table. 'Not from decent blokes anyway. Thanks, Billy.'

'Didn't cost me nowt,' he said with a shrug and what he hoped was a cheeky grin because he was feeling mightily strange down in the pit of his stomach.

'Ye're a daft sod, Billy Big Boots,' he heard Bridget say as she carried the dirty dishes out to the scullery. 'Daft, but nice.'

10

'Mam! Mam, open the door! Let us in, will ye!'

Billy had been banging on the front door for five minutes. Banging and shouting at the top of his voice until the neighbours were hanging out of their windows, despite the pouring rain, to see what all the commotion was about. Even old Mrs Turnbull from next door had stepped out on to the street, with her old woollen shawl over her head, making her look like a mean old witch, though Billy knew she had a heart of gold beneath her rough exterior.

'Billy, for Gawd's sake, lad!'

'I'm sorry, Mrs Turnbull, but I can't make me mam hear us.'

'I thought she'd given up the booze,' his neighbour said, swiping at a raindrop that had formed on the end of her long, beaky nose.

'Aye, she has an' all, but she's not been well and I'm worried in case she's passed out or something.'

The woman looked hard at Billy, who swayed before her and returned her gaze with a glassy-eyed look that shocked her.

'Billy Flynn, have *you* been drinkin', eh?'

Billy steadied himself by bracing his legs and leaning one hand up against the doorjamb. He swiped the back of the other hand across his mouth, which felt kind of numb and useless, so he figured he might be dribbling down his chin.

'Aye,' he said. 'And I'm heartily ashamed of meself, but there was a fella up at the Venerable Bede th'night buying drinks for them as couldn't go on the march and I was so damned angry at being turned down!' He turned back to the door and continued to hit it with his fist.

'Didn't they accept you for the march, then, Billy?' Mrs Turnbull asked sympathetically. 'They were supposed to be marching down to London in their hundreds.'

'Just two hundred,' Billy said, surprised at the way his words sort of ached inside his head; the unaccustomed alcohol was turning his brain into tapioca. 'I missed it by one, but they wouldn't let me sign on. Is that mad or what? I'm a lot younger and fitter than most of them that are going.'

'So you decided to get drunk and now you're keeping the whole street awake with your shenanigans.' Mrs Turnbull shook her head at him. 'I hope it's not a case of 'like mother like son', Billy. You know where it leads, eh? There's no excuse for you to go down that road. You've got more sense that that.'

'Don't worry about me on that score, Mrs Turnbull,' Billy said, belching loudly and apologizing. 'I don't even like the taste of the stuff. I was just so bliddy mad, and now I can't even get in me own house.'

'I thought you always kept a spare key under the doormat?'

'I do, but it's not there. I've looked.'

'Howay, Billy.' Mrs Turnbull beckoned to him and dodged back into her own passageway. He heard her scrabbling behind the door, then she appeared with a front-door key and held it out to him. 'I've had that spare since the day you was born. As luck would have it, yer ma nivvor changed the lock after yer da stormed off.'

'Thanks, Mrs Turnbull.'

The key was a bit stiff because it had rusted up over the years, but with some persuasion, it finally turned in the lock and the door swung open with a loud, complaining creak. He tumbled inside, his legs too wobbly from the large double whisky he had consumed, and he cursed the young man who, despite being unemployed, could still afford to buy it.

'Never again,' he muttered to himself as he felt his way along the narrow passageway, thinking how odd it was that his mother didn't have at least one low gaslight on, for she hated the dark and they could still manage a sixpence for the meter now and then. 'Mam? It's me, Billy. Are you all right?'

There was a damp chill in the house and a musty odour, though it was cleaner than it had been. When Billy had been paid off from Palmer's, he spent some time doing the housework, but he hadn't mentioned it to anybody in case they thought he was a cissy. Not even to Bridget. Not that she would have pulled his leg over it. She would have volunteered her services, more like, and she had enough on her plate looking after Laura. She also looked after the old man downstairs who owned the cobbler's shop and cleaned his place for him. The cobbler was one of the few people who still had work. Him, and one or two railway men.

Billy loved going into the cobbler's. He loved the smell of the leather and the old man, Mr Roberts, enjoyed teaching him the trade. Now, Billy could add shoe-mending and shoe-making to his list of abilities. He had made a pair of soft leather slippers for his mother only last week and she cried as he had slipped them on her cold feet and told him he was a good boy.

'Mam?' Billy found the matches and struck a light, then turned up the wick in the mantle at the top of the stairs, putting the flame to the gas that hissed out of it until it plopped into light.

Nothing. Silence. He couldn't even hear a snore coming from Maggie's room. When she was on the gin, she could snore as loud as any beer-bellied man, but as he had said to Mrs Turnbull, his mother had stopped drinking. It had happened overnight, like someone had switched her off. Now, she just sat around, staring into space, silent and miserable.

Her door was ajar. He could see that as he crept towards it, following his own long shadow until he stood just inside the room, willing his eyes to get accustomed to the combination of light and dark.

'Mam?' He called out to Maggie in a voice that had a tremor in it, for he could see her form outlined on the bed and a deep-seated fear started up in him. It worked its way from the soles of his feet to his scalp, and as he scrabbled again for the matches and felt for the light, he could hear the blood singing in his ears.

Maggie was sprawled haphazardly across the bed, all her limbs at a bizarre angle. She was naked and looked indecent to her son's eyes. Her head was turned towards him and she stared sightlessly at the wall behind him. Billy sank to his knees, gulped loudly, retched, then spewed his guts up in the nearest corner.

A few minutes later things seemed clearer to him. He saw the empty gin bottle on the floor and a brown pill bottle, also empty, on the bedside cabinet. She hadn't even left two Aspros for him to take to stop the pounding pain in his head.

'Aw, Mam . . . *Mam*!'

He clattered back down the stairs and battered on Mrs Turnbull's door. Then, leaving her to cover his mother's nakedness and give her some dignity, he dashed up to the doctor's and got the poor man out of bed, though there was nothing anybody could do, other than sign the death certificate.

★   ★   ★

By October of that year, life had changed radically for a lot of people in Jarrow, not least Billy. After his mother's death, he moved in permanently with Bridget and slept in a folding bed in her living room for a while, until old Mr Roberts died, leaving Bridget the rest of the house and his cobbler's shop to

Billy, who couldn't believe his luck.

The cobbler's shop was full of tanned leather and dyes and heavy iron lasts and nails and studs that would keep Billy happily occupied for a very long time. He was happiest when he was working with his hands. So, between his work up at the allotments, where, like a lot of men in Jarrow, he grew his own vegetables, he carried on where old Mr Roberts had left off. Nobody could afford new shoes these days, but there were still some who could manage a bob or two for repairs and Billy knew when to charge the full whack or put the amount owed on an imaginary slate. And as he worked, he played scratchy old records of brass band music on the old cobbler's gramophone, knocking in studs in time with the rousing marches.

'Eeh, yer a grand lad, Billy Flynn!' Hardly a day went by without somebody voicing those words. Billy thought how proud his mam would be if she could look down on him now and see what her runt of a son was doing with his life.

Laura was still staying with Bridget. Her presence bothered him, though he kept it to himself. Her baby girl, when it was born, was very poorly. It had not survived more than a month and died from pneumonia and some other unpronounceable complication. Laura had rallied, somewhat, since her traumatic ordeal, but she was still very quiet and kept her distance, especially when he was around, which was often, even though he now had his own living quarters at the back of the shop.

He was aware of Laura's mournful eyes following him about, but she would never look him fully in the face. Bridget said it was just Laura's way. Coming from her background, it was only to be expected. The poor woman was ashamed and her family and friends had disowned her. However, Billy still made the effort to speak and be kind to her, hoping that one day she might see him for what he was and not the scruffy little ragamuffin he had been.

'You try too hard, Billy,' Bridget said to him one day after witnessing his frustration following one of Laura's snubs.

'I don't know what you're talking about, Bridget,' he said, trimming off the excess leather on the sole of a boot he was repairing.

'Yes, you do.' Bridget responded, then quickly changed the subject and pointed to the boot on the last. 'Who does that belong to?'

'Nobody.' Billy shrugged. 'It's just a pair of boots I found down at the rubbish tip. Somebody had chucked them out, but the tops are good enough. I've repaired quite a few boots and shoes like that.'

'What are you going to do with them? Set up a shoe shop? Nobody's got money to buy shoes any more. Not even secondhand ones.'

'I know that, but I just thought . . . I thought . . . well . . . '

'Billy Flynn, are you up to something?'

Billy responded to her question with one of his enigmatic grins. 'Aye,' he said, but that's all he told her.

★   ★   ★

On 5 October 1936 the people of Jarrow gathered around the 200-strong men who were to take the petition of 11,000 names some 300 miles to London so that parliament, and the people of the south of England, would know that the men of Jarrow were serious and worthy of employment. Speeches were made in grand old rousing style, banners were waved as if victory over the Depression was already theirs. Billy watched from the sidelines, feeling his heart lift with hope and inspiration instilled by the fervour of the masses.

They marched from the town hall to Christ Church, which was packed to capacity with well-wishers. Bishop Gordon of Jarrow gave a religious blessing, and at 10.15 a.m., amidst rousing cheers and the music of the local brass band, the marchers started out on their long and arduous journey.

Led by the fiery, redheaded MP, Ellen Henderson, they marched in columns, three and four abreast, blue sashes across their proud chests, some wearing their cloth caps at a jaunty angle. One bunch of men had formed themselves into a band, playing rousing marching music on makeshift paper-and-comb instruments. One or two had real mouth organs and joined in. Others sang or whistled. People lined the streets of Jarrow, women and children mainly, cheering and waving their men off, their faces full of hope and enthusiasm for what they believed would come about because of these brave crusaders. Spirits, like hope, soared high.

Billy's heart swelled with pride as he sat on a borrowed cart, which he had adapted to his own needs. He gripped the reins of the old carthorse until his hands became tight and sweaty. As if the horse shared his impatience, it tossed its big head with a steamy snort and swayed its flanks inside the shafts, giving off an odour that was more sweet than offensive as it hit the air in front of Billy's nose.

'Hey, Billy, lad, where d'ye think ye're gannin' wi' that auld nag?'

As if it understood the insult, the horse

snorted, tossed its head again and stamped a shaggy foot in a puddle, sending up a shower of muddy water as high as its quivering withers.

'Watch your mouth, Alfie Lockhart,' Billy called back. 'Neddy here is very sensitive. I don't want nobody hurting his feelings before we even set off.'

'Set off?'

'Aye, on our way to London.'

'But, Billy, son, you was turned down for the crusade.'

'Who's talking about the crusade?' Billy pushed his cloth cap to the back of his head and stood up as proud and as tall as he could manage for a man of five feet four inches. 'Maybe I'll find me some work on the way. Nobody can stop me looking.'

'Well, I'll say this for ye, lad, ye're right tryer an' no mistake.'

'Aye,' joined in another shipyard worker who was busily saying goodbye to his pregnant wife and five little ones. 'He's a bit too trying at times. Makes the rest of us look bone idle.'

Laughter rippled through the ranks of men filing past. They all knew Billy and there wasn't one among them that could find it in his heart to resent what he had achieved in his nineteen short years. A lesser man would have been content to rest on his laurels and struggle to live on the meagre benefits doled out by the government. Not so Billy Flynn. He saw an opportunity and he took his chance, be it collecting rubbish, or working his socks off for anybody who would pay him for shifting anything from horse muck to builders' rubble. He wasn't the size of two pennorth of copper, but he had muscles on his wiry frame as strong as any knuckle fighter.

'Gan on, Billy,' cried out another voice he recognized. 'Wot ye gonna do wi' yersel' if that old bag of bones lies down with its legs in the air, eh? Pull the cart yersel' mebbe?'

'Don't you worry about Ned,' Billy defended his equine companion. 'He's good for a few hundred miles. We'll make it there and back, you'll see.'

And because he didn't want to be left out, Billy's old dog, Patches, raised his head and gave a jealous howl.

There was more laughter, then one of the men looked down the street with big eyes and pointed.

'Well, here comes another of your strays,' he said, grinning and nudging his neighbour, and then there was a group of men smirking and whispering behind their hands.

Billy, one hand on Patches' collar, looked

over his shoulder to see what they were going on about. Bridget, a bulging bag clutched to her, was hurrying towards the cart, her bright red halo of hair and the rosy face lighting up the grey morning.

'Bridget, what are you doing?' he asked, aware of a curiously uplifting feeling in his gut just at the sight of her.

'Somebody's got to look after you,' Bridget said, her face serious but her eyes full of determination. 'Move over, then. There's room enough for the three of us up on that seat.'

'She'll soon change her mind when yer horse farts in her face,' said one of the older men and there was more helpless laughter, but Bridget took no notice of them or their ribald comments as she settled herself on the other side of Patches. Billy passed her portmanteau bag back into the cart, which was got up like a wagon in the Wild West with a canvas tarpaulin stretched over wooden struts that he had fashioned himself out of pit props.

'I suppose there's no use arguing with you, is there,' he said to Bridget, who shook her head determinedly.

'Not a bit.'

'I didn't think there would be.'

'Go on, then. Let's be off before we get left behind.'

Billy had no intention of being left behind. In fact, he wanted to be in front all the way. He knew the route and the first stop on the march was to be in Chester-le-Street. They were taking the journey in stages and the first leg of the march was twelve miles. Ellen Henderson had organized things well and she was planning on marching with the men, which was cause for comment from some, since she had banned other women from marching.

A second-hand bus had been acquired to transport cooking equipment and it also carried ground sheets, which would be used for the outside rests. This, and an outside guard, was sent out ahead of the main crusader group and Billy made sure that he was sandwiched somewhere in between, for he was determined to be of use, even if the feisty little MP didn't want him there.

Bridget sat up front, proud as a peacock and twice as sassy, her arm about the neck of the old dog, who gave her a surreptitious lick from time to time, letting her know that he approved of her presence. Billy kept looking at her out of the corner of his eye and wishing he could change places with Patches. It would have been warmer, he told himself. And a cuddle from time to time, even from his lovely Bridget, wouldn't go amiss.

He always thought of her as 'his lovely Bridget', because that's what she was. A sister, a friend, a rock to which he could cling. Bridget never changed, nor would he want her to.

They had been on the road for more than an hour when Billy came out of his reverie and thought to ask Bridget what was happening to Laura. For some reason, Laura had completely faded from his mind, so content he was to be doing what he was doing, and sitting in companionable silence with the person he had admired and loved all his life.

'She's fine, Billy,' Bridget told him, not even looking at him, but fixing her gaze on the road ahead, which glistened in the morning light like a ribbon of shiny oil. 'Don't you worry yourself about her. She told me to come with you.'

'She did?'

'Aye. She was quite insistent upon it. I think she was scared you'd lose your way or something.'

Billy gave a short laugh. 'She must be feeling better,' he said. 'I'm glad about that. But will she be all right? You know . . . on her own?'

He thought he heard Bridget heave a sigh and gave her a sharp glance, but there was no change in her expression.

'She's all right, Billy,' Bridget said. 'In fact, she said she would enjoy being on her own for a while. It'll give her time to get her head put straight. Anyway, it's time you stopped worrying about Laura Caldwell. She's a grown woman, or haven't you noticed, Billy Big Boots!'

Bridget always called him that daft old nickname when she wanted to tease him. Coming from her, he sort of liked it.

They reached Chester-le-Street long before the marchers arrived. Billy set up his wagon on the outskirts of the town on a scrap of spare ground where there was a patch of green grass to bed down the horse. Bridget hadn't asked him any questions on the way, which was unusual since her curiosity and enquiring mind always got the better of her. But when he pulled his signboard out from under the tarpaulin, she stood back, hands on hips, and gave a click of her tongue.

'I knew you were up to something, Billy,' she said, nodding her head and making sparks fly as the beam from Billy's old oil lamp reflected from it. 'Here, give it to me. Look, you've spelt cobbler with only one 'b', ye silly sod.'

Billy's pride slipped an inch or two, but he wasn't one to dwell on failure.

'Never mind,' he said, with a shrug. 'Some of the lads out there probably can't read, but they'll soon find out what I do.'

He looked again at his notice, which proclaimed him to be 'Billy Flynn, Mobile Cobler — special rates to all crusaders'. He carefully drew in the missing 'b' and regarded it afresh with satisfaction. Then, as Bridget sorted out the kitchen stuff she had brought along with her so they could have a bite of supper, he got out some loose planks of wood and assembled them into a workshop. He had brought all old Mr Roberts's repair equipment — lasts, studs, nails, hammers and cutting blades — together with a selection of leather pieces, dyes, polishes, boots made and half-made, new and second-hand in varying sizes.

The time passed so quickly that he couldn't believe it when Bridget informed him that supper was ready and the appetizing smell of potato and cabbage soup was titillating his nostrils. As they were downing the last spoonful, the tramp of weary feet could be heard at the approach to the town.

'Here they come!' The shout went up among onlookers who had been assembling along the road for about an hour. 'The Jarrow Crusaders are here!'

As the first banner rounded the bend, a

234

great cheer went up. Women appeared carrying food, ready to dole it out as the hungry marchers went by. Men pushed to the front, armed with jugs of beer. And children danced excitedly, offering apples and oranges and waving victory flags, faded and in tatters, that had seen service at the end of the Great War.

'Just look at them,' Billy called out to Bridget. 'They're more knackered than my old horse. Come on, lads, where's your spunk? Have ye left it in Jarrow then?'

Grim expressions were turned his way, grimy faces, damp with perspiration, eyes big with fatigue and wide with expectation.

'Billy, don't.' Bridget tugged at his sleeve. 'They're tired.'

'Tired? They've only come twelve miles! Where's the local brass band? That would help wake them up. Come on, you lot. Think of the cause!'

'It's all right for ye, laddie,' one sour-faced marcher called out and Billy recognized Harry Brown, a senior shipyard official, whose legs were so bowed he couldn't stop a pig in a passage.

'I wanted to come,' Billy shouted back, acknowledging shouts and waves from others he knew. 'They wouldn't let me.'

'I see you came anyway, Billy Big Boots! Ye

bugger, ye! I nivvor seen a lad so anxious to be in the thick of things.'

'Glutton for punishment is Billy!'

'What are ye doing here anyway, Flynn? Ready to pick the bones of them among us what drops on the road to London, eh?'

'Whatever he's at, it looks like he's got himself a cosy billet th' night. Good on ye, Billy. I swear if ye fell in a pile of horse dung ye'd come up smelling of roses.'

'I'll remember that, Howie Majors,' Billy responded, holding his temper at bay, 'when you come to me pleading for new soles for yer boots.'

'Gawd luv us, he's a cobbler now!'

A ripple of weary laughter moved through the ranks as line after line of marchers filed past. In the middle, straggling a bit, were the group of men bearing paper and comb, but not a tune was forthcoming.

'That's what's wrong,' Billy said. 'They need music to cheer them up.'

He dug in his coat pocket and brought out his penny whistle, trilling a few jolly notes that soared bell-like in the air. Suddenly, the waiting crowd of townsfolk gathered around, clapping their hands in time to Billy's music. One or two of the younger women grabbed the nearest marchers and danced a jig with them. Not to be outdone by a young whippersnapper like Billy Flynn, the paper-and-comb band took up their instruments once more and joined in. It was an old song, 'The More We Are Together', but everyone remembered it and it seemed right for the occasion.

Like magic, the faces of the crusaders lit up and the tiredness faded. Billy marched alongside them until they reached the spot in the town where they were expected to spend the night, and then he took his leave.

'Thanks, Billy!'

'Ye're a good lad, Billy!'

'See ye in the mornin', Billy!'

It was raining as he walked back to his little campsite, still playing on his penny whistle as if he didn't know how to stop. His heart felt full and warm, despite the fine rain falling like sea fret on his shoulders. The night was bitterly cold and he felt sorry for those men who would not be lucky enough to sleep under cover, for they weren't all guaranteed lodgings.

As he turned the last corner and the cart with its makeshift tarpaulin roof came into sight, a bulky figure broke from the shadows and bowled into Billy, knocking the breath out of him as he bounced off a stone wall. He heard a deep-throated grunt, smelled the animal odour of the man, but before he could steady himself the fellow was off at a perilous speed, rocking and rolling over the greasy cobbles, his boot studs striking sparks like flints.

'Big ugly bugger!' Billy called out after him. 'Why don't you look where you're going?'

He brushed himself down, wincing slightly as he touched his elbow, grazed sore even through his clothing. The man who had run into him was now a mere lumbering shadow, picked out fleetingly by the light of the street lamps as he ran towards the town centre.

Billy stared after him and a small niggling fingernail scratched at his insides. There was something vaguely familiar about the silhouette that was growing more and more distant. When the man finally reached the end of the road and disappeared from view, Billy put the whole incident to the back of his mind and headed for the cart, where he could see a flickering light. Bridget had lit the oil lamp and was waiting for him. He quickened his step as a cold shiver went through him. It would be good to get back to the welcoming warmth of Bridget. Somehow, wherever Bridget was, it always felt like home, be it cramped terraced house or, as was the case right now, a tatty old cart.

'It's me,' he called out softly as he climbed in the back of the cart and carefully pulled down and fastened the rope ties to stop the tarpaulin from being lifted by the wind.

'Oh, Billy!'

It was such a weak, hoarse whisper that he whipped around and peered at her through the dull, yellow light. She was slumped in the far corner, her hair a tangle over a face that looked odd. As she lifted a hand and pushed back the curtain of curly tresses that had come undone, he saw blood on her arm. She leaned forward, reaching for a blanket and pulled it up to her chin. She was shaking like a leaf in a storm and her usually rosy cheeks were pale and puffy and bruised.

'Bridget?' Not wanting to believe his eyes, Billy picked up the lamp and held it so that he could see her more clearly. There was no mistaking the state of her. 'Who was it, Bridget? Who did that to you?'

She was having difficulty speaking and as she shook her head at him in despair, tears flew from her terrified eyes.

'Which one of them buggers hurt you?' Billy persisted, reaching out and gently taking her hand in his. 'Tell me his name if you know it. We'll report him to the police.'

Again she shook her head. 'No, Billy, it . . . it wasn't one of the marchers. It was . . . '

'My God, did he . . . you know . . . ?' He couldn't bring himself to say the words or the thoughts that were screaming in his head. As Bridget nodded and wept bitterly into her blanket, he felt himself fill with a red fury.

'Yes, he did. He . . . he raped me, Billy!'

He crawled over to her and took her gently in his arms. Bridget leaned all her weight against him. He could feel her heart beating, hear the sob-wracked breathing that was almost choking her. Billy didn't know what to do. This was something new, something terrible that had come into his life.

'Did you recognize him, Bridget?' he asked, not daring to tighten his hold in case he hurt her.

Bridget drew in a deep, rattling breath and curled her fingers into the lapels of his coat, holding on so tightly that he couldn't move.

'Billy . . . it was *him*! It was your father . . . Patrick Flynn . . . '

The red fury turned into white rage and then Billy knew that the man who had run into him had indeed been his father. It had been Patrick's size and shape. It had been Patrick's odious smell. For a fleeting moment, Billy had known it, but had rejected the fact out of hand. Patrick, he had thought, would be miles away, probably on the other side of the world. He was too wily a bird to come back to the north-east of England where he could be so easily recognized.

'Are you sure, Bridget?' he asked through gritted teeth and a fresh bout of tears burst from her, soaking his shirt, but still she clung to him and wouldn't let go.

'It was him, Billy,' she said, her mouth muffled as she buried her face into his neck and he found it strangely moving, even through his anger. 'How could I ever forget the man that murdered my mother?'

'Dear God, Bridget, he might have done for you too!'

'I think he would have, if he hadn't heard that penny whistle of yours.'

'But what about Patches? Didn't he make a fuss?' Billy looked around frantically, suddenly aware that there had been no welcoming bark or warm, friendly lick to greet him on his return.

Bridget lifted her head and he followed her gaze to what he had thought, from the corner of his eye, to be a bundle of rags. Patches lay, the victim of a brutal assault judging by the wounds over his back and skull, but he was feeling no pain now. Billy's old friend was no more.

'Aw, no! No!' Billy slithered over to the dog and gathered him up in his arms. Letting his own emotions take over, the tousled coat of the dog was soon wet from his tears. 'I'll kill you one day, bliddy Patrick Flynn! I'll kill ye!'

Bridget's hand found his shoulder and her fingers squeezed hard, digging into his flesh.

'No, you won't, Billy,' she sobbed. 'He's not worth going to prison for. Let the authorities deal with him.'

But the authorities showed little interest in the fact that known murderer Patrick Flynn was at large in their town. They did not seem to care that a young woman had been raped by the man. In fact, they treated poor Bridget abominably, indicating that she had probably led her attacker on, and where was the proof that it was, indeed, Patrick Flynn, since there were so many men in the town that night and what was a girl like Bridget Maguire, looking the way she looked, doing sleeping rough and attracting attention. She probably deserved all she got, they intimated. They had enough on their hands keeping the peace, what with the men of the Jarrow Crusade and the strike breakers and a whole host of other strikers and workers intent on making their presence felt.

'So you're not going to do anything about it?' Billy could not keep the disgust from his voice.

'Proof, laddie,' the desk sergeant said, snapping his report book shut and popping his pen back in its holder. 'Can't do nothin' without proof. How are we to know that the lass hasn't just been earning a bob or two on the side and one of her customers got a bit rough. Go on, the pair of you. Stop wastin' police time.'

They walked back to the wagon, dragging their feet but hand in hand. Billy was tempted to rush off and find that bastard Patrick and give him the punishment he deserved. And he would have done it, had it not been for the fact that he didn't want to leave Bridget on her own. In fact, he felt as if he would never again want to leave go of her soft warm hand. He wanted to be with her, as close as he could get, feel her body pressed against him, her head on his shoulder. It was a strange new feeling, sort of bittersweet, bringing him pleasure and pain at the same time.

'You won't do anything silly, will you, Billy?' she asked as he tucked her up once they got back to the cart and prepared to watch over her the whole night long. 'I don't want to lose you too.'

'Don't be daft, Bridget,' he said, feeling slightly uncomfortable and wishing he were more of a man of the world. 'You'll not get rid of me. You'll never get rid of me.'

'I'm glad of that.' Bridget's eyelids were drooping and she slid down into the folds of the blanket and went to sleep.

As she slept, like an exhausted child, Billy

tried to analyze his feelings. There was a great knot of something he couldn't figure out beneath his breastbone. It was sending out disturbing vibrations left, right and centre and his head was in turmoil over it. He tried to distract himself by thinking of Laura, wondering how she was faring back home on her own, whether she was still depressed, still regretting the past. But the image of Laura was constantly being pushed away, replaced by one of Bridget.

Bridget with the sun shining in her hair. Bridget with raindrops glistening on the end of her long eyelashes. And those sea-green eyes that he felt he could drown in like a deep, deep ocean. Finally, he could see her mouth, all full and rosy and inviting and he didn't know why he should, but he wanted, oh so badly, to kiss it. And he did kiss it, the touch of his lips on hers as light as the brush of a butterfly wing.

Bridget murmured in her sleep, her body stirring and dislodging the blanket. Billy swallowed dryly, feeling an odd pang of guilt, for his own body was betraying him the way it never had before. He pulled the blanket back up to her chin, took the lamp and went out in the pouring rain on that icy November night and buried his dog. Then he cried over the grave for Patches, cried for Laura and his mother and his Auntie Colleen, his brother Desmond, and the father he had never known. But most of all he cried for Bridget and the feelings he had kept hidden for her all these years without ever knowing that she occupied such a special place in his heart, and always would.

11

'Can you not get him to go a bit faster, Billy?'

Billy gave Bridget a pained look. She had been urging him on impatiently ever since they had arrived on the outskirts of the capital. Now that they could see the high, impressive skyline of London she could hardly contain her excitement and shuffled her behind next to him on the wooden slat seat.

Like the marchers, they had been travelling for twenty-five days. Nearly 300 miles had been covered, bearing the petition of 11,000 names, carefully guarded in an oak box with gold lettering. Each time they approached a town they held the box proudly aloft. Their aching limbs were forgotten when the thousands of sympathizers they encountered en route cheered them on, supporting them with food and drink and clothing as necessary.

Billy made himself popular by mending boots and shoes and, on occasion, giving out free footwear when he found that none of the men could afford to pay anything. He couldn't see his fellow workers go barefoot when he had inherited a whole cobbler's shop full of boots and leather. Bridget tried to get him to at least put something on the slate so that the men could pay him back when they got their longed-for employment, but he wouldn't have it.

'We could all be dead and buried before that happens,' he said with a sad shake of his head. 'I don't think it'll happen.'

'So what's everybody marching for?' Bridget wanted to know. 'They might as well give up now and save their energy.'

'It's the Geordie pride, Bridget,' Billy told her seriously. 'They've got to prove something, even if they're beaten at the end of the day. That petition they're so pleased about isn't enough to change their lives, but it's their moment of glory, this crusade. What kind of person would want to rob them of that? As long as a person tries, he cannot be thought of as a failure.'

'Hey, Billy, you're a lot wiser than you look, aren't you?' Bridget smiled, trying to lighten the conversation with a little of her characteristic humour. 'I'd like to write those words of yours down and shove it up Mr Bloody Baldwin's arse. And the rest of them politicians who keep telling us that everything they do is for the good of the people.'

'I thought you'd stopped using that kind of

language, Bridget Maguire.' Billy returned her smile.

'There are times when I don't know enough words to replace them', Bridget said, pulling a face and pointing a finger at the horse's rump. 'Look at that, will you. He's getting slower and slower. At this rate the marchers will be on their way back home before we get to the House of Commons.'

'Bridget,' he said, feigning irritation, but too pleased at having her returned to her normal exuberance to mean it, 'if I ask him, Neddy here will roll over and die for me, but I have too much respect and gratitude for the old fella. Besides, we need him to get us back once the petition is handed over. Mind you, I suppose I could always put you between the shafts.'

Bridget stared at him, her eyes wide, then she grinned and gave him a hefty slap that nearly knocked him from his perch.

'I just want to be there when they hand it in to the prime minister,' she said, leaning forward in her seat as if it might help push the cart into going just that bit faster. 'We will see Mr Baldwin, won't we? I mean, he can't possibly not be there after all the men have done to make him believe in them.'

'I don't know, Bridget,' Billy said, shaking his head reflectively. 'Prime ministers are busy men, I imagine.'

'I wouldn't know about that. Anyway, I'd rather see the king and queen, but I'll settle for having a look at Buckingham Palace. Do you think they really have lots of gold and jewels and thick red carpets about the place, Billy? I'd love a red carpet. You know the kind. Those that are so thick the pile comes up between your toes.'

'I shouldn't think the queen ever goes around the palace barefoot.' Billy threw his head back and laughed, then gave Neddy an encouraging click of his tongue, but the horse turned an uncharacteristic deaf ear and plodded on, his great grey haunches swinging lethargically from side to side.

'Maybe you could make King George a pair of shoes or some slippers for the queen, like mine.' Bridget was high on the adrenalin created by the end of the long journey. 'I can just see you going home to Jarrow with a brand new sign — 'Billy Flynn, Cobbler to His Majesty the King'.'

They exchanged glances, then burst out laughing. Bridget leaned towards Billy and planted an affectionate kiss on his cheek. It wasn't the first time she had kissed him, but recently there seemed to be more meaning in the gesture. Or was it that he was just beginning to notice Bridget as something more than a friend? Billy suddenly grew hot with embarrassment and quickly looked away.

'I bet Laura's missing us,' he said and immediately wished he hadn't because he felt Bridget draw away from him.

'Missing *you*, do you mean?' There was an unaccustomed sharp edge to her voice.

Billy lifted a shoulder. There had been a time when he would have given anything to be missed by Laura Caldwell. Now, he wondered if he had been crazy in the head to ever think that she could look upon him as anything other than the little lad she had saved from the murderous hands of Patrick Flynn.

And now his thoughts became dark and brooding as he was reminded of what that man had done, and what he was likely to do to others if he was left roaming freely in the streets. If he was ever caught, they'd hang him. No doubt about that. *Damn him to hell for the devil he is!*

'Billy!'

Bridget was tugging at his arm. He gave her a questioning look then realized that he had unconsciously whipped the flanks of the horse in his rage and Neddy was pushing himself into a fast trot, steaming and foaming in the midday sun that was a whole lot warmer than it ever was in Jarrow.

'Whoa! Whoa, boy!' He hauled on the reins and Neddy slowed down again, snorting and wheezing and throwing globules of foam left and right as he struggled to pull them along the Victoria Embankment.

It was fortunate that the horse stopped just then, because the crowds of spectators were becoming thick on the ground, spreading as they did all the way from the House of Commons, everyone pushing and shoving and trying to get closer so they could see the marching men from Jarrow and be well placed to witness the handing over of the all-important box containing the petition of 11,000 names.

'We'll never get through,' Bridget shouted over the noise of people hurrying past, laughing and cheering and being generally in high spirits. 'Not with the cart, Billy.'

Suddenly there was a crush of people all around them and two uniformed policemen, with truncheons waving, were ordering Billy to get his horse and cart off the road and out of the way of the traffic. Billy had been shocked at the volume of traffic in London, with trams and motor cars travelling at breakneck speed, klaxons blaring. And pedestrians in their thousands, he reckoned, scurrying this way and that, making suicidal dashes from one side of the road to the other.

'Where can we go, Officer?' Billy asked, standing up on the cart, the reins held tautly in his sweating hands. 'I can't turn around in this lot.'

'You shouldn't be here in the first place,' one big, red-faced policeman said tetchily, pushing at the horse's side and beckoning to his colleague to come and help. 'Go on, you ugly brute! Get over, will you!'

Neddy tossed his head with a snort and rolled his eyes, but only one foot lifted and gave a stubborn stamp that raised a cloud of dust. He wasn't going to budge an inch. Not for these bullying strangers dressed in black and silver. In fact, he wasn't going to move another step, not even if the devil himself gave the order. Not even for Billy could he shift his heavy, weary body, even if he wanted to.

Billy felt the cart lurch before he saw what was happening. He grabbed hold of Bridget, one arm fastened tightly about her waist, and jumped clear with her as his world of the last few weeks crashed on to the steep embankment. In a flash, he saw boots, hammers and heavy lasts tumble out of the cart and roll down the grassy bank toward the shimmering waters of the Thames. Children, seeing it as a bit of fun to brighten their day, ran after them, grabbing trophies and holding them aloft victoriously.

'Oh, Billy!'

Billy felt Bridget stir beneath him, gasping breathlessly. He scrambled off her and helped her to her feet, brushing her down, checking for injuries, of which, fortunately, there were none, other than a grazed knee and a bruised shoulder.

'Damned coppers!' Billy said through gritted teeth. 'I could have shifted Neddy if they hadn't interfered.'

'Oh, Billy!' Bridget exclaimed again and he saw her shake her head and caught the glint of a tear in her eye as she looked over his shoulder where a crowd had gathered, gawping at the new spectacle of the day. 'I don't think you could have done anything, really. Look.'

He spun around and blinked at the sight before him. The cart, as he well knew, had overturned, scattering their meagre belongings. But it was the cause of the overturning that he now sadly feasted his eyes on. Neddy, the old but proud and courageous companion of their journey, had keeled over between the shafts and was now lying in the gutter, head thrashing bemusedly, foam and steam discharging from flared nostrils and quivering mouth, equine eyes wide and wild.

'Aw, no! Not Neddy as well!' Billy had not yet got over the death of his poor dog at the brutal hands of Patrick Flynn, and now there was another tragedy to cope with. Not only that, but it was his fault.

'Is he going to die?' Bridget whispered.

Billy said nothing. He went to kneel by the head of the old horse. As he reached out to give the beast a soothing stroke, something wet fell on to the back of his hand and he realized that he was crying.

'I'm sorry, Neddy, lad,' he said hoarsely, entwining his fingers in the black mane and resting his cheek on the cheek of the horse, feeling the animal's hot, laboured breathing on his chest. 'It's my fault. I shouldn't have pushed you so far.'

'Come on, come on, you lot!' The older policeman was taking control of the crowd, pushing them away, urging them to go about their business. Then he turned to Billy and looked down at him severely, but not totally unsympathetically. 'I'm sorry, son, but we'll have to shift you from here.'

'But how . . . ?' Even as he started to ask the question, Billy felt the horse sag beneath him and when he turned his attention back to Neddy, the brown eyes gazed up at him, so trusting, so loving, then with a final sigh, the horse breathed its last.

'Ah, Gawd, that's tough,' the policeman said. 'You from up north, are you? One o' them Jarrow lads?'

'Aye,' Billy whispered, his hand stroking the horse's shoulder in long, gentle movements. 'Aye, that's where I'm from, and I wish I'd never come to London.'

'Thought it was the land of opportunity, did ye, son? Paved with gold and all that? Well, let me tell ye, it's not what they say it is down here and you'd be best advised to go back to your roots.'

'I only came down here to help the lads,' Billy told him. 'That petition's important. I wanted to be in on the glory when it's handed over. It's going to bring my people jobs and enough money to put food in their mouths and clothes on their backs.'

'If that's what you think, Geordie lad, ye're as deluded as the rest of them. Now, why don't you pack up your things and go back home.'

Billy stroked Neddy one last time and got stiffly to his feet. He squared his shoulders and pulled himself up as tall as he could manage, but he was still dwarfed by the big, brawny officer of the law.

'And how do you propose I do that, Officer?' he asked. 'My things are scattered all over the Embankment, what little I had.

Scattered and stolen. My cart is broken and my horse is dead. I suppose you expect me to put him on me shoulders and carry him back to Jarrow, eh?'

The officer put his hands on his hips and heaved a deep sigh. He ran an eye over the damage that was blocking half the road and the traffic building up nose to tail behind them. He looked at Bridget, who was quietly weeping, though Billy wasn't certain whether it was for the horse or just their general situation. He didn't like to see her cry and if he had possessed a magic wand he would have undone all the bad things that had happened to them on the journey down. But he didn't have a wand and once a bad thing had happened you couldn't undo it, so the only thing was to move forward, one way or another.

'Tell you what, son,' the policeman said, running a huge hand around his clean-shaven face. 'I've got a brother-in-law in the butchery business. I'll get word to him about the horse. He'll be glad to take it off your hands.'

'For meat, do you mean?' Billy's eyebrows shot up into his hairline. 'If he's going to make a profit out of Neddy, I'd like some of it.'

'You're not as thick as you look, are ye?' The officer gave a short laugh and delved into his pocket, bringing out a fistful of change.

'That's not enough!' It was Bridget who bellowed out the words past Billy's ear. 'There's enough meat on that horse to feed half of London.'

The policeman fixed her with a stony gaze and dug a little deeper, but didn't come up with much more. 'Come off it, love. Do you think us law enforcement officers are made of money? My brother-in-law's an old skinflint, so you won't get anything out of him. He'd want paying just to move the horse down the road.'

Billy glanced at Bridget, pleased that she should stick up for him, but he knew they were both on a losing wicket.

'Look, Officer,' he said, resignation in his voice. 'I bought Neddy for a song from the knacker's yard. He got us to London and if he'd have lived, he would have got us back home again. Just pay me enough for our train fair and a bite to eat on the way and you can have the horse and the cart with it.'

'Billy! That's your future you're giving away,' Bridget said, her voice breaking with emotion. 'How are you going to live?'

Billy shrugged and gave her a wry smile, which was so typically him. 'You know me, Bridget. I'll find something. I always do.' He turned back to the policeman. 'Well?'

'You're a bit of a hard nut, aren't ye, son?' The officer took off his helmet and scrabbled about inside the lining, then produced a five-pound note. 'Tell you what. Take this and I won't let on to my brother-in-law. I'll forget I owe him a favour and go to somebody else I know who'll give me a tenner for my trouble. How does that cap fit you, boy, eh?'

'It fits all right.' Billy nodded and held out his hand and the deal was done. 'At least the poor animal hasn't died in vain.'

'Right, now be off with you, because I don't want to have to charge you with obstruction.'

'Where are we going, Billy?' Bridget was running breathlessly beside him as they went against the flow of the crowds. 'I think we're going in the wrong direction for the House of Commons.'

'We're not going to the House of Commons.'

'But what about the petition?'

'Damn the petition. It's brought me nothing but trouble.'

'Then where . . . ?'

'I saw a little hotel down here as we passed,' Billy told her, striding out, keeping his fast pace with head bowed as if going against a strong wind. 'There was a notice that said 'Vacancies'. I thought we might get a

258

proper bed for the night and then catch the train home in the morning.'

'Oh!' Bridget stopped and her cheeks burst into flames. 'Oh, Billy!'

★ ★ ★

'Well, there you are, then.'

Billy's right shoulder lifted self-consciously. He and Bridget were standing just inside the small hotel room. Billy clutched a brown paper bag that contained a few essential belongings they had been able to recover from the embankment. It had drawn critical attention from the landlady of the establishment, but she relented when she saw that the young couple could actually afford to pay for their lodgings.

'How do you mean, Billy?' Bridget looked uneasy and a little confused. She had looked that way since Billy had signed them in as Mr and Mrs Flynn when the ferret-faced owner had told them that there was only one room available.

They were both staring hard at the double bed in the centre of the room. It was like a magnet, drawing their attention as if their eyeballs were made of metal.

'Well, you know . . . ' Another one-shoulder shrug and Billy let the sack drop at his feet,

259

making Bridget jump. 'I don't know about you, Bridget, but I'm tired.'

'Yes, me too.' Still neither of them moved. 'It must be late by now.'

The tall casement window showed squares of navy blue with a scattering of twinkling stars and clouds scudding across the face of the moon that seemed intent on peering at them through the gap of the curtains. There was still some muffled noise from the traffic, but most of the pedestrians had gone home.

'Aye.' Billy gave a short, sharp nod. 'Must be after ten. Should we draw the curtains, do you think?'

'No, leave them. It's pretty like that.'

'The bathroom's up on the next landing,' Billy said, remembering what the landlady had told them. 'You go first, if you want.'

'Yes, all right.'

When it came to be Billy's turn, he found himself spending far more time than was necessary in the big cast-iron bath with the brass taps that groaned painfully when he turned them off and on. Bridget had enthused over the novelty of having a proper bath with running hot water, but it wasn't that novelty that was keeping Billy soaking until his skin looked like a wrinkled grape.

He was scared. Somehow, he had to go back to Bridget in their shared room with that big bed and his thoughts and his feelings were terrifying him. He and Bridget had been like brother and sister all their lives, but suddenly he was seeing her, thinking about her, in quite a different way. They had snuggled up together for warmth under the tarpaulin over the cart every night for three weeks. It had been cosy, friendly, innocent. Suddenly, it wasn't so innocent any more. He didn't know how he would be able to get through another night without touching her, without wanting to hold her in his arms, crush her to him so that they would be melded together as one being.

Billy clambered reluctantly out of the bath when the water had cooled so much that he was shivering. He rubbed himself dry with a coarse towel, then wiped the steam away from a fly-spotted mirror above the washbasin. He hadn't shaved on the journey to London and now had quite a beard on him, though it was fair and baby-fluff fine. Nevertheless, it made him look older and more mature. Bridget had laughed the other day when he gave her a spontaneous kiss on the cheek. She said it had tickled, but she seemed to like it.

'You're a bloody fool, Billy Flynn,' he told his hazy reflection. 'You put one finger on Bridget and she'll have your guts for garters. What's she going to think of you, eh?'

Billy eventually crept back through the dark landing wrapped in the damp towel. He opened the door a crack and peered in. The oil lamp by the bedside was giving off a dull glow, enough to find his way about the room. Bridget made a lovely, undulating mound beneath the coverlet. She was lying with her face towards the window and a stray moonbeam caressed the fiery gold tresses that lay on the pillow. He could hear her breathing softly and thanked God that she had not stayed awake waiting for him.

Moving stealthily, Billy pulled the second pillow from the bed on to the floor and found a spare quilt in the wardrobe. He threw the damp towel over the back of a chair and, turning out the light, sank down at the foot of the bed, like a faithful dog, covering himself with the quilt.

'Billy?' Her voice was hardly more than a muffled whisper, but it made him jump. 'What are you doing?'

'I thought you were asleep,' he stuttered like some kind of imbecile. 'I didn't want to disturb you.'

'You'll disturb me if you spend the night on the floor,' she said, rising on one elbow and peering at him through the darkness.

'There's only one bed,' Billy said unnecessarily and saw her smile.

'And if you don't get into it soon, Billy Flynn, I'll want to know why . . . or is it that you don't care for me?'

Billy got to his knees, the quilt falling away. His eyes grew large as he stared at Bridget, not believing that she could possibly mean what he thought she meant.

'Bridget, what are you saying? If I get into that bed I'll . . . well, I'll . . . '

'What will you do, Billy? Will you lie quietly beside me and go to sleep?'

'If that's what you want me to do, Bridget, but it'll be hard. I don't know if I can do that.'

Bridget frowned at him over the edge of the eiderdown cover, and then she sat up more fully and he could see that she wasn't wearing her flannelette nightdress. In fact, she wasn't wearing anything at all. Her breasts were full and round like two magnificent pearls. And she was still smiling at him as she crooked a finger.

'Come here, Billy.'

He stood up, grappling to keep the quilt around his lower body and took a few stumbling steps around the bed until he was standing beside her. He felt light-headed and confused and excited all at the same time, yet still he wasn't sure what was going to come next, didn't dare think about it.

Bridget moved her legs and patted the bed beside her, inviting him to sit down. He sat, mainly because he didn't think his legs would support him for much longer.

'Do you think, Billy, that you could kiss me?' Bridget asked and he felt his heart leap, then fall with a dull thud before beating a strange tattoo in his chest. 'And give me a cuddle, maybe?'

He sat there blinking at her like a fool until she reached out, took hold of his face in both her hands and pulled him towards her.

'Bridget, I . . . '

'Sssh. I'm not asking you to do anything you haven't wanted to do for a very long time,' she whispered as she gently touched her lips to his forehead, his eyelids, his nose, his cheeks and, finally, his mouth.

As he felt the soft warmth of her mouth on his, Billy's resolve melted and he sagged inside his bones, giving himself up completely to her demands and his own submerged desires.

'I've not done this before, Bridget,' he said as he slid beneath the covers and she wrapped herself around him so naturally that they might have been doing it all their lives.

'I know,' she said and he heard her swallow, deep and resonant. 'Neither have I . . . except . . . you know . . . '

Billy knew she was remembering their first night on the road when the man he had once believed to be his father had attacked and raped her.

'You don't have to talk about that,' he said, nuzzling her neck and willing his body to be patient, but it wasn't easy. 'Never again. I'm not like *him*. I'd never do anything to hurt you, Bridget.'

'I know.'

'This time, it's going to be different.'

'You don't have to tell me that, Billy, love. You're the gentlest man I know and . . . And I love you, Billy. Oh, I love you so much. I always have.'

The silence that followed her words seemed to deafen Billy. He hadn't expected it; had never dreamed that love could creep up on him like that. There had been moments when he questioned his feelings for Bridget, but always he brushed them away as being false. For as long as he could remember, his heart had belonged to Laura.

Now, it was Laura he was pushing away to the back of his mind. He had hardly spared a thought for her since the day he and Bridget had left Jarrow. Perhaps even before that, Laura had ceased to be the centre of his hopes and dreams for the future. So when did he start loving Bridget? It was too deep and dark a secret to delve into right now, for his desire was rising to such an extent that it blocked out all thought. If he did not have Bridget now he would explode into a myriad of pieces like a shower of sparks from a Catherine wheel.

Billy had never made love before, but he found it surprisingly easy and natural the way he fitted into Bridget's willing body. She knew he could wait no longer, so she didn't hold him off. The first time was, for him, quick and wildly passionate. The second time he entered her he was able to control his rhythm to a slow, sensual movement, pleasing her even more.

'I can't believe this is happening,' Billy muttered, as he lay back, exhausted, satiated and happier than he ever imagined he could be. 'I suppose I've been in love with you too, Bridget, all this time, without knowing it.'

'I damned well hope so, Billy Flynn, or I'll send you and your big boots flying.'

★　★　★

Billy and Bridget did not return on the same train that carried the Jarrow marchers back home, their fare generously paid for them by the people of Leeds. But they did go to the station to see them off. It was the least they could do, Billy thought, after the high-and-mighty prime minister, Stanley Baldwin, who had a job and money and food in his belly, had refused to see any of the marchers' representatives.

As they waited with the disillusioned crusaders, they listened to the stories the men had to tell. Some, it seemed, were still scratching because of the bed bugs they had picked up in the local workhouses where they had been put up overnight. Others talked of the highlight of the trip — a visit to the municipal baths at Barnsley, where they had bathed in water specially heated for them. There were some ribald comments, however, about the fact that Ellen Henderson, who had accompanied them on most of the walk, had been privileged to have the women's foam bath all to herself.

'Oh, I'd have liked that,' Bridget sighed with longing and Billy gave her hand a squeeze, doing his best not to imagine too clearly what it would be like to see Bridget wallowing naked in sweet-smelling foam.

'One day, Bridget, you'll have all that,' he told her. 'Aye, and more, if I can provide it for you.'

'Really? Oh, Billy!' Her eyes were soft and dewy. 'If any man can do well for himself, I'm sure it's you.'

'I'll do it for you, Bridget,' he said, feeling strangely emotional as his heart rose into his throat, choking him slightly. 'It won't always be poverty. I promise you that.'

They waved off the men, and then walked out into the morning sunshine, hand in hand. There was time to see at least a small part of the capital city before their train was due. It would be a pity not to make the most of it, as there was no telling if they would ever be able to return to London.

There was still enough money in Billy's pocket, over and above the cost of their tickets, to buy a cup of tea and a bun, so he felt well off. It wouldn't have mattered to him if his pocket was empty, as long as he had Bridget by his side. Oddly enough, he had always felt that way, but never recognized it as love. It wasn't the same as it had been with Laura. That, he knew now, had not been love. Fascination, obsession even, but not love.

'Do you think the king and queen are in there?' Bridget asked as they stood peering through the railings that surrounded Buckingham Palace. 'I'd love to see them.'

'Would you like me to go and knock on the door, then?' Billy grinned at the shocked look on Bridget's face at the very idea of him doing such a thing.

'Ooh, Billy! You wouldn't!'

'I might,' he said, still grinning, but meaning every word, 'if you asked me to.' Then he slid an arm about her waist and pulled her tightly in to his side so that their hearts beat in unison. 'I'd do anything in the world for you, Bridget.'

'Then let's go home, Billy,' she told him, giving him a peck on the cheek, 'and you can start proving it. London's a fine city, but it's too grand for me. I can't wait to get back to Jarrow.'

'Aye, love. Me too.'

12

It was late in the evening when Billy and Bridget tumbled sleepily off the train and hitched a ride on the back of a lorry travelling from Gateshead to Jarrow. The night was cold and cheerless with a misty rain falling that fell on the couple like shards of icy glass.

By the time they reached Jarrow and were put down by the lorry driver outside Christ Church, the very spot where the crusaders had set off from, they were too tired to talk. They walked the rest of the way in companionable silence, but had just turned the corner into the street where they lived when they were jolted into life again. There was a light burning in the window above Billy's cobbler's shop and somehow, it being after midnight, it didn't seem right.

'It's not like Laura to be up at this time of night,' Bridget said.

'Maybe she just forgot to turn it off,' Billy said, though as he spoke he felt a warning twinge in his gut and quickened his step.

'I hope she's all right.' Bridget was trotting behind him, trying to keep up as he broke into a run.

The front door was wide open, hanging limply on the one hinge that had not been shattered. Billy stopped at the foot of the stairs, holding a hand out to prevent Bridget from rushing up them to check on their friend. From a room above their heads, they could hear a deep-throated muttering. In response there was only a female whimper that they recognized as Laura.

'My God! What's happening?' Bridget whispered hoarsely as she latched her fingers tightly into the back of Billy's jacket.

'You stay here, Bridget,' Billy said, starting up the stairs, but she went with him, keeping as close as she could without tripping them both up.

The voice that had been a low rumble suddenly erupted in an angry explosion of expletives. There was the sound of a slap and a pitiful cry as something thudded heavily on the floor.

'Stupid bitch! You know where they are. You'd better tell me or I'll kill ye right here and now.'

'I don't know . . . ' The voice was now clearly that of Laura, and her attacker was Patrick Flynn. 'They left . . . went to London. They're not coming back.'

'I don't believe ye!' Another thud and a groan from Laura.

'I wouldn't tell you if I knew,' Laura said with obvious difficulty. 'But I will tell the police that you're back, you murdering brute. I'll give evidence against you and I know who they'll believe.'

Billy heard the floorboards creak as Patrick shifted his weight. He waited no longer, lunging into the room and grappling with the man that was half again as big as he was. Patrick gasped with the force of the assault and looked surprised as he toppled over and hit the floor like a two-ton ox. He lay there, winded for a moment, then started to fight back.

Helpless against this giant of a man, Billy felt ashamed as he was lifted bodily into the air and thrown to one side like a rag doll. But, as lithe as he was, he was up on his feet again in an instant before Patrick had time to raise himself to his knees.

'So it's you, Little Billy Big Boots, eh?' Patrick growled out the words. 'I didn't think you would be far away. Stop that snivelling, bitch!'

He raised his fist and whipped around, intending to bring it down across Laura's bruised and bleeding face. At the same time, Billy leapt between them and caught the full force of the blow on his temple. He felt the pain, saw stars and, for a fleeting moment, everything went black. He hit the floor and heard screaming.

It was Bridget making all the noise, but Billy was having difficulty focussing his eyes. When he did he saw something that amazed him. Bridget was riding Patrick's back like a cowboy on a bucking bronco, holding on to his hair in an attempt to pull him back. In a blur, Billy struggled to his feet. Out of the corner of his eye he could see Laura. She was lying slumped in a corner of the room and if she wasn't dead, then she wasn't far off, judging by the state of her.

There was no real warning of what was about to happen. Billy was staggering forward, shouting at Bridget to let go, but she was too incensed to listen. She was the epitome of an avenging angel and he knew what was going through her mind as she pummelled, kicked and bit the big, ugly excuse for manhood that had raped her, murdered her mother, tried to murder the man she loved, and caused untold misery to countless other people.

Patrick suddenly rose up, his massive frame stretching, his mouth opening in a great roar of rage. Billy was still seeing double through a fog, but every sound was deafeningly clear and so were his thoughts. If he didn't do something now, Patrick would surely kill Bridget.

As the thought entered Billy's pounding head, Patrick swung around, dislodging Bridget from his back. He grabbed a fistful of hair and started to drag her across the room. Billy caught sight of Bridget's stricken face and all he could think of was that he had lost so much because of Patrick Flynn that he could not tolerate losing the one person that meant more than life to him.

He was still unsteady on his legs as he looked around him for something to hit the big brute with. The scullery door was open and he veered towards it, thinking that the cast-iron skillet that was hanging above the stove would make a likely weapon, but it wasn't there. What his fingers did grip was his mother's old carving knife that had been among the meagre belongings he had brought with him to Bridget's after his mother's suicide.

'No, Patrick!' Billy screamed out to a man he could no more call father than he could call God the devil incarnate. Patrick *was* the devil incarnate. 'Enough! Take your dirty hands off her.'

Patrick looked at him, a sordid sneer twisting his moist red lips. He did not loosen his hold on Bridget's hair, but reached over and took hold of a gin bottle he had obviously brought in with him. He smashed it against the edge of the table and the end broke off, leaving jagged points of glass glinting lethally in the gaslight.

He stepped forward, parrying like a swordsman, jabbing the bottle into Billy's chest. Billy felt the sharp points of the glass pierce his shirt and penetrate through to his flesh. He didn't stop to think how seriously he was hurt. All he did was follow his natural instincts and lunged forward, just as Patrick did the same. The knife was pointed and sharp from many years of kitchen usage. Without any help from Billy, the blade entered Patrick's chest and went up to the hilt, scraping on ribs as it went.

Billy looked in horror at what had happened, then gazed, mesmerized, at Patrick's warm blood flowing over his hand, which still gripped the shaft of the knife. Then he was forced to see Patrick's face as he sank to his knees. The leery expression was still there, frozen in time. The weight of the man's body forced Billy to let go of the knife and Patrick fell to his knees, then rolled over on to his side spilling blood on to the rug which Bridget had bought from the pawn shop and brought home so delightedly.

There was no question that Patrick was

dead. He was as dead as any beast hanging from a hook down in the slaughterhouse where he had started his working life. And his long history of violent crime.

★ ★ ★

Billy stood in the dock, aware of only three things. His thudding heart, Bridget's sweet face, and the words of the judge ringing in his ears like a deafening peel of reverberating bells.

'William Flynn, the jury have found you guilty of manslaughter, but have asked for clemency, given the appalling provocation that led to the killing of Patrick Flynn. I therefore sentence you to not more than eight years' confinement . . . '

'No! Oh, please . . . you can't!' Bridget screamed out and there were other voices in agreement with her. 'It was self-defence. Patrick Flynn was no good. He was a beast, a murderer! Billy's a good man. You can't put him in prison, you can't!'

The judge looked across the courtroom, peering at Bridget from beneath wiry white eyebrows. His thin lips were sucked in tightly and for a moment it looked as if he might change his mind, but it was a false hope.

'Take him down,' he said, then with a swirl

of his robe, he left, disappearing through a rear door to his chambers.

As Billy was led away, he gave one last hungry glance in Bridget's direction and saw her sink down on a bench, her face pale, her eyes full of disbelief and awash with tears. Standing beside her was Laura, equally shocked. She still bore the scars of Patrick's attack that almost killed her a year ago. It had taken that long for them to bring Billy to trial, so long had it taken to find an unbiased jury.

Before he took that last step into the highly guarded regions of the courthouse, Billy caught Bridget's eye and tried to smile some encouragement to her, but he feared that all he managed was a tight grimace. She jumped once more to her feet and reached out to him as if trying to pluck him from the scene by magic.

'Billy!' she cried, her voice cracking. 'Billy! Billy!'

★ ★ ★

From that moment on, Billy's life became something of a blur for a while. His days consisted of jangling keys, clanging metal doors, scraping bolts and the sound of other prisoners' tramping feet, the chink of a chamber pot and groans and screams through the long, dark, unbearable nights.

He told himself he ought to be afraid, only he was too numb to feel anything at first. There was a stream of solicitors who came and spoke to him, telling him that they were sure they would be able to get an appeal, but then they didn't come back and were replaced by others who were equally enthusiastic but less experienced.

Billy imagined himself growing old with nothing but iron bars and thick cement walls for company. He soon found that friends and family became sparse when they knew what had become of him. Bridget visited when she could, but it was a long way on the bus from Jarrow to the prison and it cost money she could ill afford. Laura wrote to him, once. Her words were friendly enough, but restrained, telling him all the things he knew already — that it was not his fault he was in prison, that she was very grateful to him for saving her life, and that she hoped he would one day be pardoned and free to live a life without the physical threat of Patrick Flynn hanging over him.

Bridget had delivered the letter for Laura and sat watching him closely as he skimmed the lines of neat writing.

'Well, what has she got to say for herself,

then?' Bridget's voice was a little harsh and he guessed that relations between the two women in his life were not as good as they might be.

'Oh, just the usual type of things,' Billy told her with a lift of his shoulder. 'There's nothing much she can say, really, is there?'

'She could come and visit you,' Bridget said. 'After all, if it hadn't been for her you wouldn't be in here.'

'If it hadn't been for her, Bridget,' he said with a sad smile, 'I would be dead. Patrick Flynn would have killed me the day I was born if Laura hadn't stopped him.'

He heard Bridget's impatient sigh and saw her glance from side to side, scrutinizing the other visitors who were chatting through the bars to their friends and loved ones. He knew that these visits took a lot out of her, draining her emotionally as well as financially.

'Look, Bridget, love . . . ' How he wished he could reach through to her, take her in his arms and hug her until she begged for mercy, but that was never going to happen. 'I don't think you should come in to see me again.'

'You trying to get rid of me, Billy?' She was immediately up in arms, her eyes slashing at him like sabres. 'The day I stop coming to see you will be the day the daisies grow on my grave, do you hear?'

'Well, that'll be tomorrow, because I don't want to see you here any more,' he said with a sudden show of anger, though what he was feeling inside was despair. Despair at being responsible for making Bridget unhappy. It was time for her to get on with her life without him. He would only bring her down. Even if she waited for him, what kind of life could he offer her? He would be an ex-prisoner, a lag. Nobody would want to employ him. Life would be unbearable.

'That's a horrible thing to say, Billy!'

'Bridget, go away, *please*. This godforsaken place is no place for you.'

'God might have forsaken you, Billy,' she said, shivering and pulling her coat around her as she got to her feet. 'But I won't. I won't ever forsake you and that's a promise.'

'You shouldn't make promises, Bridget. They're not always possible to keep.'

She had simply shaken her head at him and left without a further word. He had spent a long time, sitting in his cell, mulling over that conversation, his heart alternating between swelling with love for Bridget, and sinking miserably at the thought of how he was to spend the next few years incarcerated with men who were hardened criminals. And what they did to each other, and to him, didn't bear thinking about.

That last meeting with Bridget was the most memorable in Billy's mind for more reasons than one. It was the third day of September 1939, and war had just been declared against Germany.

★　★　★

'Don't you ever get tired, Bridget?'

Bridget threw a glance in Laura's direction, but went on scrubbing the kitchen bench with her usual vigour.

'Tired of what?'

'All the waiting and the hardships. Never having enough to eat, having to make do and mend.' Laura threw down the blouse she was attempting to make over so it didn't show signs of wear. 'I can't remember the last time I was able to buy myself some decent clothes.'

'Well, you're not alone in that.' Bridget's scrubbing became more methodical as her brain switched on again and she had to recognize the fact that Laura was there and in the mood to talk. 'We do all right. There are lots of people a bloody sight worse off.'

'I wish you wouldn't swear, Bridget!' Laura got up and paced the floor, hugging herself tightly with thin arms while trying to smoke at the same time. 'I thought the years of the

Depression were bad, but this war . . . '

'This war will be over one day and things will be better.' Bridget tossed her scrubbing brush into the dirty soapsuds in the sink and wiped her hands on her pinny. 'And I wish you wouldn't smoke them things. The smoke makes me cough and the house stinks because of it.'

'I'm sorry.' Laura carefully nipped out the glowing end of her precious cigarette and Bridget felt bad because she knew her friend needed the calming effect the cigarettes gave her. Laura's nerves were always on the brink of breaking.

'How's life on the farm, then?' Laura had joined the Land Army and was stationed on a farm in Northumberland. She got home quite often and Bridget didn't know whether this was because her employers were kind or whether they were influenced by Laura's general lack of application to the job.

There was a short, poignant silence, while Laura seemed to be composing herself. Her eyes flickered over Bridget's face, then her gaze dropped to the floor.

'It wouldn't be so bad if . . . ' She gave a shrug and sat down at the kitchen table, picking at the roughened skin around her broken nails. 'You see, he . . . Mr Harvey . . . he's . . . well, I . . . '

Bridget frowned and sat down in the chair opposite. Laura had been going on about Donald Harvey since the first day she went to work for him. He was a brute of a man who could be quite intimidating if he didn't get his own way. The men on the farm wouldn't cross him. He scared the women with his rages, which turned him lobster red, though he had not been known to be physically abusive.

'He hasn't laid his hands on you, Laura, has he?' Bridget never believed in beating about the bush. She wasn't one for pussy-footing around, especially when she was up to her ears in unfinished work.

'No, nothing like that, but . . . ' Laura was going pink in the face and her fingers were so agitated it was beginning to annoy Bridget.

'So what's wrong?' she asked. 'Come on, out with it. I've got to get finished here before I do my shift.'

Laura swallowed hard. 'He's asked me to marry him, Bridget. I don't know what to tell him.'

Bridget's eyes widened and her mouth cracked open into a broad smile. 'That's some problem you've got there.'

'Oh, don't laugh, Bridget. He's expecting an answer when I go back to the farm tomorrow night.'

'Aye, well, it's not something I can help you with, is it?'

'What would you do?'

'Me? I'm not like you, Laura. He wouldn't dream of asking me to marry him.'

'But if he did?'

'I can't really answer that. I'd have to be desperate, I suppose, but even then . . . no, I don't think I'd accept his proposal. As I say, I'm not you.'

'Oh, Lord!' Laura lowered her head and rested it on her hands. 'Oh, my Lord, what should I do?'

'He's more than twice your age, but he's not short of a penny, so you'll not starve.' Bridget was trying to give Laura some positive thoughts but she could see it wasn't working. 'He's not all that bad-looking and his bark's probably worse than his bite. Do you care for him, Laura?'

'Oh, no! Not at all, but . . . ' Laura raised her head and her cheeks were wet with tears. 'It's just . . . I don't want to grow old without . . . you know . . . I'm lonely, Bridget. I . . . I need somebody.'

'Don't we all,' Bridget said, her thoughts straying in the direction of her beloved Billy. He was locked behind bars with no sign of a reprieve or parole, and him refusing to see her. 'But we can't always have what we want, can we? Not in the real world, and certainly not in a world that's at war.'

'If only Billy hadn't killed that awful Patrick Flynn,' Laura said suddenly, thumping her fist on the table and making cups and saucers rattle. 'He would have married me, wouldn't he? You knew, didn't you, Bridget, that he was in love with me?'

Bridget stared at the other girl and felt her blood run cold. Her heart skipped a beat, then thudded in her chest so that when she finally spoke her voice shook discernibly.

'Laura . . . I don't know what to say, but . . . ' She drew in a deep breath and let it out slowly. How was she going to tell Laura that if Billy's heart belonged to anybody, then it belonged to her, Bridget Maguire? But Laura didn't give her the opportunity to speak further.

'You see, Bridget,' Laura said, 'silly as it sounds, I think Billy was always in love with me, even when he was a little boy. I could see it and I tried to ignore it, but when he grew up . . . well, I told myself I was being foolish. I mean, he was years younger than me and we come from different backgrounds, but . . . Oh, Bridget, I have so many regrets. And now he's in prison and . . . '

'And if you loved him you would go and

visit him,' Bridget said. 'Why don't you, Laura?'

Laura's expression revealed the revulsion she felt at going anywhere near a prison. Her reduced circumstances had not altered the way she saw life. She still had that old family snobbish pride in her that would always come to the fore.

'I . . . I wrote to him, once,' she said. 'But I couldn't find the right words to say how I felt. And now, I don't know how I feel any more. I mean . . . he's a criminal, and even when he comes out of prison he . . . Well, he'll always be an ex-convict, won't he?'

Bridget stared at her and sighed. 'I can't believe you said that, Laura,' she said. 'Especially after what he did for you.'

Laura's eyebrows went up and her shoulders with them. 'Well, it's true. Could you see yourself living with a man who's been in prison?'

'As a matter of fact, Laura,' said Bridget, meeting Laura's gaze unwaveringly, 'I could. If that man was Billy. He should never have been put away and everybody knows that, except the damned stupid jury.'

'Yes . . . well, everybody can't think the same, I suppose.' Looking thoughtful, Laura sat down at the kitchen table and her fingers beat a monotonous rhythm on its surface.

'You know what, Bridget, I think I'll accept Donald Harvey's proposal. It's got to be better than this, hasn't it?'

As she spoke, Laura's eyes swept the little kitchen that Bridget had worked so hard to make cosy and comfortable. She had taken Laura in when she had nowhere else to go, had looked after her, helped her, and supported her. This was Bridget's home and she was proud of it. Laura's words had been a cutting insult.

'Yes, Laura, I'm sure you're right,' Bridget said. 'Mr Harvey isn't a bad man. He may be a bit harsh, but he's fair, by all accounts, and honest.'

'Yes.' A bright smile of hope was spreading over Laura's long, thin face. 'And, as you say, he's not exactly penniless, either. I'm sure he would want a wife who could do him proud.'

'You'd be perfect,' Bridget told her, biting her tongue before she could say what she was really thinking. How dare the woman cast aspersions on Billy like that after he had saved her life? Billy had spent a lifetime worshipping her from afar. What a waste. *What a ruddy waste!*

Bridget rose to her feet, reached for her coat and her bag and walked on heavy feet to the back door.

'You off to the munitions factory? God, I

don't know how you stand it mingling with all those rough girls. And you come home smelling like an old potboiler. I can tell you, I'm going to get married and have a baby as soon as I can. That way, at least, I won't have to shovel out any more manure. Mr Harvey will see to that.'

Bridget gave her a pained look.

'I hope it all works out for you, Laura,' she said.

Laura rushed over to her and gave her a brief hug. 'Oh, thank you! I hope I can rely on you, Bridget. You know, to help out with the wedding breakfast?'

'Yes,' said Bridget with a weak smile. 'Yes, of course you can.'

★   ★   ★

As Bridget made her way across town to the munitions factory where she spent hour upon hour making screws and rivets for army issue rifles, she couldn't get Billy out of her mind. It hurt so much that he had turned away from her. She didn't know if, at the bottom of him, he still had those childhood dreams of Laura. If he expected Laura to be waiting for him when he was eventually released, he would be in for a sad disappointment. The thought of the pair of them ever getting together had been the cause of many a sleepless night and troubled days dealing with a heavy heart when she allowed herself to wallow in self-pity.

Always, at the bottom of her, Bridget knew that what she really felt was jealousy. Until recently she had never dared to admit it, even to herself. Not until that memorable day after she had been abused by Patrick Flynn, when Billy took her into his arms, cradling her like a hurt child, and not once did he put a finger wrong on her.

Yes, that was when she knew, without a doubt, that she not only loved Billy as a friend, but also that she was *in love* with him. And now that the way was clear to her, Billy was cutting himself off, chasing her away. It was enough to make any woman lose heart. Any woman, that was, except Bridget Maguire.

Bloody men! Bridget swore under her breath as the factory gates clanged shut behind her, very much like the gates of the prison had done. She ignored the snide remarks of her workmates and a cautionary warning about being late from her supervisor and got on with the job. It was a small but essential task all in the name of helping her country to win the war.

'You nearly got locked out this morning,'

the girl on the next bench shouted above the noise of the girlish chatter and the cacophony of machinery noises. 'Your man keep you in bed, eh?'

'She hasn't got a man, Phyllis,' mouthed another, older woman in a matching head-scarf tied, as they all wore them, as a turban to protect their hair and them from accidents. 'He's in prison, isn't he, love?'

'Yes, but he . . . ' Bridget started to plead Billy's defence, but changed her mind when another woman chipped in.

'And I bet he wasn't guilty. They all say that, of course, bloody liars.'

'Prison!' The first young woman made her mouth heard, loud and clear. 'And I bet he thinks *he's* got it hard. God in heaven. They've got it ruddy easy in there compared to our blokes fighting the bliddy Nazis.'

'Ignore her, pet,' said the second woman. 'She's just heard that her hubby's gone missing over France. Have you got any bairns, Bridget?'

Bridget looked at her, wishing that she could say yes. It would have been a bit of Billy on the outside and something for him to look forward to when they eventually let him out. Something real and solid and good to come home to. She would have put up with the shame of not being married, the humiliation of being shunned and pointed at in the street and being called names. People were already muttering behind their hands and had been ever since Billy moved in with her. In their eyes Bridget was still, and always would be, the daughter of a whore.

Bridget's eyes stung with tears, but she blinked them away. She always got emotional when she thought of her mother. How Colleen would have been up in arms at what was happening to Billy, she thought. She would have fought tooth and nail to persuade them to set him free. Colleen wouldn't have sat back and done nothing. She might have been a whore, but she was a good person with a heart of pure gold, always on the side of justice, no matter what. If Colleen had had her way, that murdering bastard Patrick would have been hung long ago and Colleen herself would still be alive.

'Damn him!' Bridget hadn't meant to speak out loud, but the woman next to her, mistaking her meaning, turned and patted her shoulder.

'Aye, pet, that's right. You get good and angry. It's the only way to get through life when you're married to a no-good hardened sinner.'

* * *

On her next day off, Bridget decided to have one more attempt at visiting Billy. After her last visit he had had time to reconsider and might just be regretting his decision to tell her not to return. She gave her name and his to the prison warden on visitor duty and waited with the other visitors, her heart fluttering in anticipation.

The prisoners filed in and settled themselves behind the barred screen, some of them talking animatedly with their visitors, others subdued and silent with downcast eyes. Whatever crimes they had committed, it didn't show. They were all just men behind bars, restricted, punished, sad, pathetic. Some of them may have committed the foulest murders; some may have burgled or dabbled in bribery and corruption. It was hard to distinguish one from the other with their shaven heads and the shapeless prison suits they were required to wear.

Some minutes passed and Bridget was the only one left standing. She hovered nervously, waiting for Billy to arrive. On the other side of the security screen there was an empty space. She glanced at the clock, then at the grim-faced guard standing by the door. He didn't look too approachable, so she decided to hang on a few minutes more before asking him what was keeping Billy.

She waited and waited. Billy didn't come. People were starting to leave, looking at her with sympathetic eyes. One woman touched her hand in passing.

'Never mind, pet. He's probably been a naughty boy and got himself put in solitary confinement. That's the best that can happen to him. It's safer in there.'

Bridget wanted to ask the woman what she meant, but there wasn't time. A phone on the wall shrilled and the guard whipped off the receiver and spoke into it at length. Bridget decided to give up and started to sidle past him as he finished his conversation. He help up a hand, staying her progress, and fixed her with a stony stare.

'You William Flynn's visitor, love?'

'Yes,' Bridget said with a nod, her voice small and scared in her constricted throat. 'He . . . he must have been delayed. I'll come back tomorrow, if I can.'

'I shouldn't bother, pet.' The guard took off his cap and wiped a grubby handkerchief around his perspiring face. 'I just got word that he's in the prison hospital. Got beaten up pretty badly last night apparently. They're not sure he'll make it.'

Bridget froze. She wanted to scream, but no sound came out of her mouth, which felt strangely paralyzed. Blackness started to crowd in on her, pinpricked with many dazzling stars. As her legs started to give way, the guard grabbed her by the arm and pushed her towards a chair. She slumped thankfully into it.

'You his wife, are you?' The guard stood over her, big and menacing in appearance, though he had spoken to her softly enough. 'You Mrs Flynn?'

'No . . . yes . . . I mean . . . ' All colour was drained from Bridget's face as she looked up and saw the moon face of the guard through the blur. 'Are you sure? I mean, are you sure it's Billy?'

'Aye, pet. There's only the one William Flynn in here. He's the one they all call Billy Big Boots, isn't he?' She nodded dumbly. 'Well, it seems he got a bit too big for them boots of his, going up against one of the old lags. Didn't like what was happening to him, so he got stroppy. The lag has lots of friends. They sorted Billy out.'

'C-can I see him, do you think?'

'No point. He's in a coma. If he comes out of it he'll be back in his cell right away. If not, well, you'll get his body for burying.' The guard's voice softened slightly and he touched her on the shoulder. 'Go on, pet. Go home. They'll let the next of kin know how things go.'

'I am Billy's next of kin,' Bridget said huskily. 'He doesn't have anybody else.'

It seemed to take forever to get home that day. And there was Laura waiting for her. She had done something to her hair and put on a little powder and lipstick and was looking quite pretty for a change. But one look at Bridget's face wiped her smile away.

'Bridget, you look like a ghost! Whatever's happened? Did you see Billy?'

'No, I didn't. Some nasty buggers have beaten him up. They say . . . ' Bridget collapsed on their overstuffed horsehair sofa and put her face in her hands, her shoulders heaving with sobs that forced their way out of her. 'Oh, Laura! They say he's in a coma and . . . They think he's going to die.'

'No!' Laura's hands flew to her mouth. 'Oh, no, it can't be true. Bridget, say it's not true, for God's sake.'

'God had nothing to do with it,' Bridget told her coldly. 'I'd like to get my hands on the ones that hurt our Billy. I'd show them what hurting is really like.'

She looked around futilely for something to throw, for words in these circumstances were simply not enough. Laura sat down beside her and flung her arms about her shoulders, hugging her tightly.

'He'll be all right, Bridget. You'll see.'

'Will I?' Bridget shook her head sadly. 'Oh, I hope you're right, Laura.'

She got up, feeling heavy and stiff, like an old woman, and went to her room to be alone. In there she could think of Billy, pray for him, even though she wasn't sure that there was a God. If there were, why would he let such awful things happen to people? Why bring down his wrath on the head of Billy Flynn, who was a better man than most? In fact, there was none better.

'Oh, Billy, love . . . ' She hugged the carved bedpost until her fingers grew numb and the bones of her knuckles shone through. At that moment the air-raid siren wailed and its morbid sound sliced through Bridget like an ice-cold knife going through her heart. 'You've got to pull through. Live, Billy, oh, please, *please, live!*'

13

The first thing that struck Billy, like someone had taken a sledge-hammer to his head, was the light. It blinded him the second the huge iron portals of the prison swung open as silently as they had closed behind him in 1937. Most of those years had been spent in a special hospital for the criminally insane. And he had been insane for a while, he told himself.

He must have been, because he had virtually no memory of what had gone before his imprisonment, and only snatches of lucid moments afterwards. What he knew was simply the facts as handed to him by the prison officials and the young barrister who had tirelessly fought his case and finally achieved his release, though it was late enough in coming.

He had been transported back to Durham pending his release. In his pocket he carried a doctor's certificate giving him a clean bill of health, except for some pockets of memory loss, which could remain with him for the rest of his life. A part of Billy wished he had no memory at all. Another part wasn't at all sure that he was ready to rejoin the real world. A lot had happened in the world, as well as in his life, since his incarceration. Most of it, he preferred not to dwell on.

'Right, Flynn!' He jumped as the guard at the gate scraped his feet and spoke loudly in his ear. 'Off you go, lad, and good luck to you. We don't want to see you back here, understand?'

Billy squinted up at the uniformed figure and gave a brief nod. Words were still not easily formed in his head and his mouth couldn't cope with them either. To all intents and purposes, he was still suffering from post-traumatic hysteria. That was how the doctors had called it. Something like that, anyway. His experiences in prison, the beating, the coma — whatever it was, it had caused amnesia, wiping out everything he knew for a while. It had been a long time before things started coming back, and then only in flashes and he would wake up bathed in his own sweat, wondering if it had been real.

He might never get total recall, they had told him. There would always be gaps. The likelihood of the nightmares continuing was pretty certain. He tried not to think about it too much. The more he tried to remember, the more it hurt his head.

The prison officer was shaking his hand and patting him amicably on the shoulder, then Billy heard the doors shut behind him and the bolts grate back into place. He was alone in an alien world. Just for an instant the silence of the morning seemed overwhelming, then a chorus of birdsong from across the street awakened his senses. It seemed abnormally loud to him, and yet it was so ordinary. Sparrows bickering over a crust of bread on a piece of wasteground. There had been a building there the day he had entered the prison, but German bombers had flattened it. He remembered the day the bomb had fallen. Prisoners, who had been told to stay in their cells during the air raids, had been shaken out of their bunks by the blast.

Billy stopped himself thinking further. It might be too much to take if things came flooding back suddenly. The constant nightmares were vivid enough. If he was to survive, he had to learn to forget many things, block them from his mind. He had to reinvent himself, be a new and different person. The only trouble was, he didn't know how to start, didn't even know where to go.

He gazed down blankly at the address scribbled almost illegibly on a piece of crumpled paper. The governor had given it to him only half an hour ago, but he had held on to it so tightly that it had formed itself into a ball in his clammy palm, the blue ink smudging. The governor had been a good enough type. He had been supportive, kind even, but he didn't always have any real knowledge of what went on among the inmates, or even the wardens, some of which were just as bad as the criminals they guarded.

With a shudder, despite the warmth of the June sun, Billy took his first steps back down the road of freedom. He had served eight long years. It had been too long.

'Give it time, Billy,' the governor had told him, placing two fatherly hands on Billy's shoulders. 'It won't be easy. Not at first. And it's a different place out there. We've had a war. People are picking themselves up, trying to go on with their lives, sometimes in the greatest of difficulties. But if anybody can make it, you can. Try not to let bitterness ruin the rest of your life. There's still a lot of goodness out there in the world. God knows, I hope you find some of it, because you deserve it.'

Remembering the man's sympathetic words now, Billy stood in the middle of a deserted crossroads, listening to the day waking up. The sparrows had been replaced by a couple of barking dogs and somewhere close there were the high-pitched voices of children playing. An engine throbbed and murmured from the distance, getting closer, until he could see where it came from. A small black motor car was chugging down the road towards him, the sun glinting on the windshield. He stood transfixed, like a rabbit in headlights, willing his legs to carry him out of its path. But he couldn't move. He just stood there and waited.

The car drew to a halt a few feet from him. The driver got out and strode towards him, hand outstretched. He recognized the man immediately and felt relieved.

'Welcome back to the world, Billy!' Andrew Graham, the young barrister who had fought tirelessly in Billy's corner, grabbed hold of him and hugged him like a brother. 'Come on, I've got a surprise for you.'

'Surprise? W-what is it?' Billy's voice was shaky. He wasn't sure that he liked surprises. He might not be able to cope with this one.

'You'll see!' As he spoke, he pointed back towards the car. 'Look.'

Someone was stepping down on to the road. It was a woman with a well-rounded figure and the brightest copper-gold hair he had ever seen. He squinted at her pretty face, felt the warmth of her smile as she came forward, arms outstretched. Something tweaked at his heart.

'Oh, Billy!'

It was as if all the years started rushing backwards, sending his brain in a dizzy whirl. He was young again, young and fit and full of hope for the future. He was back with the lads, supporting them, helping where he could as they crusaded from Jarrow to London, demanding work, fighting against poverty and the authorities in order to survive.

And she had been there with him, with her red hair and her smile and her eyes so green and sincere that they sometimes made you want to weep. It had taken Billy a long time to realize that he loved her.

'Bridget,' he whispered softly, tasting the salt of his own tears as emotion welled up and threatened to choke him if he could not let it out. 'Bridget, is it really you?'

'Silly sod,' she said, her voice cracking as she pulled him against her and hugged him so tightly that it took his breath away. 'Who else would it be?'

They clung together for a long time. The barrister stood aside, averting his gaze to give them some privacy.

'I didn't think that anybody ... that you ... ' Billy heaved a shuddering sigh. 'Oh, Bridget ... '

He waved his hands in the air to demonstrate that he could not find the words that were bursting inside his heart. During his stay in prison and the long admissions to hospital, he had been virtually silent. Even when he had been able to speak he preferred to keep his own counsel. It wasn't easy to converse with strangers, especially when there were chunks of your life missing from your memory.

'I was so scared that you wouldn't remember me, Billy,' Bridget said. 'They told me . . . you know . . . about you being in a coma and . . . and then you were moved and . . . '

'You visited me, didn't you?' There were shadowy memories of people coming and going over the years, but Bridget's face was the only one that made any sense.

'Yes, I did, in the beginning . . . but it wasn't always possible. And then you sent me away . . . refused to see me. I kept on coming, but they moved you away. It was too far to travel in a day and then there was the war and . . . Oh, Billy, love, I thought this day would never come!'

'Shall we move on?' Andrew Graham suggested with an anxious glance at his watch. 'I'm sure you're wanting to get home, Billy.'

'Home?' There was a lump the size of a baked potato in Billy's throat and he couldn't seem to swallow it back. Home, he thought. Now there was a grand word. But he couldn't bring the place to mind. Flashes of his mother's house came to him, and his mother too, but that was useless. He knew that Maggie was long dead, and didn't somebody say that the house had been condemned and pulled down?

They all looked around when a second car approached slowly and parked. Two uniformed figures got out. Not the law, but soldiers of Christ. The Salvation Army captain and his wife had kept in constant touch, having discovered him on their regular visits to comfort and counsel the prisoners. They had been good to him and now, as promised, they were there to take him into their flock of lost souls. It was the address of the Salvation Army hostel the governor had given him.

'Billy!' Captain Harry Jones extended his hand and gave Billy a firm handshake. His wife gave him a brief but genuine hug. 'I see you have some friends to greet you. That's good, son. Will you be going with them?'

Billy licked his lips, swallowed audibly and kept his eyes fixed on the captain's top button.

'No,' he said in a whisper and heard a gasp of surprise from Bridget. 'No, I'm coming with you, as we agreed . . . if that's all right?'

'Billy, why? You can come home with me.' Bridget said quickly. 'We can . . . '

'Miss Maguire . . . leave it.' The barrister had hold of Bridget's arm and was pulling her back. 'It's Billy's decision, for whatever reason. You have to respect that.'

Billy could see them out of the corner of his eye. There was something possessive about the way the man looked at Bridget, the way he put his hands on her. They were a couple and, God knew, they made a better couple than he and Bridget would ever have made. Bridget deserved the best and they didn't come any better than Andrew Graham.

'Can we go now, please?' Billy muttered to the Salvation Army captain.

Captain Jones hesitated, throwing a sympathetic glance in Bridget's and Andrew Graham's direction, then he nodded and headed for the car. The captain's wife looked as if she were struggling to subdue her emotions. There was the glisten of a tear in her eye and a quiver in her lips. She pressed her fingers into Billy's forearm as she walked with him in her husband's wake, telling him things that he didn't really hear. He just wanted to get away from that place. Away from Bridget's sad, pleading eyes.

Billy sank down gratefully on the soft leather upholstered back seat of the captain's car. One hand clutched his bag with all his worldly goods. The car coughed into life and did a U-turn before driving back down the road away from the prison. Billy fixed his eyes on the road ahead and never once looked back.

⋆   ⋆   ⋆

'I don't understand, Mr Graham.' Bridget gazed at the tail end of the other car whisking Billy away from her. 'Billy's home is with me. He doesn't have anywhere else to go.'

Andrew Graham massaged his jaw and looked reflective. 'I think I understand, Miss Maguire,' he said, and when he looked at her there was remorse in his kindly eyes. 'He told me he didn't want you to come. I'm afraid I didn't believe him. After all, what man in his right mind would turn down the opportunity of being with you.'

'What?' Bridget blinked and the barrister looked surprised at his own words.

'I'm sorry. I shouldn't have said that. This is not the time to . . . ' He stopped and indicated the waiting car. 'Shall we . . . er . . . ?'

He opened the front passenger door for her

and helped her into the car as carefully as if he were handling precious cargo. Bridget had always been struck by his politeness and his sincerity, but it had never occurred to her that he might be even remotely attracted to her. The thought crossed her mind now, then she dismissed it and sat clutching her hands in her lap all the way back home. During the thirty-minute journey the conversation was restricted to such mundane things as the traffic and the weather. Neither of them mentioned Billy.

When they arrived at Bridget's house, the barrister seemed suddenly embarrassed and she sensed his reluctance to leave her.

'It's early days, Bridget,' he said, using her first name for the first time. 'Maybe he needs time to adjust . . . you know? Think things over.'

Bridget shook her head. 'I wanted things to be so right for him, Mr Graham. I could understand him for not wanting me to visit him. He was trying to protect me. He's like that, is Billy. But not wanting to come home with me. This is where he lived. We were happy together here and I thought . . . '

'It's not always easy to pick up the pieces and continue where you left off.' Andrew Graham looked from Bridget to her front door and back again. 'Is it all right if I come in? Just for a moment?'

She didn't reply to his question, but took out her key and opened the door, leaving him to follow her into the house. The kitchen table was laid for a dinner for two. There were candles and a posy bowl of red anemones. And over the fireplace Bridget had strung a line of cardboard letters that spelled out 'Welcome home, Billy!'.

'You think I'm an idiot, don't you, Mr Graham?' she said, her arm sweeping the room in an arc. 'I even planned his favourite dinner and lashed out on a bottle of sherry. Not that Billy touches alcohol, and I've never tasted the stuff, but I thought it was a nice idea and . . . '

She sniffed and searched for her handkerchief, but couldn't find it and had to use the back of her hand to wipe away her silent tears. Suddenly she found the barrister's arm around her shoulders and he was giving her the kind of hug she had dreamed of receiving from Billy that day. Only Billy wasn't there.

'Oh, my dear, I'm so sorry. What you've done . . . it's really quite touching. You must love Billy very much.'

'I always have.' Bridget nodded and then gulped on a sob that seemed to get stuck in her windpipe. 'And I always will.'

'Give him time, Bridget.' She flinched as

the barrister planted a soft kiss on the top of her head. 'Things will work out, one way or another. You're a very strong person. You'll be all right.'

'Will I? Oh, Mr Graham, I hope you're right.'

'Look . . . ' There was a long hesitation. 'Do you think you could call me by my first name? My friends call me Andrew.'

She blinked up at him wetly, not sure how to react, but feeling the need for this new friend in her life. He was from the other side of the tracks completely, and one day he might even be an important judge. But she liked him. He spoke better than she did, but there was no edge to him. And he was kind and had tremendous understanding. Bridget had a feeling that he would always be on her side, no matter what happened in the future.

'All right, Mr . . . Andrew,' she said, accepting his pristine white handkerchief and mopping up her face with it. 'But only as a friend, mind you. Oh, God, I hope you weren't suggesting anything else, because . . . '

Had there been a slight flash of disappointment there? No matter. He had soon covered it over with a bright smile and a forefinger held to her lips to stop her rabbiting on at him.

'Just friends,' he said, though his eyes were

saying something else and Bridget felt bad about that. 'No ties, Bridget. That is, not unless you want there to be.'

'And then what?'

'Then you'll find me very receptive,' he told her, taking both her hands in his and squeezing them tightly. 'When or if that ever happens I shall be very grateful.'

He was still holding her hands and staring into her astonished eyes when the door burst open and an exuberant Laura entered the room.

'Bridget, I've finally said yes. I'm going to be Mrs Donald Harvey! Look!' Laura thrust out her left hand, exhibiting the three diamonds that glittered there. 'I've kept the poor man waiting for too long.' Then she saw the barrister. 'Oh!'

Andrew dropped Bridget's hands and his cheeks coloured as he backed away a step and allowed Laura to enter into the small room.

'I . . . er . . . was just leaving,' he said, nodding politely to Laura and smiling bashfully at Bridget. 'Don't hesitate to get in touch with me if there's anything you need, Bridget. Anything at all.'

'Yes, I will. Thank you.'

'Don't forget.'

'No . . . No, I won't.'

'Yes . . . well, I'll get off. Perhaps . . . '

'I'll see you to the door.'

'Thank you.'

At the door, and with a curious Laura shut in the kitchen, Andrew seemed to get back some of the courage he needed to speak further to Bridget.

'I sometimes go to the theatre or to a concert in Newcastle,' he said. 'It's not much fun on my own. Would you consider going with me? Of course, if you'd rather not . . . ?'

'That's very kind, but . . . '

'Not straight away, of course.' He was anxious not to seem too insistent, she could tell. 'It was just a thought. We do seem to get on well. Anyway, you think about it. I'll be in touch.'

'Yes, thank you.'

He stared at her for a long time, then gave a brief nod, touched the brim of his trilby hat and hurried to his car. Bridget did not wait for him to drive off, but returned to the kitchen where Laura was getting impatient.

'What was all that about?' she asked of Bridget, her eyes darting about expectantly.

'It was just Andrew. Mr Graham . . . being kind,' Bridget said. 'He drove me all the way back from Durham.'

'Oh, I'd forgotten. But where's Billy?'

Bridget shook her head and willed herself not to weep bitterly in front of Laura. 'He decided that it was best not to come back here.'

'Oh!' It was difficult to tell whether Laura was disappointed or pleased at the news. 'How odd. Did he say . . . ?'

'I'm sorry, Laura, but I don't want to talk about it right now.'

'All right.' Again the hand came up showing the engagement ring. 'Didn't you see what Donald gave me last night? We're finally going to be married, Bridget! Isn't it wonderful!'

'Wonderful, Laura. I'm pleased for you.'

'You don't look it. What's wrong?'

'Nothing. I'm tired.'

'I think I'll invite my family to the wedding. What do you think? I mean, I am marrying somebody they can respect, after all, even if he is old enough to be my father. They can't not speak to me for ever, can they?'

'I suppose not.' Bridget headed for the hall and the stairs. 'Excuse me, Laura, but I think I'll just go and lie down.'

She left Laura admiring her ring and locked herself in her bedroom. Sitting on the edge of her old sagging bed, Bridget thought over the events of the day and her weariness became twofold. After a while, muttering Billy's name under her breath, she crept beneath the eiderdown and cried into her pillow until she thought her heart would break.

★ ★ ★

In the Salvation Army hostel, Billy felt ill at ease, though he suspected that no place existed where he could feel comfortable. He was given a bunk bed, much the same as he had occupied in prison, and a coarse grey woollen blanket. The bed was in a dormitory shared by at least thirty other men. It was basically clean but cramped and there was an underlying smell of unwashed bodies and stale human secretions.

On the ground floor there was an eating space with long form tables and benches and men and women were installed there in small groups. Billy chose to sit alone, but was soon joined by a man called Joe, who helped in the kitchen.

'New, are ye?' The man was unshaven and had disturbing facial jerks that he tried to hide by touching his head with his hand as he spoke. 'Prison or the road?'

'Prison,' Billy told him, hoping the fellow was not one of those insistent types who let their curiosity run away with them.

'Aye. Thowt so. You have the look. Out on the road, they gets themselves a tan like they've just come back from the Riviera. What were you in for?'

Billy's mouth snapped shut and his chin jerked. He fleetingly met the man's eyes and looked rapidly away again.

'All right, son, all right,' Joe said, holding up his hands. 'It don't matter. We're all the same in here. Hapless and homeless. You hungry? There's a good stew on the menu today. Rabbit and mash.'

Billy nodded. He wasn't hungry, but if it got Joe to leave him alone it was worth accepting a meal.

'Aye, thanks.'

'The captain wants to see you after you've eaten,' Joe said, pointing to a frosted glass-panelled door through which a yellow light shone. 'That's the office over there.'

Billy picked at his food with his head bent low over his plate. He didn't want the others in the room to think that he was seeking out friendship of any kind. Sociable conversation had not been a part of his life for a number of years. He wasn't ready to enter into it now and told himself that it was nothing to do with the fact that these people were largely tramps and drunks.

In a nearby corner, he had noticed a man of indeterminate age with matted hair hanging down to his shoulders. He was rolling in his seat, waving a bottle of meths about and talking volubly to an invisible friend. The man stank to high heaven, as did many of the others, yet there were Salvationists moving among them as if they were the usual Sunday congregation down at the local place of worship.

As soon as he could, Billy pushed his plate aside and headed for the door, which was clearly marked 'Captain H. Jones'. He knocked and got a brisk command to enter. The captain was sitting at a large office desk that had seen better days. One corner had a leg missing and was propped up with a pile of old *War Cry* magazines. The surface of the desk was buried beneath a vast amount of papers and files that would have given any secretary worth her salt an anxiety attack. However, Captain Harry, as he was affectionately known, looked perfectly calm and at ease.

'Ah, Billy! Come in, come in, lad! Have a seat.'

Billy perched on the edge of a wooden kitchen chair. He was still clutching his belongings to his chest. It had been too much of a risk leaving them in the long dormitory where the locker at the side of his bed had no lock.

The captain shuffled a few batches of

papers together into well-ordered piles and placed them to one side of the desk with a grunt of satisfaction. His attention was then fully given to Billy.

'Well now, how are you settling in?'

Billy took a deep breath and swallowed, not knowing how to answer. 'It's not what I'm used to,' he said eventually and the Salvation Army officer smiled benignly.

'No, lad, I'm sure it's not, but it's a roof over your head and food in your belly until you can do better for yourself. Who was that I saw you with this morning outside the prison? A relative, perhaps?'

Billy shook his head. He didn't want to get into any in-depth discussion about Bridget. It would cut too deep.

'Just a friend.'

'Hmm. Very pretty young woman. She seemed disturbed at your choice to come with my wife and I.' Captain Harry ran a hand over his fresh-coloured face and studied Billy from beneath a pair of bushy white eyebrows. 'Was there not a chance of finding lodgings with her, or would that have been improper? I don't wish to interfere in your life, you understand, Billy, but I need to know exactly how we can help you to get re-established. With the best will in the world, life isn't easy for ex-prisoners, especially with the war still echoing in our ears.'

'I understand that, sir.' Billy dropped his gaze to the floor. 'I couldn't go back there, sir. She . . . Bridget . . . she deserves better.'

Captain Harry leaned back in his chair, tilting it dangerously and making it creak.

'And so do you, young man,' he said gently. 'So do you.' When Billy didn't respond, the captain went on: 'I know you're not a believer, Billy, but I hear you're quite a dab-hand at all sorts of things. Maybe you could earn a few shillings doing odd jobs in and around the Army and its congregation.'

Billy looked apprehensive. He had done a little training in the prison workshop. Carpentry, plumbing and general maintenance. But the thing he wanted to do most of all was get back to mending and making shoes. He loved working with leather.

'I used to be a cobbler,' he said. 'For a short while. I had my own shop, but I doubt my old customers would want their shoes mended by somebody who's been in prison.'

Captain Harry made no comment. He simply nodded sagely and sucked in his mouth. A clock somewhere ticked loudly in the silence that fell between the two men.

'Billy,' the captain said after a while, 'is it true that you have some musical ability? Somebody said you played a mean flute.'

'A flute, sir? No, not me.'

'Maybe I got it wrong, but didn't you go with the Jarrow marchers in 1936? I've spoken to a few people who told me a tale of a lad, knee high to a grasshopper, who kept everybody in good spirits with his flute playing.'

'It was a penny whistle, sir. Nothing so grand as a flute.'

'Well, that's a matter of opinion. Do you still have this penny whistle?'

'Aye. Yes, sir.' Billy rummaged about in his holdall and came up with the whistle in question. 'They used to let me play it in prison . . . and in the hospital too. The nurses said it calmed the patients.'

'Really? That's wonderful.' Captain Harry was brimming over with sudden enthusiasm. 'Perhaps you could do the same for us here. We try to organize a little entertainment for our people.'

Billy's nod of agreement was minimal. A few years ago, had he been asked to perform on his penny whistle, he would have been over the moon. Now, he wasn't sure that he was up to doing anything in public.

'Maybe,' he said. 'One day.'

Captain Harry came round the desk and gave Billy's shoulder a squeeze. 'I won't press you, lad. Take your time. After all, you've come back to a different world to the one you used to know. And quite likely, you're a different person too.'

'Aye, sir,' Billy said, a dark cloud passing over his face. 'You're right there. There's a lot I can't remember . . . some I'd rather forget. It'll be a while before I feel comfortable with myself, if you know what I mean?'

'I do, Billy. Oh, I do, believe me.' Captain Harry reached for his cap, pulled it firmly down on his head and stood before Billy, tall and proud in his uniform. 'Just you relax. Tomorrow's Sunday and the band comes here in the afternoon, together with the songsters. We have a bit of a service followed by a singsong. Everybody joins in. It's like a big family gathering.'

'I think I'll like that, Captain Harry,' Billy said, smiling for the first time since his release from prison. 'I remember the shipyard workers' band when I was a little nipper. I always wanted to play for them, but by the time I was old enough the shipyard closed and the band broke up.' A light shone in his eyes and his smile broadened. 'I've remembered something! Me collecting firewood for my mother and . . . and Bridget and her mother, who gave me my first pair of boots . . . and the band playing and marching.'

'That's grand, Billy. You concentrate on the

319

happy memories. They'll come back, gradually, I'm sure. Now, I'd better be off. I have people to visit. We try to take God to the sick, the old and the lonely.'

'If I can put my hand on some good strong wood, Captain Harry,' Billy said hastily as the captain began to leave, 'I could repair your desk for you . . . if that's all right?'

'It's more than all right, son. You go ahead. There's a yard at the back. And a shed. I'm sure you'll find all you need out there.'

Billy felt a weight lift from his shoulders as he made his way out through the back of the hostel. There were no more fellow prisoners to mock or bully him, no guards, no clanging prison doors and rattling keys and chains. The people here were perhaps worse off than he was, but they didn't seem to mind, and bore him no resentment.

The most important thing was the fact that he could make himself useful. If he could keep busy there wouldn't be time for maudlin thoughts. Maybe even the dreams and the nightmares would fade in time and he could build another life for himself some day, somewhere.

14

Christmas had always been special for Bridget. Her mother, Colleen, had made it special for her when she was a child, and even when times weren't happy, even when she could have been drowning in her own misery, Bridget had forced herself to make an effort and enter into the festive spirit. This Christmas of 1952 was no different. Well, that's what she told herself when she put the finishing touches of tinsel and cotton wool snow on the fir tree she had bought from the local greengrocer.

'Mummy, Mummy, Mummy! Come and see.'

Four-year-old Susan came running in from the street, where she had been helping to build a snowman. Her cheeks were plump and rosy; diamonds of melting snow glistened on her dark hair.

'Is he finished then?' Bridget asked, wiping her hands on a towel and allowing the little girl she loved to distraction to pull her out of the house before she had time to grab her coat.

She laughed when she saw the lumpy,

misshapen pile of snow with pieces of black coal for eyes and a carrot for a nose. She laughed even more when Andrew popped up from behind the snowman, looking just as happy and mischievous as any child there. It was undoubtedly his hat and scarf the snowman was wearing.

'Just one more thing,' he said, delving in his pocket and producing a pipe, which he stuck in the mouth of the snowman and stood back to admire his work.

'Where did you get the pipe from?' Bridget asked and he gave her a wink.

'Ask no questions and I'll tell you no lies,' he said, touching a finger to his nose. 'Suffice it to say that my father won't be angry for long. I've bought him a new one for Christmas.'

'You're mad.' Bridget smiled on him affectionately.

'But I'm quite nice with it, aren't I, Bridget?' He fixed her with a look she both liked and dreaded. 'Aren't I?'

'Come on,' she said quickly. 'If we're to go to Newcastle to see the Christmas decorations in the shops we'd better get a move on. Susan, come and get cleaned up, sweetheart. And you, crazy man Andrew — you'd better retrieve your hat and scarf if you don't want to end up with pneumonia.'

'It's all right. I brought a spare set with me. These are my old ones and I'm glad to pass them on to Mr Snow.' Andrew pulled a face. 'But don't tell my mother, will you? She knitted that scarf for me last Christmas.'

'And if what I've seen her knitting recently is anything to go by, you're going to get another one the same this year.' Bridget grinned as he threw his head back and groaned. His mother had started knitting scarves shortly after war was declared. She liked it so much she couldn't seem to stop. She wasn't exactly good at it and her choice of colours tended to be somewhat gaudy, but she meant well.

'Will there be snowmen in Newcastle, Mummy?' Susan asked as she bounced up and down in the back seat of Andrew's car like a jack-in-the-box in overdrive.

'I don't know,' Bridget told her. 'We'll just have to wait and see. I'm sure there'll be a Santa Claus.'

'The real Santa Claus?' Susan bounced even more.

'Maybe.'

'Hey, little lady, stop that bouncing.' Andrew ordered her good-humouredly. 'My poor old car gets scared enough crossing the Tyne Bridge. I bet everybody on the bridge right now can feel your vibrations.'

Susan giggled and did her best to sit still, but she found that difficult at the best of times. Bridget saw the corner of Andrew's mouth curve up and caught him glancing in the rear-view mirror. He was completely captivated by Susan. She knew exactly how to wrap him around her little finger. He was so good with her though. In fact, Andrew was good with everybody and Bridget considered that she was very lucky to have him in her life.

'Look, Susan' She pointed out of the window. 'There's the River Tyne where the big boats come in and out. And the big white birds are seagulls.'

'Ooh! They're lovely! If we had a garden, Mummy, they would come and visit and I could feed them, couldn't I?'

Andrew's parents lived in Gosforth on the outskirts of Newcastle. They had a nice Victorian redbrick house with a large garden. Susan was quite taken with the idea of a garden where she could plant flowers and feed the birds.

'I think you could charm a dinosaur to feed from your hand, Susan,' Andrew said and they all laughed.

'What's a dinosaur?' Susan wanted to know, five minutes later.

* * *

Newcastle, Bridget thought, was the best city in the world. It had everything. Andrew had introduced her to the Theatre Royal, the Royal Arcade with its antique market, and the grand stores the whole length of Northumberland Street that had everything anyone could ask for. Her favourite outing was wandering around the departments at Fenwick's, followed by lunch at the Eldon Grill. And then there was the Quayside market on a Sunday morning, which was Susan's particular favourite. The market had stalls where you could buy bed linen cheaply, where men juggled china and sold whole dinner services at ridiculous, knockdown prices.

What enthralled Susan were the stalls with puppies and kittens, sweets, candyfloss and toffee apples; and there were often clowns and acrobats. Sometimes, they would see a huge black man parading in outrageously fancy waistcoats and baggy pants, wearing a headdress of ostrich feathers. He would march up and down shouting 'I gotta horse'. Now there was a novelty. Being a port, there were often foreign sailors in evidence, but no one with skin quite as black as the flamboyant tipster, Prince Monolulu, who was famous the length and breadth of Britain's racecourses.

But today everyone was gravitating towards

the city centre where the Salvation Army band was entertaining the shoppers with Christmas carols around the tall and elegant Grey's Monument. The column stood over 130 feet tall, with the sculpture of the famous Earl Grey standing proud on the top. Down below there were Christmas trees with winking coloured lights. The organizers had done the city proud, even though the people still lived in post-war circumstances. But things were getting noticeably better.

'See that man up there,' Andrew said, directing Susan's eyes to the statue. 'That's Earl Grey. He's been up there since 1838.'

'Ooh!' was Susan's reply. 'Isn't he tired?'

'He's made of stone, Susan,' Bridget said and turned to Andrew with a grin. 'What was he famous for, anyway?'

'Well,' said Andrew, always happy to pass on his knowledge, 'he was an inventor of tea mixtures, and the prime minister of England. He was also responsible for the 1832 Reform Bill leading to modern parliament in England. A great man indeed.'

'Well, I never,' said Bridget, but her attention had been drawn to the glorious sound of the Salvation Army band giving a rousing rendition of 'Hark The Herald Angels Sing'.

People were congregating around the band

and, as they played, a few new flakes of snow began to drift down from an iron-grey sky. The bandsmen and the songsters, all in their uniforms and smiling broadly at their public, were being decorated with a sprinkling of glistening white snow, like icing sugar on their shoulders. Clouds of steam emitted from them and their instruments as their warm, damp breath hit the frozen air.

'Do you want to listen to the band, Susan?' Andrew lifted the child on to his shoulders and pushed forward through the crowd of observers.

Bridget followed in his wake, a strange, nostalgic churning in her stomach. The sound of the brass band was awakening something in her memory. She remembered the day when she and Billy had listened to the ship workers' band as they'd paraded through the streets of Jarrow. It was a long time ago. They had both been very young and innocent, though they had seen life in the raw with poverty and unemployment, before and since. Yes, she thought, and murder.

God rest Patrick Flynn's black soul, she thought. How he had wreaked havoc on her and Billy's family. It might be temporarily forgotten, until something stirred it up again, but it wasn't anything she could ever forgive, not even to please God.

Listening to the kind of music that Billy used to love, Bridget couldn't help her thoughts wandering, couldn't stop herself wondering what had become of Billy, who had turned his back on her rather than let her help him when he came out of prison.

'I hope you're looking after him, God,' she whispered under her breath, then joined Andrew and Susan in the front line of the rapt audience listening to and singing along with the Christmas carols. Susan was demanding to be put down because she had got her sights on a tangle-haired dog. The pup, for he wasn't much above a few months old, was running among the feet of the musicians, sniffing at their ankles and the frosty ground.

'Ahh!' Susan cried out, holding out her hand and clicking her fingers at the dog, which came and gave her a brief lick, then continued on his search until he stopped at the foot of a rather short individual playing a cornet. The mongrel gave a delighted yelp and tried to climb up the man's leg, bouncing on its hind legs and tugging at the loose material of the cornet player's jacket.

Bridget watched and smiled at the dog's antics. The man was doing his best to ignore the animal, but wasn't being very effective. As the piece the band was playing came to a close, the bandsman lowered his instrument and bent down to speak affectionately to the dog. They obviously belonged together.

'Hey, you scrag end. You made me play a sour note then. What are you up to, eh? Want to get me the sack?'

The dog yelped, leapt in the air and kissed the bandsman's nose. At that point, little Susan chose to rush forward to introduce herself properly to man and dog.

'Is that your doggy?' she asked in her baby, lisping voice.

'Aye, pet. It is, and he should have stayed home, but he doesn't like being left alone. I suppose he must have escaped somehow.'

'He's nice. What's his name?'

'He's called Mister Tatters on account of him being all in tatters when I found him.'

'My name's Susan.'

Bridget had held back, not daring to believe her eyes or her ears, for she knew this man, despite his being swamped in a Salvation Army uniform that was at least two sizes too big for him and a cap that came down over his eyes. She edged forward tentatively, loving the moment and yet fearing what might follow.

'You shouldn't be here on your own, pet,' Billy said as he picked the dog up and tucked it under his arm. 'Where's your mammy?'

Susan turned and pointed. 'There!'

Billy's eyes grew wide and his mouth dropped open as he saw Bridget for the first time. It had been five years since the day he walked out of prison a free man.

★ ★ ★

'Hello, Billy.'

They stared at one another like people meeting in a dream that wasn't quite real. Billy felt his heart thud, and then sink down deep inside him, like a ship plummeting to unknown depths.

'Bridget!' Her name left his numb lips like a soft breeze.

'What on earth are you doing playing for the Sally Army band?' she asked, her eyes travelling the length and breadth of him.

'I help out sometimes,' he said. 'Since the war they've been short of players.'

'It looks like they're short of uniforms too,' she said and the smile that nothing had ever been able to wipe from his memory spread out across her rosy face.

'Aye, well, things are a bit tight.'

'Which is more than I can say for that uniform of yours. There's room for two more inside, I'd say. When did you take up the trumpet?'

'It's a cornet . . . ' He stared down at the shiny instrument as if it might give him courage to go on speaking to her without a tremor in his voice. 'I used to play the penny whistle, but I've been learning this thing for a few months now.'

'So, you're a member of the Sally Army now?'

'Not exactly . . . ' He was desperately trying not to say her name again because his fractured emotions might show. 'Captain Harry and his wife have been good to me. They found me a job and lodgings. I help them out where I can.'

'Captain Harry?'

'That would be me, young lady,' said a booming voice beside her and she turned to see the ruddy-faced bandleader beaming at her. 'Haven't we met before? I seem to know your face from somewhere.'

'I don't think . . . ' Bridget started to deny that they had ever met, but Andrew stepped up and put his hand around her shoulders in that possessive way that he had.

'We were there, Captain, the day Billy was released from prison.'

'Ah, yes, of course. Plenty of water under the bridge since then. Well, if you'll excuse me . . . ' The captain touched a finger to the peak of his cap. 'I need to get the band back

331

to the City Temple. We're playing there this evening. Billy, why don't you invite your friends to come along? I'm sure they'll find seats.'

Billy nodded and they all watched in silence as Captain Harry rounded up his bandsmen and his songsters.

'Don't let us keep you, Billy . . . ' Andrew said, picking Susan up once again and placing a hand on the small of Bridget's back, urging her to go on.

Billy looked at them, his heart disintegrating. They made such a good-looking family. He shouldn't resent that. What had he ever had to offer any woman, even before prison? He had been crazy to think otherwise.

'Just a minute, Andrew.' Bridget touched the barrister's arm and turned back to Billy. 'Is everything all right, Billy? I tried to get in touch with you, but nobody seemed to know where you were living.'

'The Salvation Army sorted me out.' He blinked at her, searching for words to say. 'I'm all right. No complaints.'

'That's good to hear.'

He gave a watery smile at that. Bridget had never been of any religious persuasion and she knew that he was the same, though there had been times lately when he had found himself sitting on a precarious fence, not knowing which way to fall.

'They're good people, but I'm not one of them, except on occasions like this one, when they need an extra body in the band.' He gave a boyish grin. 'It gives me the opportunity to play some good, rousing music.'

'Don't they mind you wearing the uniform, then? Seeing as how you're not one of them?'

'No. Captain Harry thought I wouldn't stand out so much if I wore it rather than my own clothes. His wife's furious because he didn't give her enough time to do the necessary alterations.'

'So, you have yourself a family, of sorts?'

'They treat me like a son, if that's what you mean. Them and a lot of their friends. As I say, they're damned good people.'

Bridget nodded slowly and sank her teeth into her bottom lip. He could see that this meeting was uncomfortable for her too. There were so many things Billy wanted to ask, so much he wanted to say, but it wasn't the right time. He didn't know if it would ever be the right time.

The lads in the band were chivvying him to hurry and join them. He gave them a wave of acknowledgement. When he looked off to the left he could see the barrister hovering impatiently, a look of concern on his face.

'You'd better go,' Bridget said.

'Aye.' Billy shifted his hands on the cornet he was almost strangling in his edginess. 'Take care, then.'

'You too, Billy.'

He started to walk away, his heart weighing him down. The band lads were still waving to him, calling out to him to hurry. It was the hardest thing to do, putting one foot in front of the other, knowing that Bridget, who had been his whole life and who should have continued to be so till death parted them, was standing there watching him. He had wanted to touch her, hold her, kiss her till she begged him to stop, but that was never going to happen. She had moved on, made a nice life for herself, by the looks of it. She had a husband who obviously adored her and a lovely little girl. He couldn't have wished anything better for her. Bridget deserved the best and, by God, he wasn't going to spoil it for her.

'Billy!'

He hesitated a fraction of a second at the sound of her voice. Then, pretending he hadn't heard, he hurried away.

★　★　★

Late on Christmas Eve, Bridget was hurrying to wrap a last-minute present for Andrew. It was a bit of a joke, really, but she was sure he would appreciate it. For the past few weeks, with some help and encouragement from Andrew's mother, Bridget had knitted him a warm jumper in the gayest mixture of colours she could think of. The wool had been rescued from knitwear that Susan had outgrown. Pulled out, washed and dried, it was ideal for an inexperienced knitter to practise on. Bridget wasn't sure about the size — it looked big. And one sleeve was slightly longer than the other. But she was mightily proud of her first attempt and Edna had applauded when she saw it.

'Oh, I'm looking forward to seeing my dowdy son wearing that on Christmas Day,' Andrew's mother had said and they had both looked at one another and laughed.

'Hurry up, Mummy!' Susan shouted from her lookout post at the front-room window. 'He's coming.'

'Oh, lor!' Bridget's fingers got suddenly clumsy as she tied the red ribbon bow and rushed to hide the parcel with the rest of the presents in the bottom of the Welsh dresser beside the special bottle of sherry for Edna tomorrow, and a bottle of port for Andrew's father.

'Hurry, hurry, hurry!' Susan ran into the kitchen, hopping from one foot to the other and grinning all over her chubby face. 'He's got somebody with him. I can hear them talking.'

'Oh, dear.' Bridget peered into the oven, checking that the shepherd's pie she was making for supper wasn't burning. 'I hope there's enough here for four.'

'I'll open the door,' Susan said, nodding importantly and marching off down the passage, where Bridget heard the grate of the door catch. It seemed like only yesterday that Susan was too little to reach up and open the door. She had grown so much in the last few months.

Two pairs of male feet clumped down the passage and she heard Andrew calling out to her.

'I'm in the kitchen,' she shouted back and hurriedly got out another set of cutlery to make a fourth place at the table.

She was lifting the pie out of the oven, her face hot from the high temperature and her haste, when Andrew put his head around the door and gave her an uncertain smile.

'I hope you don't mind,' he said, his brows furrowing. 'I've brought someone with me. It's . . . well, you'll see.'

'Well, don't keep me in suspense,' Bridget said. 'Who is it?'

'You'd better put that dish down before

you drop it,' Andrew said and she was glad to get rid of the dish to the table, for it was burning through the tea towel and scorching her fingers.

Andrew came into the kitchen, but the other person, whoever it was, was still hanging behind, though she could hear some kind of snuffling noise and Susan, also out of sight, was chattering away ecstatically.

'Well? Who is it?'

The welcoming smile faded from Bridget's hot face, which became even hotter as she saw who their supper guest was. Billy Flynn stepped into the room and stood beside Andrew, cap in hand.

'Billy!'

'Hello, Bridget. I've brought Mister Tatters. I hope it's all right. I thought the bairn might enjoy him. You don't have to worry. He doesn't bite or anything. Too soft for that.'

Bridget swallowed and looked from him to Andrew and back again. She was saved from having to think of the right words by Susan staggering into the room, carrying the hairy mongrel that was licking her face and generally making a great fuss of his new friend.

'Look what I've got, Mummy.'

'Susan, sweetheart, put the dog down and come and wash your hands before you eat.'

'He's called Mister Tatters, Mummy. Isn't he lovely?'

'Lovely . . . yes . . . ' Bridget couldn't take her eyes off Billy.

'You can play with Tatters all you want later,' Andrew said. 'But now, young lady, hands!'

'Knees!' Susan yelled in her squeaky child's voice.

'And bumps-a-daisy!' Andrew finished off and gave her a gentle push in the direction of the sink, where she had her own special step stool to help her reach the tap.

'Would you like some shepherd's pie?' Bridget said to Billy in a voice that was slightly dazed, which was exactly how she felt. *What on earth was Andrew thinking of, bringing Billy here to her house!*

'That would be nice.' Billy nodded and sat down where she indicated, though she got the impression that he was glad not to have to stand there before her any longer.

'Andrew . . . ?'

Andrew turned from supervising Susan's hand-washing and she saw something different in his face too. 'What? Oh, not for me, Bridget. Susan and I are going to my mother's for supper. Go and get your coat, sweetheart.'

'I don't understand. Andrew, what's this all about?'

There was a poignant silence. Andrew went to stand beside Billy and laid a hand on his shoulder. There wasn't much difference in their ages, but it was something of a fatherly gesture.

'It's all about love, Bridget,' he said. 'There are different kinds of love, you know. It also has to do with being able to recognize what kind of love you're dealing with.'

'I don't understand.'

'You will. I've had a long talk with Billy here. He's a good man, Bridget, but then ... I always knew that. Just as I've always known that the pair of you belonged together.'

The two men nodded at each other, but it was obvious that there was nothing left to say. They had already said it all.

Bridget went to the door with Andrew, who had Susan in his arms.

'Andrew . . . ?'

'Billy will take it from here,' said Andrew, hugging the little girl tightly to him. 'We'll be fine, won't we, Susan? Mummy and Billy will come and spend Christmas Day with us tomorrow.'

'And Mister Tatters?'

'Him too!' Andrew's mouth quivered slightly as he kissed Susan's cheek, then bent to plant a more lingering kiss on Bridget's temple. There was a catch in his voice as he spoke. 'Bye, Bridget. See you tomorrow. My parents are looking forward to it.'

What could she say? Did Andrew know how wonderful he was? This was a big sacrifice for him. He had asked her time and time again to marry him, but although she loved him dearly, she had always held back. Her heart belonged to another, and that man was finally sitting in her kitchen, waiting to speak to her.

She closed the door behind two of the dearest souls on this earth and walked slowly back to the kitchen. She sat down opposite Billy and they stared at one another in total silence, until she remembered the shepherd's pie cooling between them. Still without a word, she took a large helping of it and piled it on a plate in front of Billy. He looked down at it briefly, then reached out and stayed her hand, gripping it so tightly that she dropped the spoon. Her heart raced, but she couldn't speak. Not yet.

'Andrew told me about you and him,' Billy said, his voice raw, his eyes brimming with emotion. 'I thought you were married and that Susan was your daughter, but you're not and . . . and she's not . . . '

'Susan is Laura's daughter, Billy.' Bridget had found her voice at last. 'Her husband was a farmer. He was much older than her. Oh, she was so happy when she knew she was pregnant, then her husband died. There were complications during the pregnancy. Laura died during childbirth, Billy. I think, somehow, she knew that something was wrong. She had left me a letter asking me to care for Susan if anything happened to her. I wanted to adopt her, but they wouldn't let me. I'm a single person, you see. But they did allow me to be her foster mother. Andrew's her godfather, along with his parents, and there's a trust fund put aside for her that she inherits when she's twenty-one. She'll never want for anything until then.'

'I can see that,' Billy said. 'She's a lucky little girl. I wish I'd been around to see her growing up.'

'Me too, but . . . Billy?' The words stuck in her throat.

'Yes?'

'Well, it's not too late. She is only four, after all.'

Billy smiled into her eyes and his grip on her fingers became even tighter.

'I can't remember if I've ever told you this, Bridget,' he said, 'but I've never stopped loving you. I think I've loved you all my life.'

'Me too,' she said, trying to stop her lips from trembling. 'But you turned me away,

341

and the other day, you walked away from me as if you didn't care.'

'You've no idea how much strength it took to do that.' Billy licked his lips and cast his gaze about the kitchen. The only sound was the ticking of the old chiming clock on the mantelpiece. 'The thing is, Bridget, I can't offer you the kind of things that you deserve. I'm in work, so I'm not destitute, but it's not enough to feed a family on. And with my past . . . ' He drew in a deep, sobbing breath and gave a hopeless shrug.

She was about to tell him how, thanks to her own hard work letting out rooms to lodgers and taking in washing and sewing, she had somehow managed to keep on his cobbler's shop. However, before she could speak, there was a loud rattling at the front door. She frowned, and so did Billy at having to release his hold on her hand.

On the pavement outside there was a group of people, men and women, most of whom she knew from years back. They were stamping their feet to keep warm as the icy December wind blew down the street, bringing with it a flurry of thick snowflakes.

'Bridget!' Mrs Turnbull, the old neighbour of Billy's from Dawson Street, was obviously their self-appointed spokeswoman. She stepped forward, arms crossed beneath her sagging breasts and fixed Bridget with a determined eye. 'We've just heard that Billy Flynn is back.'

'And what of it?' Bridget pulled herself up to her full height and got ready to launch herself into Billy's defence. There had been some cruel people in the past, speaking ill of Billy and his whole family. She had stood up for him then and she would do so again.

'Nothing, pet.' The woman's face softened. 'Except to say that we're very glad to hear it. It's time we had a decent cobbler in these parts instead of having to traipse all the way to Gateshead to get out boots and shoes mended. Just tell him from us that if he's willing, he's already got a bevy of customers waiting for him to get started. You'll do that, will you, lass?'

Bridget bit down hard on her lip and spoke through the lump in her throat. She hadn't expected such kindness and was totally overwhelmed.

'I will . . . and . . . thank you. Thank you all.'

The crowd nodded, grinning, then moved off, calling out their Christmas wishes to her. She couldn't respond because she was crying too hard and her hankie was soaked with her tears by the time she went back to Billy in the kitchen.

'Did you hear that, Billy?'

'Aye,' he said, swiping at his own damp eyes with a shaking finger. 'I should have come out and thanked them, but . . . ' He choked on his words.

'So, Billy Flynn, will you be staying?'

He looked at her and said nothing for a long time and her heart all but stopped beating. Then she saw his face crumple and the tears roll freely down his face.

'If you want me to, Bridget.'

'Silly sod! Come here!'

Almost knocking the kitchen table down in their haste, they rushed into one another's arms and clung together as if in that one gesture was the meaning of life, and of love.

When the sun rose and spilled pink and gold over the thick blanket of snow on Christmas morning, Billy opened his eyes and looked at the beautiful face of Bridget as she slept, still snuggled in to his side. Outside, there was birdsong and, in the distance, the sound of a brass band playing Christmas carols. They were the sweetest voices of the morning bringing him untold joy. The past no longer mattered for this blessed, wonderful day was the first day of the rest of his life.

We do hope that you have enjoyed reading this large print book.

Did you know that all of our titles are available for purchase?

We publish a wide range of high quality large print books including:
Romances, Mysteries, Classics
General Fiction
Non Fiction and Westerns

Special interest titles available in large print are:
The Little Oxford Dictionary
Music Book
Song Book
Hymn Book
Service Book

Also available from us courtesy of Oxford University Press:
Young Readers' Dictionary
(large print edition)
Young Readers' Thesaurus
(large print edition)

For further information or a free brochure, please contact us at:
Ulverscroft Large Print Books Ltd.,
The Green, Bradgate Road, Anstey,
Leicester, LE7 7FU, England.
Tel: (00 44) 0116 236 4325
Fax: (00 44) 0116 234 0205

Other titles published by
The House of Ulverscroft:

TO THE ENDS OF THE EARTH

June Gadsby

Wild and beautiful Gwyneth Johnns is a Patagonian with a past that shocks the Victorian ladies of the small pioneering town in the Valdes Peninsula. She has sworn never to let any man get close, but a handsome Spaniard, Miguel, weakens her resolve. Then, new immigrants arrive from England. Gentle giant Rob, his brother, Davy, and the hard-drinking, amoral Matt with his young wife. Gwyneth is called upon to teach them how to be *gauchos*. Reluctantly, she accepts the challenge. But now she risks losing her life and newfound love to the cold glaciers of the Andes . . .